Whackadoodle Times Two

Also by Kim Antieau

Novels

The Blue Tail • *Broken Moon* • *Butch*
Church of the Old Mermaids • *Coyote Cowgirl* • *Deathmark*
The Desert Siren • *The Fish Wife: an Old Mermaids Novel*
The Gaia Websters • *Her Frozen Wild* • *Jewelweed Station*
The Jigsaw Woman • *Mercy, Unbound*
The Monster's Daughter • *Ruby's Imagine*
Swans in Winter • *The Rift* • *Whackadoodle Times*

Nonfiction

Answering the Creative Call
Certified
Counting on Wildflowers
The Old Mermaids Book of Days and Nights
*The Old Mermaids Book of Days and Nights: A Year
and a Day Journal*
An Old Mermaid Journal
The Salmon Mysteries
Under the Tucson Moon

Short Story Collections

Entangled Realities (with Mario Milosevic)
The First Book of Old Mermaids Tales
Tales Fabulous and Fairy
Trudging to Eden

Chapbook

Blossoms

Cartoons

Fun With Vic and Jane

Blog

www.kimantieau.com

WHACKADOODLE TIMES TWO

KIM ANTIEAU

Green Snake
PUBLISHING

Whackadoodle Times Two
by Kim Antieau

Copyright © 2015 by Kim Antieau

ISBN-13: 978-1-949644-08-1

Cover image copyright © Inara Prusakova | Dreamstime
Book design by Mario Milosevic and Kim Antieau.

Thanks to Nancy Milosevic

Thanks to Lisa Mills Walters
lisawaltersediting.com

Published by Green Snake Publishing
www.greensnakepublishing.com

For Mario

I can pinpoint exactly when things began to go whackadoodle again. Later, everyone else said it had something to do with a peculiar full moon. It was green, blue, or so close to the earth you could French kiss the man in the moon. For me, it began and ended with my daughter dearest who was trying to blackmail me as we sat in Juliet's eating breakfast together.

It was already shaping up to be one of those weeks, and it was only Wednesday. They were supposed to start shooting *Beauty and the Zombie Part Two: Escape from Alcatraz* soon, and I hadn't finished the script yet. All the studio and the director had seen was my treatment—which wasn't as detailed as it should be. Sally St. James, the studio head, called me every fifteen minutes to ask about it. My fourteen-year-old son, David, kept nagging his father, Hayword, and me about his science project presentation coming up in school Friday. He seemed almost desperate to have us there. I secretly hoped he wasn't planning on blowing up his school. Not that he would do something like that on purpose. Plus my man Mark Pantano's restaurant was opening this weekend. In our house.

Now Fern was trying to blackmail or coerce or guilt me into attending some AFT function that I couldn't care less about. I hated those phony baloney Hollywood parties where everyone pretended to love everyone else when in truth they were all fucking each other's spouses and/or stabbing each other in the back over some new or old development deal. It was one of the reasons Hayword and I ended our marriage—even though we were still not technically divorced. He enjoyed all the schmoozing. I did not.

In the last two years, I had been to more Hollywood functions than I'd been to in the previous twenty years—I was now on the A-list because *Beauty and the Zombie* had been such a big hit. I was invited everywhere and sometimes I said yes.

So now Fern wanted me to go to this party and talk to some new up-and-coming writers. I didn't have anything to say to them except: run for the hills. I could warn them against trying to fuck their way to the top. A writer could stumble to the top, but she could stumble right back down, too. Besides, Hollywood hated writers. The general culture here loathed us. The powerbrokers knew they needed us—kind of like a junkie needs their drug dealer—but they still hated us.

Writers weren't as pretty, we weren't as rich, and we were smarter than all of them put together, and we knew it. At least, that's what the studio heads and producers thought we thought. They believed they could get anyone to do anything by either fucking them or bribing them (or both), and most of the EPs thought writers were too ugly to fuck.

Truly.

God's honest truth. I'd had more than one EP—executive producer—tell me that. First they'd say something along these lines: "This doesn't apply to you, of course, because Jesus, you are more than fuckable. But most writers . . ." You get the gist.

And then I'd say something like, "You, on the other hand, are just too *stupid* to fuck. So let's call the whole thing off."

I really hated producers. As a rule. Except Hayword, who longed to be a producer and was finally one for *Powerbreakers* and *Beauty and the Zombie*. He did a good job. Sally St. James was an okay producer, too. I guess. For me, producers do a good job if they leave me alone.

Hayword and I had just separated when they began filming *Beauty and the Zombie*. Now we've been apart for two years. We still work together, but we don't have sex. I don't have to pretend I want to have sex with him anymore. Gawd. What a fucking relief. I don't have to wipe his tears or prop up his fragile writer's ego. And and and I don't have to pretend I don't miss our son Alberto who died when he was an infant. He wasn't actually Hayword's son by blood, but I'm not going to go through that story all over again. If you want to know more, go read my first foray into memoir, *Whackadoodle Times*, and then come back here. Enough to know Alberto's death haunted our entire family for many years. I became a drunk and a fucker. David got neurotic. Fern . . . well, Fern burned down our house so we'd have to move, but she was a kid so you can't blame her.

I'm still hoping no one will or can charge her with anything should it ever come to light that she was a bit of an arsonist when she was a child.

Fern worked for AFT now, against my wishes, for Sally St. James, who was as talented as a studio head can get. Sally wanted to do good work, she wanted to treat people well, she wanted to have a life separate from her job—at least she said she did. She said she didn't want to work so much, but she made excuses to stay at the office too many nights. She said she wanted to be monogamous, but over the last couple of years, she had tried to seduce me more than once, usually when she was drunk. And I'd tell her I didn't do women anymore.

In fact, I didn't do men anymore either, except for Mark Pantano, my plumber turned restaurateur. Or about to be restaurateur. He had studied to be a chef before he settled for the plumbing life, and I was helping him achieve his dream of having his own restaurant.

Did I mention the restaurant was slated to open in about four days (Sunday), two days before David's science project (Friday), one day before my script deadline (Saturday), and three days after the party (Thursday) Fern was blackmailing me to attend?

Perhaps "blackmailing" was too strong a word. Guilting?

We were sitting in Juliet's when Fern started asking me all sorts of stupid questions. You remember Juliet's. It's the restaurant where movie people go who are pretending they don't want to be seen. So they go to Juliet's to be seen by other people who pretend they don't want to be seen. I went there because I'd been going there for a long time. It was where Sally St. James talked me into script-doctoring Hayword's zombie movie. I told her I thought zombies were stupid. She said she wanted a sexy zombie movie: She wanted me to sex up zombies the way other writers had sexed up werewolves and vampires.

Gotta tell you I didn't see any way to make zombies sexy.

Until I did.

I made it into a love story. *Beauty and the Zombie*.

Yep.

AFT made the movie. Jonny Black played Thomas, the alien zombie who supposedly betrayed the heroine of the piece, Colleen Kelly (who was played by Kate Becker). Colleen is who we see pregnant in the last frame of the movie.

Sequel heaven.

Both Kate Becker and Jonny Black were on board and ready for filming the sequel.

If I could just write the damn thing.

Now at Juliet's, Fern was drinking Bloody Marys at eleven a.m.

"Don't do the 'like mother like daughter' thing," I told her after the waiter took our food order. He was a cutey patootie, and we both watched him walk away.

"What are you talking about?" Fern asked as she stirred her drink with a celery stick. Organic celery stick, mind you. We might get fucked up at eleven a.m. here in la-la land, but we do it organically.

"This is fucking health food," she said.

Oh gawd. She was trying to be a tough guy. It just didn't suit her. She wasn't really tough. She was angry. She was smart as hell. But I had damaged her clear to the marrow, and that had let all the true toughness leak out. Sometimes, like right this moment, I wanted to take her in my arms and squeeze all the shit out of her. Make it better. Make her all better. When her brother Alberto died, I was depressed for a long time. In Fern's addled pre-teen brain, she thought the family would be better off if we could leave the house where her brother had died. So she set the house on fire. We didn't know it at the time. Didn't know until about two years ago when she confessed to me and her father. Since then we'd offered to go to therapy with her. Offered to do whatever she needed to feel better.

She said a job made her feel better. Making something of her life made her feel better.

Didn't quite sound right, but my brain had been pickled from years on alcohol and drugs. Might just be getting right about now, I supposed, so I wasn't positive sure about anything.

"Darlin'," I said to Fern as she sipped her Bloody Mary. "Please don't try to be like me. Live your life opposite to mine. Do everything differently from what I did and you should be fine."

She put down her glass and rolled her eyes. "Mother, how

you do or don't live your life doesn't come into my mind at all, ever."

"Maybe it should," I said, "so you can avoid my mistakes. I drank because I'd lost a son. I drank because I was monumentally unhappy living this Hollywood life. Why are you drinking?"

"I'm not drinking, Mother," she said. "I am having *a* drink. Because it tastes good. Especially with scrambled eggs. Would you like a sip?" She held the glass out to me.

For a moment, I wanted to smash the glass out of her hand. Man, she could piss me off more than any other human being alive.

For another moment, I wanted to take a sip.

I didn't like that feeling. Much better to feel angry than . . . to want to drink. I didn't like seeing my daughter try to tempt an alkie back to the bottle.

"Really, Fern?" I said.

Her eyes widened for a moment, as though she hadn't realized what she was doing. She set the glass down again and then pushed it away from her. Then, as if realizing she had pushed it toward me, she grabbed it and slid it toward her again.

"I'm just tired, Mom," she said. "Work has been rough lately."

"I accept your apology," I said.

She started to say something else—I could tell it was a mean smart-ass remark—but she stopped herself. She wanted something from me, and she wanted it badly. She was even wearing the blue and green swan pin I had given her after Alberto died. He had loved that pin—or loved the way it sparkled in the light because he always reached for it when I wore it. Always tried to pull it from my shirt or sweater, whatever I had pinned it to. We could never figure out how the swan had gotten green and blue. When my mother had given it to me when I was a teen, it had been white. Then one day it was blue and green. Figured I must have washed it with something that ran, but who knew?

"You're wearing the swan," I said.

"What?" Fern said. "Oh, the pin. Yes, I was thinking of Alberto this morning, so I wore it."

I didn't believe her. She wore the pin to try to manipulate me.

She smiled. "I miss him."

We were silent for a moment.

"So did you always want to be a writer?" she asked.

Okay. Now we were back to her asking me bizarrely stupid questions.

I could play along.

"As long as I can remember," I said. On some days, I couldn't remember a whole lot. That ole pickling of the brain. Some experts said my brain would eventually return to normal, whatever that was. Other specialists said it wouldn't. If it wouldn't return to normal, why the fuck had I bothered to quit drinking in the first place? No. I couldn't think like that. I kept telling myself my brain *was* healing. It was learning to produce its own opiates. Or whatever it was missing. Sometimes I imagined my brain as a black hole that was slowly filling up with good times. Or chocolate. Or love. Sometimes I had to think good thoughts—even though that was antithetical to who I was now.

Sometimes I just had to *not* think good thoughts.

Reality was reality, man, and we had to face it.

"And Dad, too?" she asked. "He always wanted to be a writer?"

"And Toto, too," I said.

She looked at me and made a face.

"Did you hear about this weird full moon tomorrow?" Fern asked. "Or late tonight."

"Just something about it being very close to Earth," I said, "and some people are afraid its pull will awaken the undead."

She smiled grimly.

"And Mercury is in retrograde," she said. "A shit storm of misunderstandings, miscommunication, and crazies coming up. At least that's what I've been hearing."

"Some of the more New Age radio stations have been telling people to pay attention," I said, "because something really good or really bad is going to happen." I laughed. "You could pretty much say that any time, couldn't you? What the hell is Mercury retrograde, anyway? I've never understood it. The planet goes backward but doesn't really. It just looks like it. What does that mean? It does a moon walk?"

Fern shrugged. "I don't know. I wish I'd paid attention earlier though. I would have changed my plans."

"You mean this breakfast?"

"No! I've been looking forward to this breakfast."

"Darlin', just ask me what you have to ask me," I said. "You don't have to butter me up. For one thing, you really suck at it. If you're going to stay in this business, you'll probably have to work on your sucking up skills."

She bit the inside of her lip.

"Look, Mother."

Oh, so we were back to Mother instead of Mom.

"I know you've really been trying these last couple of years," she said, "and I appreciate it. I know it's been tough. You've had to change everything about your life. Tough work."

She didn't mean it. She didn't really think it was tough.

"I've changed, too," she said. "I'm no longer protesting corporations, I'm working for one. I'm trying to keep it a good business."

Christ on a bender. She was falling into the same trap her

father and I had fallen into when we first came to Hollywood: We thought we could change it, make it kinder, gentler.

"Good god, daughter," I said. "Learn from our mistakes. This business will suck the motherfucking life out of you. Unless you're careful. It's like any relationship. It's best to see it truthfully and not try to change it—because it will not go gently into that good night."

"Hollywood isn't a person," she said. "It's just a place. It's a company town, and I happen to work for that company."

"It's actually a two-company town," I said. "If you count rehab."

"Mom, could you just shut up and let me finish," she said. "Please."

The cute waiter brought our meals: Fern got scrambled eggs, potatoes, and sausage, and I got a mushroom omelette. I suddenly craved a glass of champagne, but I bit my tongue before I asked for one. What was with me? I go two years without a single craving, and now in the space of five minutes, I had two?

If I were prone, I would have broken out into a sweat just then.

We watched the waiter walk away again.

"Sally is feeling a bit vulnerable," Fern said quietly. "I'm not sure why. She's the damn studio head. But Irving Jackson seems to be causing trouble. Not sure how. He's nice to me, but Sally doesn't trust him. They're really counting on your movie and Daddy's new movie. With me there, it's like our family is the heart and soul of AFT. Sally is counting on us. I think we need to nurture some new talent. We can't rely solely on you and Dad."

"Because we're old and feeble and likely to die soon?"

I began eating the omelette. Lovely. So nice to have my sense of taste back.

"Yes, that," she said, "and you keep saying you're not going to work in Hollywood anymore. We can't rely on you to continue to produce work."

I made a noise. "I've been saying that for years," I said. "Now that I'm sober and in a happy relationship, I'm having fun writing."

Oh crap. I had said that out loud. Never, *ever* say publicly that you're in a good relationship or you're with the love of your life. Or whatever. Not in Hollywood. Within minutes, hours, days, you'll be eating your words. Trust me on this. The evil eye was now going to come snatch away my sobriety and/or my relationship.

"Not that I'm really that sober and my relationship with Mark pretty much sucks."

"What?"

"Nothing," I said. "I was just taking it all back."

"But you're *not* writing," she said. "I bet you a year's salary you haven't even started on the new *Beauty and the Zombie* script. You did the treatment and that's it."

"Let's move on," I said. "What is it you want from me?"

"Just come to this party," she said. "It's on Thursday, tomorrow, so you won't even need to think about it ahead of time. Talk with these writers. They're young. They've got ideas. I think they could work for us and with us. But they need convincing."

"Convincing? Write them a check. That will be all the convincing they need."

"Mom, please just come," she said. "If you don't, I'm going to tell Dad that you and Sally had an affair."

I glanced around the restaurant. She had said that last bit a little louder than I liked. It wasn't that I had suddenly become discreet. That ship had long ago sailed—and foundered, and sank with all aboard. But Fern was just starting out. She didn't want to get a reputation for . . . anything . . . but most of all, she didn't want a reputation as a gossip.

"So that's how you're going to get me to do something for you," I said. "You're going to try blackmail? Lordy, sister, I've done so many things worse than that. Not that that was especially bad, or anything. I'm sure your father knew, and if he didn't, he wouldn't care now. I tried making amends to him, but he didn't want a whole list or anything. It was enough that I apologized and meant it. Why would you want to open his wounds to get me to come to a party? None of this conversation is making me want to come. Why the desperation? Are you dating one of these writers?"

"Mother, that's insulting."

"Why? I assume you wouldn't try to blackmail your old mother over just any schlub."

"No one is a schlub," she said. She took a couple of bites of her scrambled eggs. She blushed, put down her fork, then picked up her Bloody Mary and drained the glass.

"All right," I said. "I'll go to this party. Is your dad coming? Maybe we can go together." Mark didn't like industry parties.

"Yes, I think he's coming," she said. "You'll talk nice to the writers? You'll encourage them to work for us?"

"Sure," I said. "On one condition."

She rolled her eyes. She really needed to stop doing that. It was a teenager's gesture, not something an adult did on a regular basis.

"You don't have anything to drink from now until the party is over," I said.

"So now *you're* resorting to blackmail," she said.

"I wouldn't call this blackmail," I said. "Just honest deal brokering."

She pressed her lips together. Then she shrugged and said, "Okay, sure. Why not? Not all of us are lushes like you, Mom. I can stop any time."

"You have such a charming way with words, my daughter," I said.

"I learned from the best," she said.

Her version of a compliment.

Just then, two gunmen burst into the restaurant.

Seriously.

They were both dressed all in black, with Ninja masks covering their faces.

The dozen or so patrons in the restaurant gasped. I did, too. But I wasn't afraid. Not sure why.

One of the gunmen locked the restaurant door. Turned the deadbolt.

The maitre d' just stood there, dumbstruck.

"What the—?" Fern said.

"Everyone stay still and no one will get hurt!" the taller gunman shouted. He held his gun high.

His yellow gun.

What?

"Don't anyone look at us!" the other one shouted. He had a black gun.

They were moving all over the small restaurant, quickly, restlessly, as though searching for something or someone. Fern looked over at me.

"Don't worry," I whispered. "It's not real."

"What?" she whispered loudly.

"No talking!" The shorter one was at our table.

He had the bluest eyes. And the slightest of accents.

He had the bluest familiar eyes.

He looked at me and squinted.

"Enrique?" I whispered to the gunman. Enrique deChamp had been the leading man in our first movie, *Love and Other Insanities*. He had been a rising star then and had taken a chance on our indie movie. He had taken a chance on two new writers and a movie few people thought would go anywhere. It had paid off for all of us. At least it had then. I hadn't seen much of Enrique in quite a few years. Had heard rumors of drug and/or alcohol abuse.

A fellow lost soul on this rocky sober road?

"Brooke?" he whispered, leaning down to get a better look at me. "God damn!"

"No talking!" the other man screamed. "Everyone under the tables!"

"Mom!" Fern said. She ducked under our table.

"It's fine, Fern," I said.

"It's not fine! We're being held hostage!"

"I know this man," I said.

"Now he'll have to kill us!"

"Sense the room, Fern," I said. "He's holding a fucking squirt gun."

"Which could be filled with poison!" she said.

"Enrique," I said, "what the fuck are you doing?"

I got under the table, too, and Enrique squatted next to us. I glanced up and saw a phone number scratched into the underneath of the table. "Julia. Will work for oranges. Call xxx xxx-xxxx."

Really? Who did she think would see her number there? Why had *she* been under the table?

"The police are going to be here in two seconds," I said to Enrique. "You've got to get out of here."

"It's not a real robbery," Enrique said. "It's an audition. No one has called the cops."

"An audition!" I said. "Christ! Every single person in here has a cellphone. The cops *are* coming!"

"John Maloney was supposed to be here," Enrique said.

"John Maloney, the director?" I whispered. "He's not here!"

I glanced around the room, although it was difficult to see everyone who was underneath a table at this point.

"He's casting for that new thriller," Enrique said. "*Ten Most Wanted.* About a serial killer who kills people on the FBI's top ten wanted list. I want to be that killer. So I thought this would be a good way to show him my range. Since *Love and Other Insanities*, I've been typecast. Everyone thinks I'm gay."

"You weren't gay in that movie," I said.

"No, I was hetero sensitive," he said. "Same thing."

"But aren't you gay in real life?" Fern asked.

"No," he said. "I've got a family to feed, and I haven't had an acting job in a couple of years."

"Gay people have families to feed, too," Fern said.

"Oh my god," I said. "Can we have this conversation later? John Maloney isn't here and you're about to be arrested for kidnapping or whatever and grand larceny." I glanced over at the other guy. He was taking jewelry from the restaurant customers. "Is he an actor, too?"

"Sure," Enrique said.

"Don't tell me his name," I said. "Come on. Let me get you out of here."

"Mom!" Fern said. "What are you doing? They're criminals. You can't *help* them!"

"They're not criminals," I said. "Those aren't even prop guns. I told you. They're fucking squirt guns. I promise." I shook my head. "Christ, Enrique, how stupid can someone be?"

I heard sirens.

Enrique's baby blues suddenly looked terrified.

I got up from underneath the table.

"Hey, you!" the other gunman shouted at me.

"Hey, you!" I shouted back.

Enrique stood, too, and motioned to his partner. I leaned down and said to Fern, "Stay here. I won't be long." I hurried to the rear of the restaurant and through the doors into the kitchen with Enrique and his friend following close behind me. For some reason, the kitchen was completely empty. Maybe everyone had run away?

"My god," I said, when the doors swung closed behind us. "How could you think this was a good idea in this day and age when crazy people are running around everywhere shooting people in malls and restaurants and schools? That's just fucking stupid. And it's not very nice."

Enrique pulled off his mask and shook his head. "No one would have been hurt. It was all planned! Maloney was supposed to be here with a big group. Our friend Manny arranged it for us. We'd pretend to be bad guys, and then we'd give the director our cards and say it was an audition."

"Worst idea ever," I said. "You know directors. Biggest control freaks on the fucking planet. You think anyone likes to have the shit scared out of them?"

"But Maloney is supposed to be a man's man," Enrique said. "He'd understand. I know he'd understand."

"Couldn't your agent get you an audition?"

"She dropped me."

"I didn't see Manny," the other man said. He reached up to take off his hood.

"Leave it on," I said. "I don't want to know who you are."

But it was too late. The hood was off. The other burglar was a nondescript twenty-something man.

I put my hand up. "Don't tell me your name. I'll just call you John Doe. You both have got to get out of here now. You could go to prison for a long time if they catch you."

John Doe started pulling out jewelry and watches from his pockets. He held them out to me.

"Jesus," I said as I took the jewelry from him.

"It worked," he said. "They believed me. They fucking believed me as a thief. I've never stolen anything in my life. I *am* a fucking good actor."

He raised his gloved hand in anticipation of a high five from Enrique.

Enrique gave him one.

At least they had worn gloves.

"You've got to go," I said. "Out the back, near the overturned milk crates, there's a gate. Go through that and then get out of fucking Dodge. And don't ever do anything like this again."

"What about the guns?" Enrique said. "Should we leave them here? It's proof we weren't really robbing the place."

They handed me their guns, and then they were out the door, after Enrique shouted, "Call me!"

I looked down at the guns and jewels in my hands. I set the jewels on the island counter. Then I grabbed a towel and wiped down the plastic guns, just in case. I picked up everything again and walked back through the swinging doors and into the dining room.

"It's okay," I said. "You can get up now. They're gone. Here are your jewels and watches." I held them up. "Someone should let the police in before they batter down the doors."

The diners emerged from under their protective tables.

"You saved us," one of them said.

Someone else said, "It's Brooke McMurphy. The writer. She saved the day."

Someone knew what a writer looked like? Someone knew what *I* looked like?

People began to clap. Several uniformed cops came through the door. Fern was watching me, shaking her head.

"No," I said. "I didn't save anyone. They weren't real robbers. It was an audition gone bad. You know actors. Kind of stupid sometimes."

"What?" someone said. "What did she say?"

Two of the policemen pulled out their guns and pointed them

at me. They were shouting. Goddamn it, they were shouting so loudly that I could barely understand.

"No, no, you assholes," I heard someone say. "She's not the criminal. She fucking saved all these people." Then the someone stepped between me and the boys in blue.

My daughter, Fern.

Several other people did the same thing.

"No, she's one of *us*," one of them said. "The robbers went out the back."

I said, "They aren't robbers. See, I've got all the stuff."

The cops ran past me. I was tempted to trip them, but I realized in time that would be wrong. Customers came up to me and took back their jewelry. I had no idea if everyone got back their right jewels. Another cop tried to stop them, saying something about evidence. But my hands were soon empty. Even the squirt guns were gone. I think I accidentally on purpose dropped them into the garbage.

More than one person came by to say thank you. I saw admiration in their eyes, and that made me uncomfortable. I straightened my little red dress—why had I worn a dress?—and said, "It was nothing. They were actors. It was an audition."

I felt a lot of goodwill in that room.

I should have known it would not last.

TWO

The cops talked to all of us for far too long. They interviewed me longer than anyone else. I kept saying, "They were actors. It was an audition. They didn't mean to scare anyone."

"How do you know?"

"They told me."

"Why did they tell *you*? Did you know them?"

"No! I saw they had fucking squirt guns," I said. "I figured they were out of their depth. I just wanted them gone so I could finish my breakfast, which is cold now, thank you very much."

In fact, it was way into the lunch hour.

Donna, the owner of Juliet's—she always wanted to be a Juliet—had her crew make us another breakfast, after she found them. They had all run off when they'd heard the gunmen come into the restaurant.

The media showed up. The paps and legit apparently. (They all look alike these days.) The maitre d' kept them out, but Donna asked if I would go talk to them.

"Me?" I said. "Why would they want to talk to me? No! I don't want to talk to them."

"Mom," Fern said, "this could be good publicity for the movie. You know the old saying, all publicity is good publicity."

"That is complete and utter bullshit," I said. "Whoever told you that is full of shit." I held up my hand. "If you're going to tell me I said that, I plead drunkenness."

She shook her head. "Sally said it."

"Sally is full of shit."

Donna was still standing next to our table, waiting. Apparently my "no" hadn't been adamant enough for her. She must be one of these people who believed everyone secretly wanted to be famous.

Let me tell you: I did not secretly or openly want to be famous. I wanted people to know my writing—people who could hire me for a job. But that was about it.

"No, Donna, I do not want to talk to the press," I said.

Donna shrugged and walked away. I continued noshing on my now fresh mushroom omelette.

"Mom, you could mention the movie," Fern said. "You could say this has given you ideas for the movie."

"The movie that I've supposedly already written?" I said. "The script the actors are waiting for? I can't go out and admit I haven't written a word of it."

"Are you kidding me?" Fern said. "Not a word?"

I shook my head.

"Don't worry," I said. "I've done this before."

"That's not reassuring," she said. "A lot of people are counting on you."

"I understand that completely," I said.

Donna came back to the table and cleared her throat. We looked at her.

"There's a Ruby Shirley out there," she said. "She says she knows you."

I sighed. Yes, Ruby was a friend from way back. She'd been kind to me during some tough times in my life: She never wrote about my . . . lifestyle. Neither did anyone else, but she knew the life I was leading.

I glanced at Fern. She mouthed, "Please." I shrugged.

"Okay," I said. "She can come join us. But no cameras."

"Of course," Donna said. "No cameras are ever allowed in here."

"Except for the hundreds of cell phones with cameras," I murmured as she walked away.

Soon Ruby Shirley was walking toward us. I smiled, got up, and embraced the woman. She was a little older than I was, small, curly graying hair, wide grin.

"You look good," she said to me. "Sobriety becomes you."

"You look like a Jewish grandma," I said. "Trolling for gossip becomes you."

She smiled.

"Sit," I said. "Ruby, this is my daughter, Fern Lightman."

The waiter brought Ruby a coffee, and then she asked us what happened. We told her. I left out the part about knowing the "actor" who pulled the stunt. Fern didn't say anything either.

"See," I said. "It's not newsworthy. Just a stupid kid who believed he could get a director's attention. No harm, no foul."

"Except no directors were here," Ruby said. "In fact, I got the list of people who were here and you two are the only movie people. The police told me you'd mentioned John Maloney, so I called his office. He's never even heard of Juliet's."

"I heard the man say John Maloney," Fern said.

"Look, Ruby," I said, "There's no story here. Now, tell me what you've been up to."

She put down her long reporter's pad. (Yep, she still used one.)

"You keep saying there's no story," she said. "That must mean there's a story."

We looked at each other for some long seconds. Then I smiled and said, "No, I'm just trying to extricate myself from this thing. I've got a deadline to finish up the sequel to *Beauty and the Zombie*, and I can't get hooked into anything else. Although this gives me ideas. Perhaps I'll have to add a scene in a place like Juliet's."

"I thought you were finished with *Escape from Alcatraz*," she said.

A fan then?

"You know, a writer's work is never done," I said.

Ruby looked over at Fern. She seemed to be about to ask Fern something and then decided against it.

"I'd love to get a backstage pass to the filming," Ruby said. "Jack Meredith directing this one too?"

I smiled. She knew the answer to that.

"Of course," I said.

"Bet that was tricky," she said.

"Why?" I asked. I glanced at Fern.

Ruby shrugged. "Heard you two had history."

"If my mother wasn't able to work with people she had 'history' with," Fern said, "she wouldn't be able to work. In the end, everyone loves my mother. Including Jack Meredith."

I looked at my daughter and then over at Ruby. Ruby smiled.

"She knows whereof she speaks," I said. "But no, we didn't have any trouble getting Meredith back. He loved the first script. He made a lot of money on the first one—we all did—and he'll make a lot on this one."

Although Jack Meredith was pissed that he hadn't seen a script yet. I had several unanswered texts from him.

"I can get you a pass," I said. "Sure." I wasn't sure, but I didn't want to talk about the robbery anymore. I wasn't a very good liar. Wasn't particularly good at secrets either. I didn't want to blurt out Enrique's name.

"Okay," Ruby said. "Doesn't look like there's anything to see here. Maybe we should have a bunch of directors do a PSA warning actors not to do stupid things like this." She picked up her notebook and then stood. She held out her hand. "It's nice seeing you again, Brooke. I'm glad you're doing so well. You deserve it."

We shook hands, she said goodbye to Fern, and then she left. Fern motioned the waiter over and ordered another Bloody Mary. When he was gone, she said, "Why was she so nice to you?"

"When Alberto died, she was one of the reporters they sent out to dog us. The others were assholes. She was kind. We became friends of a sort. I gave her a couple of exclusives and nudged others in her direction when she was having a difficult time a few years ago. She still tries to do journalism even though she's covering Hollywood."

"We don't want any real journalism, Mom," Fern said. "We don't want them to know the truth."

The waiter brought her drink, and she took a gulp. Then she looked at me.

"No, I'm not giving up drinking," she said. "I don't have to. But you have to come to my party. You owe me after entangling me in your little lie. Why the hell didn't you just keep quiet and let the police come and take them away?"

"Because I know what it's like to feel desperate," I said. "Enrique is making decisions from that desperate part of his brain. I've been lucky, Fern. You've been lucky. Your dad has been lucky. We're working. We can pay our bills. Enrique did a stupid thing, but he didn't deserve to go to jail. I wish he had called me. I would have put him in the film. Or talked Jack Meredith or your dad into giving him a part. He could be the alien leader."

"You mean Jonny Black's part?" she asked.

"No! Jonny's boss, if you will," I said. "The real alien leader. I could make him very bad."

"Are you seriously thinking of writing a part for him?" she asked.

"I might," I said.

Fern looked nervous. "I don't like the police involved," she said.

"Who does?" I said. "But Enrique and his accomplice were stupid not to figure the cops would come."

She nodded. She looked like there was something else she wanted to say.

"I didn't think they'd question *me*," she said. "I'm worried. I'm worried they might go back to the arson."

"There was no arson," I said quietly. "There was just a kid who didn't know any better. You're safe, Fern. There's no evidence, and no one is looking into it. They've built another house where the old one was. You're okay, darlin'. I wouldn't let any harm come to you."

She looked at me. We both knew I had let harm come to Alberto, her baby brother. I hadn't been able to stop SIDS. But I could stop an arson investigation should one begin. Couldn't I? Maybe not, but I was confident no one was going to go digging into the truth about a house fire that happened over ten years ago.

"This will all blow over," I said. "Betcha."

"But you're coming to the damn party?" Fern said.

"Yes, I'm coming to the damn party."

We finished breakfast, talked a bit about her brother who was now a teenaged boy without an ounce of obnoxiousness in his soul. Seemed Fern had gotten the whole kit and kaboodle when it came to teenage rebellion. Only she was no longer a teenager—although when she was around me, she certainly acted like one.

I hadn't been much of a mother when Fern was going through her tweens and teens. I barely remembered her childhood, but I couldn't admit that to her. She'd never let me live it down.

"Hey, Mom," Fern said as we got ready to leave, "I saw Mark the other day at Surfas. Did he mention it?"

"No," I said.

"Yeah," she said. "He was with some woman and a kid. A boy."

"You mean Ian?" I asked. "Was it his son Ian? You've met him. He's about 10 years old."

"I don't know," she said. "The woman was pretty."

I kept eating my omelette.

"I've met his ex," I said. "She is quite attractive. A nice woman. A little blond for my taste, but you know."

"She wasn't blond," Fern said.

I glanced at my daughter. What was she trying to do? I thought she had come to terms with her father and me being apart. In fact, I figured she thought it was better if we were apart since clearly, I didn't deserve the love of a good man like Hayword Lightman.

"She had dark brown hair," she said. "They were laughing and having a good ole time."

"Good," I said. "I wouldn't want him to be having a bad ole time. It was probably his sister."

"Really? They didn't seem like brother and sister."

My eyes narrowed. If Fern had been a friend, I would have said, "What the fuck are you trying to do? I'm not the jealous type, remember. I fucked half of Hollywood and never cared if they all were fucking the other half of Hollywood."

"Wait," I said. "Surfas? That's a little chichi for Mark."

She shrugged. "I wonder why he didn't tell you he'd seen me. You think there was something going on?"

"Fern," I said, "why are you trying to stir up trouble? I thought you liked Mark."

"I do like Mark," she said.

"Oh, so the implication is that you don't like me," I said.

"I just thought you'd want to know," she said. "The woman looked more like she was his age."

I started to laugh. "Fern, you are about as subtle as a Mack truck. Yes, I am older than Mark. But, we only fuck in the dark, so he can't really tell how old I am and vice versa."

"Mom, someone is going to hear you."

"You started it," I said. "Don't try to bust my balls, cuz honey, I don't have anything that easily crushed."

She put up a hand. "Just trying to help out."

"No, you weren't," I said. "You were being passive aggressive. If you're pissed at me, be pissed at me. If you have something to say to me, say it. This constant poking me, trying to get a reaction, is just fucking tiresome."

"I am not passive aggressive," she said. "I would never be passive aggressive. That would be following in your footsteps."

"What are you talking about?" I asked. "I've never been passive aggressive in my life."

"What do you call drinking?" she asked. "What do you call having sex with every other person you meet? Weren't you trying to get back at Dad? Weren't you trying to get back at us?"

"What?" I said. "Trying to get back at *you*? You mean you and David? No! Why would I want to get back at you? For what?"

"For surviving," she said. "For not being Alberto."

"Good grief," I said. "No. I wasn't trying to get back at your dad. Not really. I was trying to get back at myself. Trying to drown the pain. Or myself. I don't know. Fern, addiction is so complicated."

"And yet so simply destructive," she said.

"Yes," I said. "I am so sorry for the damage I did to you and your brother. But you know, honey, it's a disease. A brain disease. In many ways, I didn't have any control."

She rolled her eyes. I hated when she did that.

"Fern," I said. "I'm trying to talk to you about something important. You can be angry at me all you want. But I'm trying to tell you that addiction isn't much different from diabetes or asthma. Cancer. It's a disease. I can send you the studies. I blamed myself—I still blame myself—but one thing I learned in rehab is that it's not about willpower. It's about brain chemistry."

"I don't understand that," Fern said. "If it's a disease, why don't they just give you a pill? Why then does the addict have to decide to stop in order to get better?"

"That's confusing to me, too," I said. "I think it's because they don't really have a pill to make you stop. But every day, I have to decide not to follow the destructive messages from my brain. I have to decide not to drink. That's not always easy."

"You make it look easy," she said. "You never talk about it. I never see you go to AA. Most alkies I know talk about it all the time."

"I know," I said. I shrugged. "I figured you're not interested in my life. Why should I burden you with my struggles?"

"I wouldn't mind," Fern said. "I mean, you always look like things are so easy for you."

I laughed. "That is the art of an addict," I said. "We thrive on making everything look easy. Easy does it."

"I don't think that's what addicts say," Fern said. "Isn't that what they say in AA?"

"Um, everyone in AA is an addict, darlin'," I said. "So tomato, tomahto."

"I thought we were having an honest conversation."

"Sorry," I said. "Just habit. Trying to get out before I get speared by you."

Fern made a face. She used to make the same face when she was a kid, when I had caught her doing something wrong.

"So tell me how work has been," I said. Perfect parental dodge. It was either that or ask her how her car was running.

Fern looked at me. For an instant, I thought she was going to launch a stream of invectives at me. Instead, she said, "Except for Sally stressing out about being toppled from power, it's been going all right. We've got some new projects I'm excited about."

As she talked, I tried to figure out who Fern had seen Mark with. Didn't like that I was even wondering about it. A dark-haired woman his age or younger. Could be Sherry. She was the general manager at Mark's new restaurant. Marco's End of the Road Cafe. Yep. The café—and my house—was on a street called End of the Road. Someone had a stupid sense of humor when they named it. Or else, they had just run out of . . . imagination. Mark's childhood nickname was Marco. His mom and sister sometimes still called him that. So, there you go.

Anyway, Sherry Burns was his general manager. Not sure he really needed a GM for a place that pretty much only served breakfast, but I didn't know nothing about running no restaurant, so I kept my mouth shut. Sherry was nice enough. Used to be an actor until she gave up the life to have a kid and live the quiet life.

Like me.

Only I hadn't really lived the quiet life. I sometimes wondered if she had either. If I were truthful—and I tried to be nowadays—I'd have to admit I didn't really like her. She smiled too much. She seemed too upbeat. She was never sarcastic.

I didn't really understand her at all. Didn't trust her as far as I could see her. But I never suspected anything was going on between her and Mark.

I was sure it wasn't. They were probably just getting supplies.

"Sherry Burns," I said, interrupting Fern's description of an upcoming project at AFT.

"What?" she said.

"I bet he was with Sherry Burns," I said. "His general manager. She has dark hair, and she's got a kid. Of the boy variety, I think. Yep. Bet they were shopping for restaurant things."

Fern raised an eyebrow. "I thought you didn't care who it was?"

"I didn't," I said. "It just got stuck in my head."

She smiled. A triumphant smile.

"What?" I said.

"It's good to see you're human," she said.

"What else would I be?" I asked. "A zombie from one of my movies? Of course I'm human."

She shrugged. "Just saying."

"Sometimes you're a mean kid," I said.

"Like I said, I learned from the best."

After we finished our meal and I paid the tab, we walked out to the parking lot, kissed the air next to our cheeks, and then started toward our separate vehicles. But then I stopped and turned in her direction. "Hey, kiddo," I called.

"What?" She stopped and looked at me.

I smiled and held out my arms to her. She rolled her eyes, but she came over to me. I wrapped her up and held her close. I rocked her and buried my face in her neck and breathed deeply. "I love you, baby girl."

She sighed and did not put her arms around me.

"I'm not a baby girl," she said.

I kissed her on the cheek, she flinched, and I let her go. She hurried toward her car, as though it was 30 below zero and she had to get to some warm protected place before she froze to death. When she got to her car, she shouted, "I love you, too, old woman."

I flipped her off.

"Nice, Mom."

I smiled and got in my car.

It was good we were finally establishing a solid mother-daughter relationship. I knew my mother had wanted to flip me off most of my life and never had.

It was early enough that I could either go to my writing studio (the former love nest) or to the ocean house without encountering much traffic.

I should go to the studio and write the damn script.

But I wasn't in the mood.

I drove home.

Hardly any traffic and soon enough I could feel the difference in the air, in the world. And then there was the Pacific Ocean. I breathed deeply.

Just then someone on the radio said, "Don't breathe too deeply, friends. The radiation is hitting the coast just about now. Get out those Geiger counters. Check your fish. Your greens. Stay out of the rain. Or just ignore all of this and pretend we are not living in the end times. It's all whackadoodle, my lovelies."

I glanced at my radio. "Who are you?" I asked.

Must be talking about the plume of radiation leaking from the nuclear power plant in Japan. I thought that had come and gone. I shook my head. I should really get my children away from this place.

"Ain't nowhere else to go," the radio said. "We're going to hell in a handbasket. Bet you wish you hadn't quit drinking after all. We're all zombies, baby."

"What the fuck?" I said. I pushed the button on the radio and changed the station to some old time rock 'n' roll. Led Zeppelin. No DJ.

I parked the car behind my house and then walked up the drive to the café, which was on the bottom floor. Mark's pickup was at the front of the house, so I knew he was there.

I opened the front door—and smiled. The place smelled of fresh bread and basil. Or butter. Even from here, at the front door, I could see the ocean stretching out beyond us.

"Mark?"

I heard music coming from the kitchen. I glanced around the dining room—tasteful and small—and walked to the kitchen. The cooler door was open and Mark was bending over to retrieve something inside. I came up behind him and grabbed his ass.

"Hey there, superman," I said.

And then I knew something was off. Mark's ass had suddenly gotten flabby.

The man at the fridge jumped and turned around.

I laughed.

It wasn't Mark.

It was his brother-in-law, Giovanni, holding a cooked chicken leg in his right hand.

"Sorry about that," I said. "You and Mark have very similar asses."

"Uh, thank you, I think," Giovanni said. He was clearly embarrassed. I was amused.

"I was just—" he started.

"Sampling the food?" I asked. "He's a great cook, isn't he?"

Giovanni had worked at AFT for almost two years, but then he got fired or laid off. Or maybe he quit. I couldn't be sure. He was a lawyer, had passed the bar and everything, but he couldn't seem to hold on to a job to save his life.

"Yeah, sure," he said. "Great cook. He's around here somewhere. Said I could raid the fridge."

Giovanni always acted like he had just gotten caught with his hand in the cookie jar. He never seemed comfortable around me.

Wasn't quite sure why. Maybe he sensed I thought he was a loser. People knew when someone wasn't on their side. I was actually. I rooted for him. I wanted him to succeed because he was part of Mark's family. But he made one bad choice after another.

Of course, right this second I couldn't think of what other bad choices he had made, besides blowing a gig at AFT. Sally tended to surround herself with people she liked and trusted—people who did good work and were loyal. All Giovanni needed to do was be good at his job. But something had gone wrong, and he no longer worked at AFT. I didn't ask him why. Wasn't my business.

Mark came into the kitchen. He put his arm around my waist, and we kissed.

"I just grabbed your bro-in-law's ass," I said. "Mistook it."

"Mistook it for mine?" He leaned around as if trying to look at Giovanni's ass. "I have a much better ass than that."

"Fer sure," I said.

"All right," Giovanni said. "Can we move on?"

"Gee is helping me tie up some loose ends here," Mark said.

I didn't remember Giovanni being particularly handy. In fact, he was kind of a klutz at home repair. The first time I met him, he was working on the kitchen sink at Mark's mother's house, and he practically flooded her out of home and house.

"Don't you have a contractor for that?" I asked.

Mark shrugged and looked away from me. Ah, something else was going on here. I'd ask him later. I put my arm around Mark's waist, and we walked into the small dining room.

"You wouldn't believe the morning I had," I said.

"You were with Fern," he said. "So I'd pretty much believe anything."

I laughed. "Actually didn't have anything to do with her," I said. "Two actors pretended to rob Juliet's as an audition for a movie role. And on the way home, some guy on the radio seemed to be talking to me."

"How does someone pretend to rob a restaurant? And what was the radio guy talking to you about?"

"They had squirt guns," I said. "And once I figured that out, I asked them what was going on and one of them told me it was an audition."

"Crazy ass actors," he said.

"No shit," I said. "And Mark, I knew—"

Just then Sherry came into the restaurant, hurrying through the front door.

"You're on the news, Brooke," Sherry said. "They say you're some kind of hero." She came over to us and showed us her big screen phone. I didn't really understand why these phones kept getting bigger. Pretty soon people were going to be walking around with big screen phones in their overly large purses. Until the trend changed and everyone had a tiny phone again.

Couldn't keep up.

On the screen, I saw some blow-dried Botoxed woman with breasts out to there looking at some blow-dried Botoxed man with no soul in his eyes as he said, "Yes, Jenna, that old saying that writers will save the world came true today, didn't it?" Then they laughed. Jenna said, "Maybe Brooke McMurphy will once again save us from the zombies in her upcoming movie *Beauty and the Zombies Part Two: Escape from Alcatraz*. I for one can't wait. I toured Alcatraz once. Just fabulous."

"And there you have it, folks," the man said. "We have our own escapee from Alcatraz in this studio. Maybe she'll get a part in *Beauty and the Zombie Part Two*. Me, I'm holding out for Part Three."

Then they laughed.

Sherry tapped the screen, and it went dark.

"You wrestled guns from robbers?" Sherry asked. Her eyes were wide.

"No!" I said. "They were actors."

"They didn't mention that," Sherry said. "Just said the bad guys escaped but not before you got all the stolen goods back."

Mark looked at me. I dropped my arm from his waist.

"That's not what happened," I said. "This is why I hate the media. They get everything wrong."

"Aren't you part of the media?" Sherry asked.

"No," I said, "I am part of the *entertainment* industry. Completely different. We just make stuff up."

"Sounds like that's what they did, too," Mark said.

"Yep," I said.

"How exciting!" Sherry said. "Were you scared?"

"No," I said. "I was annoyed."

Sherry was smiling at me. She wanted to hear more. I'd already told the tale to the police. I didn't feel like telling it again, at least not to her. To Mark, Hayword, David. Maybe. Might stress out David. He was always worrying about the end of the world.

"Hey, Sherry and I have a meeting," Mark said. "Big opening coming up soon."

"Yes, I know," I said. I smiled. "You kids go have fun. I'll see you for dinner?" Mark nodded and kissed me.

"I want to hear all about your adventure later," Sherry said.

I gave her the thumbs up sign. "Can't wait to tell you."

Mark gave me a look. I shrugged, almost imperceptibly. I got my keys and went to the locked door that opened on the stairs leading up to my apartment. I could get into my apartment this way or go around to the back.

Now I unlocked the door, started up the steps, then closed the door behind me. I hurried up the rest of the stairs to our place. Truth to tell, I wasn't sure I really wanted a restaurant in my home. When I'd bought this place, I thought it would be perfect for Mark and me. He'd have his restaurant; I'd have my peace and quiet. But how much peace and quiet would I have with a restaurant below me? It was only going to be open four hours a day, five days a week. So that wouldn't be too bad. At least, that was what I told myself. It had been my idea, so I couldn't back out now.

My phone was buzzing in my purse. The house phone was ringing. (Yes, I still had a landline. I liked it better than the cell phone. Cell phones were turning us into zombies.)

I pulled out my cell phone. David.

As I answered it, I walked over to the landline to see who was calling.

The police.

The police?

"David, hang on," I said. Then I picked up the other phone. "Hang on," I said. "I've got my son on the other phone." Back to the cell phone. "Everything okay, David?"

"You were robbed?"

"No!" I said. "I thought the school confiscated cell phones at the beginning of the day."

"We were in the computer lab," he said.

They still had computer labs?

"No, I wasn't robbed, honey," I said. I could hear the panic in his voice.

"And the radiation is coming," he said. "They found a two-headed whale."

"I bet that didn't have anything to do with the radiation," I said. "Darlin', I've got another call, but I promise you everything is okay. I can come pick you up from school today, if you want. I'll text your dad."

"Okay," he said.

He ended the call. I put the other phone to my ear.

"This is Brooke McMurphy," I said.

"This is Detective Alex Baxter," he said. "I have some questions for you about today's robbery at Juliet's. Can you come down to the station?"

"I was just in the city," I said. "I answered questions already. Don't you have the notes? It wasn't a robbery. It was a job audition. A screwed-up job audition."

"But there was no one to audition for," he said, "except for you and your daughter."

"My daughter?" I felt a knot in my stomach. "My daughter is an assistant to a studio head. She doesn't have any power. And I'm a freaking writer. No one listens to us. I don't hire actors. This was *not* for my benefit!"

"But you figured out it was an audition," he said. "You helped them escape."

"I figured out it was something besides a robbery when I saw the squirt guns," I said.

"No one else figured that out?"

"It happened so quickly," I said. "One of the guys told me it was an audition, and then I took them to the back room. They gave me the jewelry and stuff and left. End of story. Don't you have real crimes to investigate?"

How to win friends and influence people.

"This is a crime, Mrs. McMurphy," Baxter said.

"I don't have time for this," I said.

"You better make time," he said. "And you might want to bring along your lawyer."

"My lawyer?" I said. "What for? I didn't do anything wrong."

"You helped two felons escape from the scene of a crime," Baxter said.

"No," I said, "I did no such thing. I encouraged two actors to stop being stupid and to leave the premises."

"The truth of all of that is yet to be determined," he said. "Maybe a jury will have to sort it out."

"Are you calling me a liar?" I asked.

He didn't say anything.

I made a noise. "Look, do you know Philip Case? He works in Major Crimes. Or major case. I don't know what they call it. He knows me. He'll vouch for me."

"It doesn't really work that way, ma'am," Baxter said.

"Can't you just call him?" I asked. "He'd tell you I'm the last person who would go out of my way to help someone, especially a criminal. I'm law-abiding. Keep my nose clean. Etc."

"I do know Phil," he said. "I'll call him. But just because he *knows* you, it doesn't mean he knows you. Everyone has their dark side."

"I know," I said. "That is my dark side. I don't go out of my way to help anyone. And I don't think we're supposed to say dark side. That's equating darkness with evil, and that's racist. Maybe we should say anti-social? Or our criminal side?"

"The media is calling you a hero," he said. "We hate heroes."

"I hate the media," I said.

"I thought all you movie types loved the media."

"I'm not a movie type," I said. "I'm a writer. I don't like the glitz and glory. I don't even know how the media got this story."

"You did that zombie movie," he said.

"Yes." I hesitated. Did he love it or hate it?

"I don't really understand zombies," Baxter said.

"Me neither," I said. "That's why I made them into aliens."

"Yeah, that makes a little more sense."

"I wrote *Love and Other Insanities*," I said. "Many lifetimes ago."

"I saw that," he said. "Really liked it. Took my wife to it early on, when we were dating. Seemed like an honest film."

One thing I loved about Los Angeles—and sometimes hated about it—was that you could go anywhere and talk about movies to anyone. Everyone had an opinion. It was such a company town.

"Thanks," I said.

"Being in love is a little bit like insanity," Baxter said.

"Yes."

How could I get out of this?

"But zombies?" he said.

"My husband asked me to help him out with the script," I said. "I didn't want to do it, but I wanted to make him happy. Love and other insanities, you know."

"It was kind of . . . cute," he said. "My wife is really looking forward to the next one."

I wanted to offer to get him opening night tickets, but I had enough sense to keep my mouth shut. I didn't want to sound like I was trying to bribe him.

"I'll call Phil and then get back with you," he said.

"Thank you, Detective Baxter," I said. "I appreciate it."

Since I had stopped drinking my head was so much clearer: I could actually remember names, places, times.

People seemed to appreciate being remembered.

"Thank you, Mrs. McMurphy," the cop said. I didn't correct him. I wasn't Mrs. anyone. Never had been.

I was glad the call was over. Two other people had called my cell phone while I was on the phone with the cop. Media outlets.

Man. The longer I was in the media spotlight, I knew, the worse it was going to be. I hadn't done anything wrong. Not really. But I knew that in the media one could go from hero to whore in about 60 seconds flat. My 60 seconds were just about over.

THREE

I didn't want to interrupt Mark's meeting—or deal with Sherry's cheerfulness—so I texted Mark I was leaving, texted Hayword I was picking up David, and then I went out the back way to my car.

I hadn't even been home ten minutes.

Fern called me before I was out the driveway. I sat still and listened to her yell at me.

"Mother! What have you done? The police want to talk to me. They think we had something to do with this. Why did you lie?"

"Fern," I said, "I did not lie. Can we talk in person or on one of my burner phones." Was that what they called them? "Just in case someone is listening. You don't have to talk to the police. You didn't do anything wrong. Just tell them you're too busy to talk to them."

"I am too busy!"

"There you go," I said. "I just talked to the detective on the case. I told him you had nothing to do with it. I told him I had nothing to do with it. That's the truth, Fern."

"Okay, okay," she said. "Sally is ecstatic."

"Did you say *ecstatic*?"

"Yes! It was all over the news, and most of the reports mentioned the movie. Great free publicity. They're calling you a hero."

I didn't mention that the detective was not calling me a hero. In fact, he seemed to be calling me an accomplice. I was going to kill Enrique.

"I gotta get David," I said. "He heard about it and is a bit scared. Heard about the radiation coming, too."

"Little freak," Fern said. "We're all going to fucking die anyway, what's his problem?"

"His problem is he's 14 years old and he shouldn't have to worry about radiation or maniacs coming into restaurants threatening to kill everyone."

"They didn't actually threaten to kill anyone," she said.

"What?"

"They didn't threaten to kill anyone," she said.

What was going on here? Suddenly she was defending the faux robbers?

"So you don't think I need to go talk to the cops again?" Fern asked.

"No," I said, "but ask Sally, and ask for the company lawyer if you do go. Remember, you didn't know the so-called gunmen. You'd never seen them before."

"I don't know them!" she said.

"Good," I said. "I was just reminding you."

Christ. Why was every conversation with my daughter so fraught with . . . peril, nuance, atomic war, end of life as we knew it?

Soon enough, we ended the phone call, and I headed back to

my own 'hood, sort of, to pick up David at his school. My phone kept vibrating, but I didn't answer. I had promised David years ago that I wouldn't talk and drive. I also promised him I wouldn't drink and drive. I didn't do that either. Anymore.

I was a few minutes early, so I parked the car under the tall eucalyptus trees near the school and sat back in my seat and closed my eyes. When I lived at the big house with Hayword and the children, I had gotten more down time than I did now. We had a huge back yard—beautiful back yard—and a garden house. Even though I was drunk for most of the time I lived there, I still appreciated the solitude and quietude. Plus it was across the street from Joan Donning, who was the closest thing I had to a best friend. She was completely fucked up—as most of us are—but she was fun to be around, even now that I wasn't drinking. And now that I wasn't drinking, she didn't seem as stupid. Or more to the point, I tried not to categorize people as stupid or not stupid. Perhaps I was just a wee bit more compassionate than I had been in the past.

Maybe not.

The phone buzzed and would not stop.

I finally answered it.

"What the fuck?" Hayword's voice.

"Hello to you, husband o' mine," I said.

"You were robbed?"

"I wasn't robbed," I said. Gawd. How often was I going to have to tell this story? "They were actors trying to audition for a role, only the director they were auditioning for wasn't there. I sent them on their way and all was well."

"Not *that* well," he said. "Philip just called and said some detective Baxter called him and wanted Phil to vouch for you, vouch for you that you wouldn't be involved in helping criminals escape the long arm of the law. Philip didn't know what to say."

"What do you mean he didn't know what to say?" I sat up

in my seat. The kids were beginning to stream out of the school. "He better have said all good things. You've gotten him more consulting jobs on more shows than I can shake a stick at."

Granted not a great metaphor, but I was rattled.

"In other words, we've made him rich," I said.

"Not quite," Hayword said. "He did say nice things about you to this Baxter, but he wants to talk to you later. You're not mixed up with anything, are you?"

"Hayword," I said. "That's a stupid question."

"Doesn't it all seem strange to you?"

"Actors always seem strange to me," I said. "Maybe they were high or on drugs. I don't know. I just know they didn't really have guns, and everyone got back their jewelry and whatnots."

I saw David coming out of the school building. I stuck my hand out the window and waved. It was February, but it was warm out for a Midwestern gal like me, so I had driven up the hill with my windows down.

"I see David," I said. "You at the house? I'll be up in a bit."

Hayword was saying something, but it was too late. I had already pushed end call.

"Hiya, sugar," I called to David. He grinned and waved. He always looked glad to see me. I loved that about him. I did him a favor, though. I didn't get out of the car and hug and kiss him in front of all of his friends. He did have friends now. He had his own group of fellow geeks—if that was even what they called smart technologically capable people these days. Maybe they were just called teens. In any case, some of David's anxieties had lifted once he had more friends. And then he got a girlfriend and then later another girlfriend. Although now he had a different set of anxieties.

He was so gorgeous. Looked a lot like his father with some of my softening features to make him drop-dead gorgeous. My guess was that once he reached sixteen, the girls (and some of the boys) would be swooning over him.

He got in the passenger seat next to me.

"Hey, Mom," he said.

"Hey, kiddo," I said. I started up the car and drove us carefully around the other kids looking for their rides. David's school didn't have any buses. Buses were for the poor or for parents who didn't care enough about their kids to pick them up. Yep. That was the attitude.

"So what happened?" David asked. "Why were you in the news?"

"I was in the news because there are hardly any true journalists left in the world," I said, "and certainly none in Hollywood." Maybe Ruby. "There were two actors who were trying out for a role, so they were pretending to be criminals."

"How'd you figure it out?" he asked. "Were you afraid?"

"I wasn't afraid," I said.

I didn't get afraid like that. The worst thing had happened— one of my children had died—so I didn't sweat the small or big stuff. Of course, I had been afraid something might happen to my other kids, afraid something might happen to Hayword, and afraid of feeling my grief and despair over Alberto's death for a long while. But that was different. I didn't have the free-floating anxiety that haunted David.

If I had it at one time, I didn't remember anymore. Now I was more afraid of taking a drink than I was of radiation, climate change, or creeps with guns. Didn't know what to do about any of it, anyway, so why be afraid?

I did feel some responsibility in fixing these things so that my kids didn't have to live their lives in fear and misery. So I gave money here and there, and I tried to live the simple life. As simple as a Hollywood mogul can live.

Not that I was a mogul.

With David, we had tried to change his diet, had sent him to a therapist, had put him on medication. He was better, but he still had these attacks of anxiety, and we weren't sure why.

Maybe because he was the only one in the family who was actually paying attention.

I had had some anxiety attacks after Alberto died, but I had buried those with medication. After a time, they stopped. Maybe because I drank them away.

"Did you hear about the moon?" David asked. "It's so close to the Earth they think the tides might be really high and low. We should go to the ocean and see. Could be so low some ancient civilization might be uncovered."

"I thought the full moon meant the undead would roam the planet," I said.

"Who told you that?" David asked.

I laughed. "I heard it through the grapevine. Or maybe I'm just trying to get in the mood to write my script."

"Maybe that's why you were robbed today," he said.

"I wasn't actually robbed," I said, "but, hell, let's blame the full moon and Mercury retrograde on people being stupid."

"Can we do that every month?" David asked.

"Done!" I said.

"I did find a place online that said there was an ancient prophecy about this time of year and this moon and some other astrological things," David said. "Mountains will fall and the earth will open. And that which was dead will come alive."

"See," I said. "I told you I heard it through the grapevine."

"I don't believe it," David said. "They were vague about who the prophets were. One place said it was a Vedic prophecy, and another place said it was Navajo. I've decided it is bullshit."

"Good decision," I said. "One less thing to worry about."

Joanie was walking up our drive when I pulled in. She waved with the hand that was holding the martini.

David started talking before he was out of the car. "Aunt Joanie, Mom got robbed by two actors. It's all over the news. They're calling her a hero."

"Hi, David," Joanie said. "She's not a hero anymore."

I got out of the car. "What are you talking about?"

David pulled out his pad and looked at it. The three of us walked toward the house as the front door opened and Hayword stepped out.

"She's right, Mom," David said. "It's trending away from hero. Now they're saying the police suspect it was a publicity stunt—and you're part of it."

"What?"

"I just heard," Hayword said. "Come in. All of you."

For an instant I wanted to snap at him, "It's my goddam house, too," but then I remembered I was the one who had left the house and the marriage. I was the one who was living at the seaside with the man I had been fucking for a year, more or less, before I finally left Hayword. Before I finally stopped drinking—and then left Hayword.

Hayword wasn't a bad man. He was a good man, actually. Even though I had caught him fucking some blonde bimbo right after Alberto died. That image was seared into my brain. Granted, I had already cheated on him—that's how we got Alberto in the first place—but it didn't matter. He screwed some woman with fake breasts, and I had wanted to kill them both.

Instead, I stayed with Hayword and cheated on him nearly every day of the next ten years, more or less. Publicly. I mean, I didn't hide it from him or anyone else, really.

To this day, I couldn't forgive him for the image in my brain of him fucking that woman up against the wall, or up against the copy machine, or wherever it had been. It seemed so crass and brutal and animal-like.

So I started drinking. Not that I blamed him for my drinking. Not anymore. Maybe I started drinking before that. When Alberto died.

It didn't matter. None of that mattered.

I went into the house with Hayword, Joanie, and David. Violeta—who had been our housekeeper before I left—wasn't there. Someone still came in to clean and cook occasionally, but we—or they—didn't have full-time help any longer. We figured we all needed to learn to take care of ourselves. Violeta had her own housekeeping company now, so she still worked for us, sort of, even though we seldom saw her anymore.

"Brooke," Hayword said, touching my elbow. "Phil wants you to call him ASAP." He handed me his phone. Phil's number was right there. I walked away from the chatter in the kitchen.

"Phil," I said when he answered. "This is Brooke."

"I heard you had an adventure today," Philip said.

"I wouldn't call it that," I said. "It's turning into a big pain in the ass. Can you get the police off my case?"

"I talked to Baxter," he said. "He's an okay guy."

"They're saying in the news that police think I had something to do with it," I said. "Phil, you've known me forever. When have I tried to get publicity for anything?"

"You might want to get your publicist on this," Phil said. "An hour ago, the media was singing your praises. Now they're talking about your imminent arrest."

"Arrest?" I must have yelled this because everyone else stopped talking. I glanced toward the kitchen. They were all looking at me. I waved them away and then walked into Hayword's office and closed the door behind me. "What could they arrest me for? I don't have a fucking publicist! Phil, I don't want publicity!"

"Then the studio you work for," he said. "Something. You need to get on top of this."

"This is crazy," I said. "I didn't do anything except tell two actors to quit being assholes. I stopped what was happening! I got all the jewelry back from the fake robbery. No one was hurt. What did I do wrong?"

"They could charge you with aiding and abetting," he said.

"But I didn't do that," I said.

"That's what we have a court system for," he said.

"Oh my god," I said. "Can't you do something? David is already a wreck about it." Okay, so I exaggerated. But I wasn't afraid of using my children in this small way if it meant it could help me avoid jail.

"I wish I could," he said. "I spoke up for you. The problem is that all the jewelry wasn't returned. One woman says she is missing a bracelet worth ten thousand dollars."

Oh Christ.

"Maybe she's lying," I said. "Maybe it's insurance fraud."

"Maybe," he said. "It's not my case. But when I suggested the woman might be lying to Baxter, he suggested *you* might be lying."

"Fuck, fuck, fuck," I said.

Philip didn't have an answer to that.

"Do you have any suggestions?" I asked.

"Get a lawyer," he said, "and talk to your studio. Maybe they can spin this back in your favor. It is Hollywood, you know."

Christ on a stick.

"Okay," I said. "I appreciate all you did, Phil. Thank you."

I stared at the phone. Now what was I going to do? Had Enrique or his friend actually pocketed someone's bracelet? This was why I should never get involved in anyone else's life. I should have just let the police storm the restaurant and arrest them.

Clare Boothe Luce was right: "No good deed goes unpunished."

Now I'd have to find Enrique and get the damn bracelet, and I'd have to talk to Sally St. James about all of this. But I couldn't.

I couldn't let her know I had actually helped these people because I knew one of them.

Stupid. I had thought Enrique was stupid. Lord love a duck. *I* had not acted very intelligently either.

First, I needed to reassure my son, and then I needed to do some major damage control.

I went into the kitchen. Hayword opened his arms to give me a hug. Normally, I didn't want to get that close to Hayword. It was just too familiar. Too strange. Right this minute, I felt a wee bit vulnerable—which in the past would have caused me to act nastiest to the person who was being nicest to me. But I went into Hayword's arms. It did feel familiar, and it did feel nice.

"Okay," Joanie said after a bit, "get a room. Or tell me what's going on."

David said, "Yeah."

I laughed and pulled away from my husband.

"It'll be fine," I said. "I was a witness to an audition, but the cops believe it was an attempted robbery." I didn't say they believed this because a ten thousand dollar bracelet was missing. "It'll all get straightened out. I probably need to talk to Sally, though. David, you want me to make you a snack?"

David rolled his eyes, and Hayword laughed.

"Hey, I can put peanut butter and jelly on a piece of bread as well as the next person."

"Darling," Joanie said, "that's what we have maids for."

"We don't have a maid," I said.

"Mom, I don't eat peanut butter," David said. "It can have a fungus that causes liver cancer."

"David, you have got to stop reading that shit," I said. "We buy only organic peanut butter."

He shook his head. "Nope. Doesn't matter. Peanuts—"

Hayword held up his hand. He and I both knew this listing of toxins in the environment meant David was stressed. Probably worried about me going to jail.

"I will make us all a snack," Hayword said. "Joanie, you want to stay? Brooke, go make your phone calls."

Hayword went to the fridge. Joanie sat on one of the kitchen stools and sipped her martini.

I put my arm around David's waist. "How's your science project coming?"

He nodded. "It's good," he said.

"You want to tell us about it?" I asked.

"Not yet," he said.

"You're not going to make zombies of us all, are you?" I asked.

"Too late," David said.

He was smiling. I squeezed him and then let him go.

"I'm actually looking for a cure for zombies," he said, "so you can use it in the movie."

"Cool," I said. "I'll steal any good idea. I might even steal some bad ideas. Just pitch them to me."

"I think you should have her alien zombie baby burst out of her belly like in *Alien*," Joanie said. "At the very beginning of the movie."

"That would mean she'd die," I said, "at the very beginning of the movie. She's a big star. We want her for the third movie."

Oh good grief. I was talking like Sally St. James—like a studio head. I was talent. I was the writer. I couldn't think like an exec.

"She *can't* die!" David said. "Why'd you make her pregnant anyway, Mom? You always said it was lazy writing when writers could only think of two things to do to a woman: rape her or get her pregnant. Wouldn't she have used protection, especially in a world where people were dying of a mysterious contagious illness?"

I leaned against the counter and glanced at Hayword. He smiled and shrugged as he peeled carrots.

"I didn't say it was *always* bad writing. But often. I just loved the shot, though. I loved how the camera came around and then you saw she was pregnant. Chilling."

David and Joanie nodded.

"Yes, I'm sure she used protection, David, my son. But such things are not always 100 percent."

"Besides," Joanie said, "we don't know about alien sperm. They could have eaten right through any condoms."

"Alien zombie sperm," I said.

"Okay, I give," David said. "No more talking about sperm, sex, or condoms."

I laughed. David was beginning to relax, so now I could, too.

"I'll make these calls and be right back," I said.

I went up the stairs to my old office. I hadn't used it when I lived here, and it was still unused. Hayword hadn't changed a thing. It was a shrine to . . . me. To me not using it. I sat at the desk and called Sally St. James.

"What the fuck, Brooke?" Sally said. "You go to lunch and now there's an international scandal. You know, you were a lot more discreet when you were drinking."

"Fuck you," I said. "First my daughter tries to get me to drink and now you."

"Really? Geez. I was just kidding. We've got our lawyer, Stanley Takata, standing by to go with you to the police station. You remember Stan, don't you? Good guy."

"I don't want to go," I said.

"Why? If you didn't do anything wrong—"

"I can't believe you just said that. Lots of people who 'don't do anything wrong' end up in jail. I gave the police a statement at the time. If they want to charge me with something, show me the evidence and charge me. Otherwise, I don't want to go down there."

Sally made a noise. "Brooke, can't you ever do anything the easy way?"

I thought for a moment, and then I said, "I do lots of things the easy way. That's how I often get in trouble."

"Okay, I'll have Stan talk to the police on your behalf," Sally said. "On the behalf of AFT. He'll tell them that this wasn't a publicity stunt. You'd never be involved in anything like this, and we'd never be involved in anything like this." She paused. "You weren't involved in this, were you?"

"Of course not!" I said. "Like I want any publicity."

"You've got it," Sally said. "The publicity, I mean. First there was this nice photo of you and Hayword. You look so much like middle America. They talked about *Love and Other Insanities*. Then an hour later, the photo they showed was one taken right before rehab. I don't know where they got it. You look like hell. They noted your stint in rehab. Noted the monstrous success of *Beauty and the Zombie*. But they said you had a reputation for living *la vida loca*."

"Oh Christ on a freaking cross," I said.

I was mortified.

"Maybe it's only on the local news," I said. "I mean, who the hell cares about this kind of stuff?"

"Wish I could reassure you," Sally said. "But the media smells a scandal. *TMSleez* and *ET* are both running with it. They called AFT and asked us for a comment. Don't worry, we didn't have one—beyond saying we had complete confidence in you. I'm surprised they haven't called you. But I know how protective you are about who gets your phone number."

"This is really stressing David out," I said. "I'm going to go home for a while to be with him, let him see all is well."

"At the beach?"

"No," I said, "at the house. Ah, at Hayword's place." *Our* place? We owned the damn house together still. But it wasn't *our* place. It was strange how I felt possessive over it even though I had never liked it. Thought it was ostentatious.

"Stan Takata will help," Sally said, "and if you could get this all to calm down, that would be great."

She sounded a little off. I remembered what Fern had said: Sally's position was tenuous at AFT. Or Sally was worried her position was tenuous. Everyone in Hollywood was paranoid, and everyone thought they were about to become obscure and unimportant—if they actually were important—and they were right. I mean, come on, we were all about to become dust in the wind.

Especially with this drought.

And since the radiation from Japan was coming our way, we'd become radioactive dust in the wind.

"Sally, this has gone from me being great to me being scum in about two hours. Maybe it'll go back to me being a hero in the same amount of time. Or better, they'll forget about me."

"Hero is better," Sally said. "I didn't want to mention this to you, but the suits are iffy about *Beauty and the Zombie Part Two*."

"The suits?" I said. "I thought you were the suits."

She made a noise.

"I'm serious," I said. "And beyond that, *Beauty and the Zombie* was the highest grossing—"

"Yeah, yeah," Sally said, "I know all that. But they're not sure they want to be associated with the franchise any longer."

"Fine," I said. "Any studio in town would snatch it up."

"I think they'd tie it up for years," Sally said, "until it was dead, dead, dead. Just for spite."

I shrugged. "So what? I'd be okay. Hayword would be okay. You'd be okay." But I did feel butterflies in my stomach. Did this physical response mean I actually wanted to write the script? I had fun with the last one. I wanted to have fun with this one. In fact, *Beauty and the Zombie* had been the best work experience of my life, from beginning to end.

"Damn it," I said. "What can I do?"

"Turn this around," she said. "Get it out of the news or change the story so you're the good guy again."

"You always said all publicity was good publicity," I said. "I don't understand."

"The entertainment media is so different now," Sally said. "I don't think you understand."

I rolled my eyes. I wasn't an ignorant child.

Although I did tend to ignore the rest of the world.

"If the media decides to go after you," Sally said, "it won't be pretty. They'll dredge up everything, Brooke. *Everything.*"

I groaned. My past wasn't pretty, but it also wasn't public. How could they find out anything unless people talked? Most of the people involved in my past wouldn't want to discuss our relationship. It wasn't like Sally was going to blab about our love affair. Our sex affair. But there were all the others. Someone at rehab could talk. They weren't supposed to but they might.

No. Couldn't jump to the future.

It was all about now, babies. All about now. I closed my eyes. Had to get this under control.

"You have a morals clause," Sally said.

"No, I don't," I said. "I wouldn't have signed such a thing."

"You've got it," she said. "We all have it."

"For stuff I did before I was under contract?" I said. "I doubt it. What the fuck, Sally. AFT is supposed to be all about the artist. It was created for us. The talent, man."

"I'm just saying there are some forces at work who aren't happy with me," Sally said. "It's sexist bullshit. Or some kind of bullshit. I don't know what's happening yet. But they could use this to get rid of you and then get rid of me."

And then where would Fern be? Working at AFT was the only thing that had ever made her even vaguely happy.

Fuck, fuck, fuck.

"They might even look at the fire, you know," Sally said.

That woke me up.

Why was she mentioning the fire?

"What do you mean?" I asked. I could hear how much higher my voice had gotten. "What about the fire? My fucking house burned down not long after my baby died of SIDS. Why would they look at that?"

"Jesus, Brooke," Sally said. "Calm down. I just mean they might go back to that time. You know, Alberto. Might even dredge up your affair with Alberto's father."

What?

"You knew about that?" I said.

It had been a fucking state secret.

"Yeah," she said. "You told me. One of the times, you know, one of the times we were naked together."

"Christ, Sally," I said. "When did you get demure? Are you saying I told you Ryan Nichols was Alberto's blood daddy when you and I were fucking?"

"Drunk and fucking," she said.

I closed my eyes. Ryan Nichols. I hadn't thought about him in a long time. I didn't know where he was. He'd been an assistant director on one of Hayword's movie. I didn't know if he'd actually gone on to be a director or a producer. Maybe he got out of movies. I only knew I fell for him hard, got knocked up, and then he deserted me. Left me broken. Open. Never had been in love like that before or after. Maybe not even during. Hayword didn't care about me cheating on him or even about being pregnant. He cared about us staying together, no matter what. So we did.

Which was why I was so shocked the day I saw him fucking the blonde. The day of the funeral. Couldn't have been that exact day. Could it? In my memory it feels like the day of the funeral.

Every time I think I've let go of that memory, it pops up again.

Hated that.

Now, I had to concentrate.

Had to go to a meeting. AA. Work the program, man.

No, wait. First I had to find Enrique and get the fucking diamond bracelet back. Somehow get the bracelet back to Juliet's. Get someone to find it. Then the police couldn't say anything had been stolen.

"Okay, Sally," I said, "I'll do the best I can."

"You're magic, baby," Sally said. "Always have been."

I ended the call by setting the phone face down.

Wished I could end the whole day.

I went back into the kitchen.

"Okay, here's the buzz, peeps," I said. "Don't anyone panic." I looked at David. "It's not a tragedy. As an old friend of mine used to say, 'no one is bleeding.' But I need to go back to the city. Gotta put the kibosh on this, whatever it is. If anyone calls you or comes up to you on the street and asks you anything about anything, don't talk to them. You have no comment." I looked directly at Joanie.

"What?" she said. "I don't talk to anyone. And what street? You think some reporter is going to come down this road? I don't think so."

"Just in case," I said. "Don't talk to anyone about me or the family. Not the guy who reads the meter. Not Maria." (Joanie's maid.) "Not anyone."

"Not anyone?" David asked. He thought about it. "Okay, okay, I can talk to my friends about regular things but not about you. If someone asks me if you're a hero or not, I don't say anything."

I laughed. "That's right. Although if you slip and say I'm always your hero, that would be all right."

"But that would be a lie, Mom," he said.

The kitchen got very quiet. I stared at my son. He looked dead serious. Except for the glint in his eyes.

I laughed. David laughed, too, and Hayword and Joanie breathed.

"For yo momma," I said, "a little fiction might be a good idea."

Hayword had put out a plate of veggies and hummus.

"Stay for a snack," Hayword said. "Or stay for dinner. You leave now and you're gonna be in traffic for hours."

He was smiling. How happy he was when we were all together. If Fern showed up, and we were all nice to each other, he would be in heaven. Until he got restless, and then he'd have to call one of his Hollywood friends and talk about his latest project. Get reassurances now from someone besides me.

I wondered why he was so mellow.

Maybe he was seeing someone. Sex always calmed him.

"No," I said, "as tempting as that is. I better git."

"Mom," David said, "at least go to a meeting."

"Or call Mark," Hayword said.

Joanie emptied her martini glass, crossed her pajama-draped legs, and nodded.

I laughed. "Um, don't be telling me what I need to do. What's wrong with you guys?"

"It's got to be a bit strange," Hayword said. "All this. I mean, I kind of shivered listening to it."

"I haven't heard any of it," I said. "Are they saying I have horns? That I'm a zombie? That I beat my children?"

"No, nothing like that," Joanie said. "Just that you might be a thief."

I made a noise. "That is not going to cause me to drink," I said. "Geez Louise."

"You were shouting when you were on the phone," Joanie said. "Reminded me of the bad old days." She shrugged. "Or the good old days. We did have some times."

Hayword gave her a look. They did all handle me with kid gloves, still, sometimes. As though I was a bomb just about to go off, but if they talked quietly, sweetly, that would disarm me.

I didn't feel like a bomb. Didn't feel like I was going to blow up.

I just needed to take care of some things.

Like find Enrique and wring his freaking neck.

"Mom, do you think those two-headed whales are because of the radiation?" David asked. He was looking down at his phone. Should never have let him have a phone.

"There aren't any two-headed whales," I said.

He glanced up at me. "But if there are," he said. "Should we move? Go live with Grandma and Grandpa?"

My parents. In Michigan.

No.

"It'll get in the rain, won't it?" he said. "It'll be everywhere. Nowhere will be safe."

"Honey," Joanie said, "nowhere is safe."

"And this is nowhere," I said, "so it is safe." I gave Joanie the nastiest look I could manage. "David, your dad and I will protect you. I wish you'd stop worrying about that stuff. It's good to know what's going on in the world, but concentrate on the stuff you can actually change or fix. Try to look for inspiring things. That will help your body chemistry. Then your stress level will go down. And then you can eventually come up with solutions to all this stuff. When you're older."

The room was very quiet again, and the three of them were watching me.

"What?" I said. "I learn stuff. How do you think I've stayed sober for two years? This constant overload of news and media crap isn't good for us. You pick a problem and then you work on it. Right?"

Hayword put his arm across my shoulders and squeezed me.

"Right."

I squinted at him. Why was he being so tender with me? I wasn't a melon they could bruise. I shook my head. Who cared? He could be nice to me if he wanted to.

"Okay, I'll stay and snack," I said, "but David has to put away his phone and each of us has to tell a funny and inspiring story. No tragedies. No end of the world scenarios. Deal?"

"Deal," David said. Hayword and Joanie nodded.

"Okay," I said. "David, you start."

"Can I look something up first?" he asked, staring down at his phone. I snatched it away from him.

"No," I said. "Just start. Once upon a time. Or there are seven continents. This story comes from the eighth continent."

David nodded. "All right. There are seven continents," he said. "This story comes from the thirteenth continent."

I grinned. "That's my boy."

FOUR

After I left my family and Joanie, I sat in my car for a moment and breathed—and listened to the sound of my breathing. Normally if something like this had happened, I would be sitting in my car drinking and making a date.

Normally in the *past*. But this wasn't the past. It was here and now. What did I need to do *now*?

First up, I had to get the diamond bracelet from Enrique. I shouldn't call him on my phone just in case the police one day got a hold of my phone records. I had disposable phones down at my writing studio—old ones that I had when I was drinking and screwing. In my former life as a double-lifer.

I drove down the hill to the writing studio, parked the car, and went inside. I hadn't been for a couple weeks so the air was stale. I felt anxious. Even though I had redone the place since it was my love nest, even though I'd been here many times in the last two years, I had mixed feelings about it. Sometimes—not certain why—I walked in the door and recalled all the lovers who had come through that door. I remembered—or didn't—all the nights and days that I had drunk my weight in booze. Or close to it. I remembered bringing Mark here. For a year or more, this place had been our place. Our love nest. It was here that I first decided maybe I did have a drinking problem. It was here that my daughter admitted setting fire to our house after her brother died, when she was a pre-teen.

Sometimes I felt sad here. Sometimes I felt peaceful. Sometimes I felt incredibly happy.

I suppose that was just life, eh?

At the ocean house, I still felt like a stranger. I did worry about the radioactive sea water, although I'd never tell my kids that. The radiation was from the plant in Japan that had been leaking for . . . years? Decades? Some scientists said it was going to be the end of the world as we knew it. Others said the leaking radiation meant nothing; we'd be fine.

I figured it was somewhere in the middle. We were living in a fucking cesspool, and we couldn't do anything about it now.

I couldn't focus on that or else I'd want to drink.

So when I looked out at the ocean, I tried not to think about Japan. Or radiation. Or the sea of plastic. Or the level of toxicity in the great mammals that lived in the ocean.

When I was a kid, I had worried about living in a science fiction future of a polluted toxic world. Now here I was, living in a polluted toxic world.

Fucking whackadoodle times.

I dropped my keys on the counter and shook my head.

Nope. Wasn't gonna go there. Everything was not bad. Everything was not lost.

I got one of the burner phones from the junk drawer and plugged it in to charge it up. Then I went on the computer and tracked down Enrique's number. Didn't take much. I cleared all evidence of my search—I hoped. I also searched my own name under news.

I was not happy with what I found.

Several short articles had been posted on how I had thwarted a robbery at Juliet's. Each article mentioned I was coauthor of *Love and Other Insanities* and *Beauty and the Zombie*, and that was about it. Some sites had that same article with an update above the original article: "Police sources now say they suspect Brooke McMurphy may have been involved in the attempted robbery at Juliet's restaurant off Sunset Blvd. McMurphy is the cowriter with her estranged husband of *Love and Other Insanities*. She is also the scriptwriter of *Beauty and the Zombie*, which came out after McMurphy's stint in rehab."

Crap.

How the hell did they know I'd been in rehab?

Not that I was surprised they knew it. But how did this all blow up so quickly? It wasn't overnight. It was over a freaking hour!

I shouldn't exaggerate. It hadn't blown up. Just a few . . . *dozen* articles.

Ugh.

I started to turn on the TV but decided against it.

I got the burner phone and called Enrique.

"Hello?" He sounded so cheerful. Didn't he understand the shit storm he had generated for me?

It suddenly occurred to me that Enrique's phone records might be examined should the police come to suspect him. This phone couldn't be traced to me. Could it? Crap. I couldn't remember if I had bought it with cash or a credit card. At the time I wasn't worried about the police; I was just trying to keep my sexual escapades private.

"Hello?" he said again.

"Enrique," I said. "You have ruined my life."

Ah, the drama queen was never far beneath the surface, was she?

"Brooke? What's going on? It was great seeing you today."

"Ricky!" I said. "We didn't just run into each other. You tried to rob the restaurant where I was having breakfast."

"No, no," he said. "It was an audition. An audition!"

"Please tell me you haven't told anyone about what you and your friend did."

"Besides Manny?"

"Manny?"

"He was our inside man at Juliet's," Enrique said, "even though he wasn't there. Remember? I told you."

"I wish I could forget this entire thing," I said. "Listen to me. They're calling it a robbery. They're saying I was in on it. They're talking about me on the news. The studio head believes they're going to dig up everything they can on my private life."

"No worries there," he said brightly. "You've had a blessed life."

Blessed?

I had never heard that word in relation to me before.

"Blessed? What the hell, Ricky. You found god or something since I last saw you?"

He laughed. "Naw. Just AA. I'm straight as an arrow now. You're a friend of Bill, too, I hear."

"Who'd you hear that from?" I hadn't seen the man for fifteen years, give or take. How could he know anything about me?

"I don't remember," he said. "Just heard it. Am I wrong?"

"Look, Ricky," I said, "you've got to make this right. The police told me there's a ten thousand dollar diamond bracelet missing."

"What?" He actually sounded surprised. "We didn't steal anything. We gave everything back to you."

"No, you didn't," I said. "Or your *friend* didn't."

"Maybe the woman is lying," he said. "I didn't take any bracelets from anyone."

"Okay, so I'll go to the police and say, 'I'm sure the woman is lying because the robbers said they didn't steal any bracelet.' Ricky, they might charge me with aiding and abetting!"

"What? You didn't have anything to do with it. I mean, you helped us get away, so I guess they could argue you were aiding us."

I groaned. "No, I did not *help* you get away! I got the loot from you and pointed you to the door. I was trying to end the whole thing. If this ever becomes public, you can't say I helped you!"

"What does abetting mean?" he said.

That stopped me. I had to think about it.

"I think it means aid or help," I said.

"That's pretty redundant then isn't it?"

I'd never realized how irritating he was. Maybe he hadn't been back then. Twenty years of pickling his brain with alcohol might have changed him.

"I have to have that bracelet back," I said. "Now. Today."

"I can talk to—to my friend," he said. "I can't believe he'd do that, but I'll see. Are you going to take it to the police and turn us in?"

"No," I said. "I'll take it back to Juliet's and leave it someplace and hope someone finds it."

Or something. I'd figure it out once I got there.

"Do you know this guy well?" I asked.

"Well enough," he said. "We've been to a lot of auditions together. For different parts, of course. He's—"

"Naw, remember, don't want to know him. Just get the bracelet back, Ricky. If you don't have it, he does. If he doesn't, we might all be in a lot of trouble. Right now, I might be able to make it right. Call me back on this phone."

I ended the call. I wasn't sure where to go or what to do. I was not made for the life of a criminal. I wanted to fix this now, get it taken care of now, get it off my plate *now*.

The AA people talk about being in the now. I was in the now *now* and I wanted this shit done.

But I had no control over what was going to happen next. My day wasn't even half over and I was ready for a nap.

I stayed in my studio for a couple of hours waiting for a call from Enrique and looking over the original treatment for *Beauty and the Zombie: Part Two*. The movie opens with Colleen Kelly giving birth to her alien baby. The alien father is still in prison, but he feels some kind of shift in the world. In the first *Beauty and the Zombie*, Thomas had been a good guy and then a bad guy who tricked Colleen Kelly into having sex with him—and into vouching for the aliens, telling everyone they would cause no harm. Only they were causing harm. Colleen woke up one morning to discover she had the deadly alien plague that turned humans into zombies. Thomas and the other alien zombies had spread the plague on purpose, to kill off the human race.

Only in the end of the movie, as Thomas is going off to jail, he says that he loves Colleen. She doesn't hear him—or at least the viewer doesn't think she hears him.

So now I was supposed to continue the love story between a mass murderer and Colleen Kelly, the scientist who was duped by the mass murderer and who actually ended up pregnant by him.

I should have never done that. The pregnancy made her weak. No way of getting around that. I was pregnant three times. I birthed three children. Although it was the most powerful thing a human being could do—create life—on the screen, pregnant women were not often the heroes of the piece.

Maybe I should change all that. Maybe she shouldn't deliver until later in the movie. Make her like Ripley in *Alien*. Kicking some ass and taking names.

Except Colleen was a scientist. She was a peaceful person.

She had figured out how to save humans from the plague (a combination of dirt and sunlight). She had literally saved the world. All without any gunfire on her part.

No. I'd stick with the treatment. She would give birth to the child immediately. Then all hell would break loose. I wasn't sure how yet. In the treatment, the alien zombies attack the earth again, but I wasn't sure I cared for that plot line anymore. Lots of shit blowing up would make it popular. What about the human element?

I laughed at myself and pushed the laptop away from me. The movie was supposed to be loud and funny and fast-moving. I could sandwich some human element in-between all that.

I took a break and checked online to see if the media was still discussing me. Apparently they were. I was "trending." I made the mistake of going to some of the sites. Most had added this line, "Two years ago, McMurphy went to rehab for alcohol and drug abuse and sexual addiction."

"I did not go to rehab for sexual addiction, you assholes," I said. "Or drug abuse. Unless you count alcohol as a drug, which I suppose I do."

The comments were wild and rude. All about how nasty Hollywood people are. We're all a bunch of drinkers, druggers, and whores, according to the commenters. Several posts were about how "fucking ugly" I was, so they couldn't understand how I had gotten any partners for my sex addiction.

The only photograph on any of these sites was the one of me going into rehab. Or leaving? In any case, I wasn't ugly. I just looked like a normal woman. One or two commenters said, "I'd do her." Which was more upsetting than the comments about how ugly I was.

Not that I was seriously upset.

Just kind of pissed me off.

I wanted to call Mark, but I was annoyed he hadn't called me to see how I was doing now that my name was mud. Guess he was too wrapped up in his meeting with what's her face.

I rubbed my forehead. I couldn't believe Fern had put that idea in my head and now I couldn't get it out: about Mark all cozied up to Sherry at some store.

Wasn't like me to be jealous. Sure, I'd punished Hayword a good ten years for fucking some bimbo on the day we buried my son, but that wasn't jealousy. That was fury. I knew Mark loved me, and he wasn't the cheating kind.

End of story.

Of course, Hayword hadn't been the cheating kind either.

No! Wasn't the same thing. Mark and I were committed to one another. We lived together. Most of the time. He still had his house. He usually stayed there when he had his son, Ian. Ian liked my house, but it was away from all of his sports and his friends. He came over now more often, now that the restaurant was almost open.

Sunday was opening day. That's when everything would change. Again. The restaurant had been turning our lives a bit upside down for the last year. Sometimes I thought Mark was doing it all just to please me.

"It's okay to have a plumber as a lover," Mark had said to me more than once, "but not as a permanent boyfriend or husband."

"What the hell are you talking about?" I'd say. "I don't care what you do for a living—as long as you can dedicate nearly every waking hour to me."

That would usually end the conversation or we'd continue it in the bedroom.

The docs and therapists at rehab had warned me not to ruminate. Rumination was a trigger for depressives. And that's what I was. Or had been. Suffering from depression. Rumination just made everything worse. But ruminating about Mark and me having sex was kind of fun.

I heard the key in the back door. In another moment I heard the door open.

"Anyone home?" Mark.

I got up and went into the kitchen. Mark was carrying a bag of groceries. I grinned.

"Hey, baby," I said, "I was just thinking about you."

"Was I naked or clothed?" he asked as he put the bag on the counter.

I went to him, and we kissed and then embraced.

"You started out clothed," I said, "but you ended up naked. Just like now."

He laughed. I took his hand, and we went into the bedroom.

Where we tripped the light fantastic.

You don't need the details. Suffice to say, everyone was very happy at the end of it all.

After I stopped drinking, sex wasn't that much fun for a time. Actually, I didn't have any sex for a while, but once I got back on the horse—so to speak—or back on Mark, or vice versa, sex seemed muted or something. I was incredibly self-conscious. I'd been drinking so long that I couldn't remember if I had been self-conscious before I started drinking. Probably not. Except for Alberto's biological father, Ryan Nichols. I'd been sober then and the sex had been amazing. Quick, but amazing. We weren't together long enough for it to get routine. Weren't together long enough for the milk in the refrigerator to go bad.

In other words, we lusted, we had sex a few times, I fell in love—it was like being drunk, that feeling just before you go over the edge and you know you've had too much to drink and you're gonna be sick soon. I doubt we would have stayed together if I hadn't gotten preggers. But once I told him I was pregnant, he left town. Or the country. I didn't try to track him down—not after I called his phone and discovered it was no longer in service. Hayword could have found him, if I had asked. But I didn't ask. I just threw up a lot, told Hayword about the baby—and the fact that he was not the baby daddy—and we went on with our lives.

Sort of. Then baby Alberto died and the house burned down and we moved into the canyon, into one of those obscenely ostentatious mansions, and I became a drunk who slept with everyone and anyone I could. At least, it felt like that sometimes. The sex always seemed great. Now I understood that was my alcohol besotted brain changing reality for me, but sometimes I missed how alcohol relaxed me. Got rid of my inhibitions. I didn't do anything freaky or kinky—I liked face-to-face sex—but I had sex often and in a variety of places until I settled on the love nest, aka my studio.

I was thinking about all of this while Mark made us omelettes. Ordinarily I didn't like thinking about the past so much. It was done and over. It couldn't hurt me anymore. I had dealt with it. But now, thinking of the past was making me nostalgic for my drinking days. Thinking that sex while drunk was better than sex while sober was a lie the alcohol was telling me—or a lie the part of me who wanted the alcohol was telling: Sex had *not* been better then.

Right?

Right.

Now, sex was just sex. It was fun. But I pretty much did it to get off. The intimate part where you hugged and talked about your deepest feelings—you know that part?—that was not what I longed for or even wanted after sex. I wanted to do the deed and then move on.

Remember that scene in *Network* when the filmmakers were trying to demonstrate how bad—evil really—Faye Dunaway's character was because when she had sex she wanted to get on, get off, and then get off? I remember seeing that at some film festival at college with a group of friends. Afterward, everyone was talking about how disgusting the Faye Dunaway character was. How she was the bane of civilization. I didn't particularly like her, but when my friends kept bringing up how she used men to have sex, I didn't understand: I didn't think she was bad or evil because of that, and I didn't understand the outrage. She was efficient. She did what she had to do, and then she moved on.

Point being, sex was still fun sober, but it wasn't one of the central pillars of my life as it had been before. Mark understood that I wasn't prone to spilling my guts after we had sex. Or any other time, actually. I did try to be more honest and open about my feelings these days—even though I still didn't often recognize when I was actually having feelings.

So after sex—or after we made love—we'd hug for a few minutes while our heartbeats went back to normal, and then we'd get up and carry on. I liked it best when we carried on in the kitchen.

This time Mark made us omelettes filled with mushrooms and spinach and who knows what else. It melted in my mouth. No one could make breakfast quite like Mark. Which was probably why his restaurant was going to be a breakfast place, mostly.

We sat next to one another at the counter. We could see the backyard from our perches. Wasn't much going on there, but it was green and wild-looking.

"So why didn't you let me know what was happening?" Mark asked. "My mother called and told me they were accusing you of being part of some robbery."

"I bet she loved that," I said. "Good excuse for you to dump me."

"Where the hell did that come from? My mother loves you."

I looked at him. "She thinks I'm the whore of Babylon."

Mark laughed. "She certainly does not. She was worried

about you. She asked me to tell you to call her later if you need someone to talk to."

I nodded. "Sorry. I am feeling a bit raw. I'm not sure what happened. The studio is telling me I have to take care of this or they might dump Sally and the movie. And the police want to interrogate me."

"Okay," Mark said, "how much of all that is just a horror story you're telling yourself? My guess is that Sally encouraged you to do something to stop the bad press, and the police just want to talk to you."

"I wish it was all exaggeration," I said. "I talked to the police— some detective named Baxter—and I tried to explain that the so-called robbers were just actors. They weren't actually robbing anyone, but he told me one of the customers at Juliet's claims she is missing a ten thousand dollar bracelet."

Mark shook his head and made a noise.

"I know what you're thinking," I said.

He raised an eyebrow. "I bet you don't."

I leaned into him and laughed. "Bet I do. Hundred bucks?"

He shrugged. "Bet."

"You're thinking what the fuck is someone doing with a ten thousand dollar bracelet."

He laughed. "Dead on. You're a scary woman, reading my mind. Guess that means I should take back the diamond bracelet I got you to celebrate my grand opening."

"You know how I love the bling," I said.

Mark smiled and pushed away his empty plate.

"I wonder if it is just someone trying to hit up the insurance companies," I said.

"The police will investigate to see whether she actually owned a bracelet like that, right?"

"I assume so," I said, "but I better call someone and make sure."

I went to the couch, retrieved my phone, and texted the lawyer via Sally's number. I saw there were several texts I hadn't read. Must have turned the sound down again.

I scanned the texts quickly. Four from Fern. One from Irving Jackson. What the hell could he want? One from David. I checked the kids' messages. David was reminding me again about coming to his school on Friday. He was being a little weirder than usual about this. And Fern: "WTF, Mom. What's going on?" "They're going to dig up dirt." "Brooke! Where the fuck are you?"

I sighed.

"Mark, I've got to call my daughter," I said. I went into the bedroom and shut the door. Fern answered on the first ring. She sounded panicked.

"Mom," she said. "They're saying terrible things about you."

"No, they're not," I said, trying to calm her. "They just say the police suspect I had something to do with it. And that's not true."

"But you talked to the robbers! You know them! What am I going to say if the police ask me?"

She sounded . . . hysterical.

"Honey, tell them the truth," I said. "I *didn't* have anything to do with it."

"What would they do to you if they thought you did have something to do with it?" she asked.

"I don't know," I said. "I can't imagine it would ever go to trial." Actually I *could* imagine it. Wouldn't be fun. But would they really send me to jail for showing those two idiots the door? "If they don't drop it, they'd probably try to make a deal with me if I'd tell them who the robbers were."

"Actors," she said. "You said they were *actors*."

"Yes," I said, "and if I have to choose between going to jail or giving up—" I started to say Enrique's name. But I stopped.

Maybe Fern had never heard me say it when we were under the table together. Or maybe she'd forgotten. She had been under stress. "I'd give up the person I knew," I said. "That's the truth of it, honey. I know it's not courageous. But it was an asshole thing for them to have done."

"People do stupid things," she said.

"You have sympathy for them?" I asked. "I figured eventually you'd get around to blaming me for the whole thing."

"Why?" she asked. "You didn't do anything."

She was still sucking up to me. Probably wanted to make sure I'd show up to the party tomorrow.

"You still having the party?" I asked.

"Of course," she said. "Sure." She sounded uncertain, or far away. "Mom, one of the media outlets—I forget which one—mentioned Alberto's death."

"What?" I sat on the bed. I felt rage rising. I stood again.

"In what fucking context?" I asked.

"They mentioned you had gone to rehab," she said, "and that ten years earlier your son had died from SIDS. They didn't mention the house burning. Mom, what happens if they start looking into the house?"

"So what if they mention the house?" I said. "It was just a family tragedy." Hmmm, did a burning house constitute a tragedy? A baby dying was definitely a tragedy. But a house? "A family hardship." Hardship? Really? We went out and bought a more expensive house. Fortunately most of our photographs and important papers had been conveniently stored in the garage. Amazing how a kid her age had the presence of mind to put that stuff in the garage—before she set the house on fire.

"Besides," I said, "I don't think they can do anything about someone burning down their own house."

Well, except for insurance fraud.

"It wasn't *my* house," she said.

"Sure it was," I said. "It was our house."

"So when you and Dad finally divorce," she said, "and you sell this house, will I get a quarter of the money?" She was slurring her words.

"Fern, are you okay?" I asked. I knew if I asked her if she was drunk, she'd deny it. She'd say she was just tired; that's why she was slurring her words.

At least that's what I had always told people when I was drunk.

"Just worried," she said.

"You're slurring your words." I couldn't resist.

"I'm fucking tired," she said. "Sally works my ass off. What if the police didn't offer you a deal? What if it went to trial? What if they found you guilty?"

She sounded frightened. Did that mean in her heart of hearts she actually loved me and wished the best for me? I knew she did, really, but sometimes it was difficult to tell.

"Darlin', I am not going to jail."

"You are not listening to me, Mother," she said.

Now I was "mother" again. She was back to being pissed at me.

She continued, "What kind of sentence would you get for aiding and abetting?"

"How the fuck should I know! Do I look like a lawyer?" Fern was an adult. Couldn't she clue into the fact that I might be a little worried myself about going to jail?

"Mother, do you remember the time when we were kids and David said the word *butt*, and I said to him, 'It's not *butt*, it's *bottom*.' Do you remember what you said?"

I sighed. "No, but I can tell this is going to be a bad parent story."

"You said, 'It's not *butt* or *bottom*. The proper word is *ass*.'"

I laughed. "And your point is?"

She *was* drunk. She didn't have a point.

"My point is you are being a butt, bottom, and ass. I'm giving you the same look I gave you back then."

"You better not be driving anywhere," I said. "It's a little early in the day to be drunk on your bottom, isn't it?"

"Hah! The black cat calling the kettle a cauldron. Or something like that." She laughed. "I'll see you at the party tomorrow. I'll text you the address. Love you, ass mom."

I stared at the phone. Now that had been a weird ass conversation. What was going on with my daughter? I needed to talk to Hayword about her. Or Sally.

I looked at the text from Irving Jackson. He was creative director or something at AFT. Their titles always confused me. His in particular since he didn't seem very creative. He acted like a suit, even though he rarely wore one.

"Need to speak with you ASAP," his text read.

Probably just wanted to rag on me about the media coverage of the robbery.

Crap. Now *I* was calling it a robbery.

I went back into the other room.

"Your omelette is cold," Mark said. "You want me to heat it up?"

I shook my head and sat next to him. "Your food is delish cold or hot." I stuck my fork into the omelette and then brought a piece to my mouth. Wasn't actually very good cold. Mark got up, went around the counter and into the kitchen, and leaned over and grabbed my plate.

"No," I whined. "I hate microwaved food. Eggs get so rubbery."

He gave me a look, and then he slid the omelette back into the pan. Like he would ever microwave something he had made for me.

He stayed at the stove, not looking at me, and said, "Honey, something else is going on here. The police may not know it, but I can tell." He turned to look at me.

I shook my head. "There's nothing. Nothing I can tell you." He made a noise and turned back to the stove. "Look, Mark, if this goes to trial, they could call you as a witness, and then you'd have to tell them what I said."

He flipped over the half eaten omelette and then looked at me again. "I'd lie," he said.

"You wouldn't really," I said.

"To protect you? Sure."

"Mark, how would our justice system ever work if people went around lying all the time?"

He laughed. "Lordy, woman, you can surprise me."

He brought the pan over to me and slipped the omelette back onto my plate. Man, some champagne and orange juice would be good right about now.

"Okay, if you won't let me lie—"

"You continue to surprise me, Mr. Upstanding citizen."

"If you won't let me lie," he said, "then marry me. They couldn't force me to testify against you then."

I laughed, my mouth full.

"Then I'd be a bigamist," I said.

"Yeah, what's up with that?" he asked.

"You want to have this conversation now?"

"I'm just saying," he said. "We never talk about it. Why are you still married?"

"Because the split would be horrible," I said. "The money thing. The house the kids grew up in."

"People do it all the time," he said. "I did it. If you don't want the family to lose the house, just let Hayword have it. You've got enough money."

I ate in silence. I didn't like anyone nosing around my business, even Mark. If I'd been a cat, my hair would have stood on end.

"Unless we're not making a life together," he said. "Unless we're just playing. Then that's a different story."

"Do you want to get married?" I asked.

He sat next to me. He was silent for a moment, and then he said, "Yes, I do. I love you."

"But why should that mean marriage? It's a lousy institution."

He put up a hand. "Okay. You're right. We can talk about this another time. We can expound on our philosophies of marriage later."

"You saw how I treated Hayword," I said. "I wouldn't want to do that to you."

"Then don't," he said. He looked at me and shrugged. "Then don't. It's your choice."

I nodded.

"So what can't you tell me about the robbery?"

"I know one of the robbers," I said. "It was Enrique deChamp. He was one of the leads in *Love and Other Insanities*. He played Daniel."

"You're kidding!"

I shook my head. "No. He said it was an audition gone wrong and I believe him. I don't know the other guy. Thank god, I don't know two people who are *that* idiotic. I took them in the back and showed them the door. I wanted them gone so that things wouldn't go bad. One of the patrons could have had a real gun. The cops could have stormed the place. So I helped them leave. It didn't dawn on me that that was a crime. I got all the jewelry back. Or I thought I did. The police told me a $10,000 bracelet is missing. I called Enrique and told him he better get the bracelet back come hell or high water."

"Oh crap."

"Understatement of the century," I said. "But I concur."

"What are you going to do with the bracelet if Enrique does give it to you? Then you'll be in possession of stolen merchandise."

"Oh crap."

"There's only one thing we can do," Mark said.

"Leave the country? Confess? Throw myself on the mercy of the court?"

"AA meeting."

"Good idea," I said, "but I don't want to go around here. Too many rich people."

He laughed. "And that's bad because you hate rich alcoholics?"

"No, I'm always afraid I'll meet someone I slept with and don't remember."

"Don't know what to say to that," he said.

"Why do you think I picked you?" I asked. "I had run through most of the rich people around here."

"Ah, the romance never ends with you."

FIVE

I started to relax as I sat in the truck next to Mark, heading somewhere in the dark. I didn't care where. Mark still had his truck—his plumber's truck—because he continued to work as a plumber, part-time. He said he liked it. And he needed the money for the restaurant, although I told him I would finance it. I mean, I owned the building. The rest was gravy, right? Not right. Renovating and opening a restaurant was a lot more expensive than I ever thought it would be.

Not that I had ever thought about that. I encouraged Mark to follow his dream. If his dream was to open a restaurant, I was right there with him. What else was I going to do with the money from *Beauty and the Zombie*? I had points, man, and AFT actually did honest accounting, so Hayword and I were rich all over again and again.

We all got rich from that movie. That was why I wasn't convinced AFT would dump Sally and me just because of some silly misunderstanding about a robbery. A non-robbery.

Anyway, I didn't mind riding around in Mark's truck anymore, even though he did have a car—an electric one—which I wished he would get in the habit of driving.

"You wanna go out to eat?" he asked. "Or we could get take-out and hang out at my place for a while, after AA."

"Is that where we're going?"

Mark laughed. I knew why. I didn't always know where I was. Even though I'd been to Mark's house many times over the last two years, I couldn't find it on my own, not without GPS. I could get to my house at the beach and in the canyon, could get to any of the studios or downtown Los Angeles, could get around Brentwood where we used to live, but that was about it. The valley, the 401, or any of the burbs—yes, Mark still called them that—were a complete mystery to me. It was like asking me to drive to *The Twilight Zone*. How could you drive to *The Twilight Zone*? It wasn't a fucking destination. Same with Mark's house.

"You should be fucking ashamed of yourself," Mark said, laughing. "You should know the land beneath your feet."

I shrugged. "I do. I know my place, baby. I know my pla*ces*. This ain't my place."

"It's my place," he said. He sounded vaguely hurt. I looked over at him.

"Really?" I said. "Dude, you know who I am. These kinds of neighborhoods creep me out." I looked out the window, but it was dark and I couldn't see anything.

"What are you talking about?"

"You know," I said, "places with basketball hoops on the garage. Cars up on blocks. Women exchanging casseroles. Creepy, creepy, creepy."

"Um, that's pretty much how I grew up," he said.

"So did I," I said. "I never wanted any of it. That kind of lower middle-class suburbia nightmare. Gawd."

"I like how I grew up," he said.

I shivered. "No roots. No culture. No tradition. Just . . . zombies."

"Seriously?"

I looked at him. "Seriously. Hey, I'm glad you had a great childhood. So did I, I guess. But it had no depth. No ritual, no ceremony. Don't you ever wonder about that? Big fucking surprise that I became an alcoholic. Something terrible happened in my life and I had absolutely no backbone—if that was the right word—nothing to fall back on. Nothing to hold me up. Nothing to hang on to. No traditions, no community. When I finally called my mother to tell her about Alberto, she said, 'That happened to Aunt Jane, too. Never got over it.' Really, Mom? Fucking really?"

"We had Christmas," Mark said. "Easter. Halloween."

"All consumer holidays," I said. "Presents on Christmas. Eating jelly beans and chocolate eggs pooped out by some Easter bunny to celebrate the Jewish zombie. Bunnies don't lay eggs, you know. So those eggs were pure shit. Maybe even literally. And Halloween: more candy. Although the undercurrent of Halloween is very cool. Honoring and celebrating the dead."

Mark glanced over at me. He was frowning. Then he looked back at the road.

"What's going on, Brooke?" he asked.

I looked out into the darkness. What *was* going on? I was suddenly sounding bitter and angry. Too much thinking about the past today. My conversation with Fern had been weird. My mother and I never talked to one another like Fern and I did. We never talked period.

I could feel myself wanting to pull away from everything and everyone. I didn't want to fight this battle—or whatever it was—about the robbery. It would have been so much simpler if I'd kept my nose out of the whole fucking thing.

"I feel like I'm starting to fall away," I said.

Fuck. I hoped that old bugaboo depression wasn't about to raise its ugly fucking devouring head again.

"I don't want to deal with this," I said. "There's too much going on. I feel overloaded."

"You're not still hungry?" he asked.

I laughed. "No, I'm not hungry. I am a little angry." Maybe a lot angry. "I'm not lonely." Well, maybe a bit. I was always a little lonely. "I am tired. I've been tired since 1980, I think."

That was an AA thing: H.A.L.T. If you were feeling hungry, angry, lonely, or tired, you could be, would be, might be . . . you were vulnerable for relapse.

Fuck, fuck, fuck.

"This will help, baby," he said. "You can't focus on the negative."

That was unlike Mark. He didn't usually give me advice. Must be seeing signs that scared him. And *that* scared me.

"You thought I'd already been drinking," I said. "Didn't you?" I could hear how pissed I sounded and I didn't know where it was coming from.

"No," he said. "But you know, you never mentioned Alberto's birthday this year. That was just a week ago, right?"

"Oh fuck," I said. "Oh my god. I completely forgot. How could I have forgotten?"

I had never forgotten Alberto's birthday.

"That means they all forgot," I said. "The entire fucking family."

"Or maybe they just didn't mention it because in the past you've had such a difficult time."

Mark stopped the truck in some parking lot next to what looked like a church. I hated AA meetings in churches. Always felt there was something a little judgmental about AA meetings in churches, as though someone was listening just outside the door to discover what our sins were.

I felt a wave of panic. Was there something wrong with my brain that I'd forgotten Alberto's birthday? Or was there something morally bereft about me that I could forget my own son's birthday? My *dead* son's birthday.

The jury had long ago come back on the morally bereft question.

"It's okay," Mark said. "It doesn't mean anything except that you've had a lot going on."

"But I haven't," I said. "You've had a lot going on. You and Sherry. And Fern and Sally are busy at AFT. David and Hayword are busy with their lives. I have not been busy. I know I'm supposed to be working on the screenplay, but it hasn't happened. I've been busy avoiding my work. That's no excuse for forgetting my son's birthday. No kid likes to be forgotten."

"I'm sure if he were alive, you wouldn't have forgotten."

"But that's kind of the point, isn't it? He's dead."

Gawd. I felt like I was going to throw up. Either that or take a drink. I didn't want to go to this meeting.

"Brooke," Mark said.

I looked over at him. "What?"

"Are we going in? Do you need to talk?"

"Nothing to talk about," I said. "The past is past. Live in the now, baby. Isn't that what we're supposed to do?"

I didn't feel as sanguine as I tried to sound.

I got out of the truck and closed the door. I felt like I was in a bit of a fog. Mark came around the truck to me. He reached for my hand and I let him have it. I even leaned on him as we went up the walk and into the church and then down the steps to the basement. Lovely. I hated being in basements more than I hated being in churches. What a banner day.

I was being too negative. Too critical. I was thinking too much about what I didn't want. What I didn't like. I had to change my thought patterns.

Think about what I did want. Living children, for one. Except for the dead one, I could check that off: I had two living children. A sober life. Check. Satisfying work. Check. Safe and beautiful home. Check. Good health. Check. Except for this panic and depression. Hated that these feelings—or whatever they were—could descend almost without warning.

But there had been warning. I should have been paying attention. When the media accused me of being a criminal and then brought up my dead son's name, I should have realized that might trigger a reaction in me.

Or maybe it didn't have anything to do with that. Perhaps it was seeing what Enrique had been reduced to because he couldn't get a job.

I'd always liked Enrique. But we hadn't kept in touch, probably because he had been friends with Ryan Nichols. I never knew if Enrique had been aware of our affair or not.

Things had seemed so normal this morning at breakfast as I parried with my daughter. How easily they could go askew.

The entire basement of the church was filled. Lots of people I didn't know milling around. I felt a jolt of panic.

"I'm gonna make a call," I said. "I'll be right back."

Mark kept a hold of my fingers for a moment, as if trying to tug me back to the meeting. I didn't look at him. I didn't acknowledge that I was having a difficult time. I didn't even snatch my fingers away. I just squeezed his hand, let go of him, and then hurried up the steps again to the foyer of the church. Only they don't call it that, do they? What was it? The lobby. Vestibule. That word came into my brain, and I was grateful for it. Perhaps I could stave off this panic attack after all.

So I stood in the vestibule with people streaming in around me to get to the AA meeting. Like fish to slaughter. . . . No, like fish to their freedom. *Come on, Brooke.*

This must be a popular group. I didn't actually like big AA meetings.

Didn't much like little ones either.

Right now I couldn't think of anything I liked.

Except a drink. I would like a drink.

I called Hayword's phone.

I glanced up at the people coming in as I heard Hayword say, "Hey, Brooke." One of the men walking past looked exactly like Ryan Nichols, Alberto's baby daddy. I blinked, and he was gone, or he morphed into another man. Christ on a stick. Now I was having hallucinations.

"Hayword, I feel strange," I said.

"What's wrong?" he asked.

"I feel panicky," I said. "Don't know why. Started in the car. Don't know why I'm calling you." Should be calling my sponsor. Or a doctor. Or something.

"Something's gonna happen," I said. "I'm sure of it."

"It already happened," Hayword said. "Probably all the media stuff."

I backed myself into a corner away from everyone. I whispered, "One of the media outlets mentioned Alberto. They fucking mentioned Alberto!"

"I know," he said. "I saw it."

"I forgot Alberto's birthday!" I said. "I fucking forgot his birthday."

"Oh Christ," he said. "I did, too."

"What a couple of lousy parents," I said.

"Because we forgot our dead son's birthday?" He sounded hurt.

"We're still his parents," I said. "You don't stop being a child's parent just because he dies. Hayword—" I felt like I was going to start crying. "Today. Today I saw Enrique. I can't tell you where. But I think seeing him brought up some old shit." To Hayword.

I didn't normally spill my guts. Or as my therapist would say, I didn't normally "share." I knew I was supposed to—it was one of those things that could help me not drink. But I was not very good at it.

"I keep thinking of Ryan Nichols," I said. "In fact, I thought I just saw him. Can you fucking believe that? I think I'd kill him if I really ever saw him. Kill him fucking dead."

"Brooke," Hayword said, "you didn't see him. You're at a meeting? Why not go and talk. Is someone with you? Is Mark there? I'm gonna call AFT and see if they can pull some strings to stop the media from digging up our past."

I didn't tell him AFT had asked me to clean up this mess. I didn't tell him anything. It just felt good to hear his voice. We had been together for so long—before we weren't—and we had known each other for so long.

Or something.

"Breathe," he said. "Go find Mark."

"Why are you telling me to go find Mark?" I asked. "Isn't he the man who stole me away from you?" He hadn't, actually.

"No, I think that was Ryan Nichols," he said. "Or, more to the point, me. I pushed you away by being an asshole."

"You weren't an asshole," I said.

"But you always say I am," he said.

"You are now," I said, "but you weren't then." I laughed. "Love you, Hayword. Thanks."

Okay. I was feeling better. The people were all gone. The meeting must have started. I walked quietly down the stairs. The welcome was over, and now a woman was walking up to the front of the group to share.

I spotted Mark. He had saved a seat at the end of the row so I easily slid in next to him.

He took my hand and whispered, "Are you okay?"

I nodded.

The woman said, "Hello, my name is Nicole, and I'm an alcoholic."

"Hello, Nicole," we all said.

"Did you see that moon?" she asked. "Wow. Felt looney all the way over here."

We laughed. So I wasn't the only one. I began to relax. Nicole talked for a while about her struggles. Then she sat down and someone else came up. By the fourth share, I was completely relaxed. It wasn't so bad being in such a big group. I could be more anonymous than usual. The media talking about me or my dead son meant nothing. I hadn't done anything wrong, at least not today, and today was all that counted.

I closed my eyes and leaned against Mark. All was well in the world, all was well. I could almost take a nap. But then I remembered I should be paying attention. This wasn't just about me. It was about the other people in the room.

Except I had to pee. The next alkie hadn't gone up to speak yet, so I got up quickly and hurried to the back, found a hallway and then the bathrooms. Went in. Did the deed, quickly. Was tempted to turn my phone back on but didn't. Heard a muted "hello" from the crowd. Washed my hands. Left the bathroom, went down the hall, stepped into the gathering room again, the meeting place, the come to God or come to our senses room. Looked down and noticed I had splashed some water on my shirt near the waist, and I uselessly wiped it away.

Then I heard, ". . . found out my son died today. I don't mean he died today. I didn't know he was dead. Didn't even know he was a son."

I looked up.

I couldn't fucking believe it.

My knees almost buckled.

The room tilted.

I almost threw up.

Or maybe I did throw up.

Maybe I did buckle.

Maybe I grew a spine of steel and just stood there staring at Ryan Nichols, the father of my dead son Alberto. The man who left town without a forwarding address once I told him I was pregnant, like some kind of teenage boy who had gotten caught with his pants down.

He looked the same. It had been over a decade, but he looked the same. Maybe some gray. Yes, gray. Of course. But no pot belly. No wrinkles I could discern from here.

Or was I hallucinating? I blinked. Hard. No, everyone was looking at him. A woman got up and started to walk by me to the restrooms. I whispered to her, "Did that man say something about a dead son?"

She nodded—and frowned. She must have thought I was looney tunes.

"Do you remember what his name was?"

"Ryan," she said. "Or Bryan. Yep, that was it. Or Ryan."

I let her go her way.

"I didn't even know he'd been born," he continued. "Or that he was real. It's a long story."

I was riveted in place. It wasn't really a long story. He fucked me, I got pregnant, and he fucked me again by running away.

I stared at him. I couldn't hear what else he was saying. If I'd had a gun, I might have shot him. Or not. I wasn't a particularly violent person. Except my wit. My sharp wit. Could I cut him down with that? Could I ruin his life with that?

I could see tears in his eyes, but I couldn't focus on what he was saying. Tears? Twelve years too late. Maybe they weren't tears. Maybe they were some kind of lights. The weird full moon had caused the earth to open up and release all kinds of monsters into the world.

Not that he was a monster. As far as I knew.

I started to laugh. I did. Right out loud. In the middle of an AA meeting. Loudly. Everyone turned around and looked at me. I kept laughing. I couldn't help it. Ryan stopped speaking. He looked at me. At least I thought he was looking at me. I assumed he was looking at the crazy woman at the other end of the room.

I saw someone out of the corner of my eye get up. To take me away no doubt.

Did Ryan open his mouth and say, "Brooke?" Or maybe he said, "Brooke!" Or maybe it was an anguished cry indicating how fucked up his life had been since he left me. "Brooke."

I tried to stop laughing.

I finally choked out, "I'm so sorry. I'm sure I'll be blackballed from every AA group in LA and environs, but this man has no right to talk about my dead son. You have no right to talk about him, you asshole. He wasn't *your* son. He was *my* fucking son, and yes, he did die. You didn't know because you never bothered to find out if he'd ever even been born!"

I saw Mark now coming toward me. Someone else I didn't know, too. I heard someone else whispering, "I love coming to this group. It's fucking theater every time."

Heard someone else say, "Fucking full moon. Should never go to a meeting during the full moon. Every alcoholic has a little werewolf in their blood."

It was as if I suddenly had amazing hearing. A pin actually dropped somewhere in the room. Ryan blinked and the sound of his eyelids over his eyes sounded like sandpaper. He sucked in his breath as I talked, and I couldn't think what that sounded like. A death rattle?

Mark was next to me. He didn't try to stop me or touch me. He was just there. My fucking stalwart man. My wing man. My troops.

The other person—was she male or female?—said, "You need to take it outside."

My spine of steel wobbled a bit then. Or the room stopped tilting.

Because I nodded. Then I headed toward the stairs, with Mark right beside me. I started up. Stopped at the third step. Turned around and said, "You are not his father, motherfucker. I hope you drink yourself blind tonight because of this."

I think everyone in the room gasped or choked. Even Mark? Maybe even me.

With my curse thrown, I hurried up the stairs, through the vestibule, and out into the night.

I started pacing the parking lot near Mark's truck as I pulled out my phone and called Hayword. I tried to look at Mark or the truck, but I could only focus on the darkness. It was so dark. I could not wait for spring. I could not wait for fucking spring.

"Brooke?"

"Hayword," I said. "Hayword, he's here. He's fucking here. And he's talking about Alberto as if he has a right to speak about him."

"Who is there?" Hayword said. It pissed me off that he sounded so confused. He should *know*. He should know. He should fucking know!

"Ryan Nichols!"

"Ryan Nichols?" I could hear in his voice that he didn't know who that was. That made me almost angrier at him than at Ryan.

"Oh my god," he said.

"Yes, yes," I said.

"He's at the AA meeting?" he asked. "Did he follow you?"

"No," I said. "He couldn't have. I've never been here before. Mark brought me, and Ryan—" I could barely say his name. Each time I said it, I felt sick to my stomach. Revulsion. Yes, that was it. I felt revulsion. "Ryan was inside before I was."

"Do you want me to come there?"

"No," I said. "I don't even know where here is. Somewhere in hell, I think." Or near Mark's house. Same thing? Yikes! Was that what I really thought?

"But find out why he's here," I said, "if you can. Is he in town for a job? Is he even still in the biz? I want to know why all the characters from my past are showing up today."

"They're not actually characters," Hayword said.

"Really, Hayword? Is that really what you want to say to me right this second?"

"Yeah, I know. Sorry."

"I'll talk to you later."

I ended the conversation and looked up. Mark was standing next to me. I hadn't known that. Had not been able to see him until this moment.

"I know him," Mark said.

I was so stunned I couldn't move.

"He lives in this area," Mark said. "Maybe for the last year or so. Has a house not far from mine. But he calls himself Bryan Nichols. I never made the connection—although even if he called himself Ryan I probably wouldn't have made the connection since I've only heard you mention his name once."

Yep. Once, when I told him that Hayword wasn't Alberto's biological father.

"I've played poker with him," he said. "Once or twice. I've seen him at a meeting now and again. Played basketball in his driveway. Doesn't say much. I think he lives alone. Gone a lot."

He kept talking, as though anticipating all of my questions.

"If I mentioned you," he said, "I probably only said your first name and there are lots of Brookes in the world."

Yes, that would have been my next question.

My heartbeat was starting to slow again. The world was beginning to look normal again. The big old moon in the sky was vaguely green. I had an urge to reach up and grab it, take it down, and eat it.

I heard footsteps and turned away from the moon.

"Brooke." It was Ryan. I stepped back as he got closer. "Brooke," he said again.

I remembered how Ryan used to whisper my name when we made love. I hadn't liked my name when I was a kid, had tolerated it when I was an adult, but when he said it, I had loved it. It was as if the wind itself were whispering it, and that wind loved and wanted me more than life itself.

"Stop saying my name," I said.

I could feel Mark next to me, could feel he wanted to say something, *do* something. But he let me do my thing, as always.

"Hello, Mark," he said. "I remember you mentioning a Brooke, but it never occurred to me it was this Brooke."

"Hello, Bryan," Mark said.

Ryan looked at me. "That's my real name. Bryan. When I'm working I use Ryan. Always thought that was more interesting." He smiled. Did he really think I would find this confession charming? "Although I've never heard of a director changing his name. At least not someone who is only a director." He shook his head. "I'm babbling. I'm scared. I don't know what to say, Brooke, except that I am so so sorry. I had no idea."

"What? No idea that you provided the sperm for a boy who was born and then who died some months later? That's because you ran away with your tail between your legs like some dog who had pissed on the carpet."

I really wanted to end this conversation.

I really wanted a drink.

"Yes, of course I'm sorry about that," he said. "I heard on the news today about the robbery, and they mentioned you and your son."

I shook my head. "They had no right."

"No," he said, "they didn't. They said he died of SIDS."

Why was I still standing there?

I nodded.

"When I heard that—" He shook his head. "I'm just so sorry, Brooke. You weren't a drinker then, I know, and I—I was always drinking. You just went along, I know."

"What the fuck are you talking about?" I asked. "I've never gone along with anything. I didn't drink then."

His head moved slightly, as though he wanted to correct me, but he didn't know how.

"Brooke, we drank every time we were together."

"We didn't," I said, "and even if we did, you think you were so special that you could force me to drink? You're at an AA meeting. You must know the drill."

"I know, I know," he said. "But the baby. Gawd. I was just stupid and careless."

"What are you talking about?" I said.

"You said he died of SIDS," he said.

I looked at Mark and then at Ryan again.

"So what? What are you trying to say?"

"When the mother drinks during pregnancy," he said, "their infant is more likely to die of SIDS."

I slugged him. In the face. I had never slugged anyone before so it turned into a kind of slap. But it was hard, and he backed away, moaned, put his hand up to his face.

And my hand hurt.

"You motherfucker," I said. "You learn my child died of

SIDS a few hours ago and then you come here to tell me you've figured it all out. I drank so my son died? You blame me for my son's death!"

"No," he said. "Me. I—"

"You cock-sucking motherfucking asshole." I was in his face now. "How about this? Maybe he died because his father was a cowardly bastard with defective sperm?"

"Brooke." Mark's voice.

"I did *not* fucking drink with you," I said. "At least not to excess. And I didn't drink when I was pregnant. So get the fuck out of my life. Get the fuck off the planet. We'd all be better for it."

I turned around. Thankfully the truck was right there. I opened the door and got in. Wished I had the keys so I could just drive away. Mark got in next to me, started the truck, and roared away. That's what it seemed like. I closed my eyes and listened to the roar.

I felt or heard a phone vibrating. I looked down at my phone. It wasn't mine. Mark was staring at the road as though he were in shock. The sound kept coming. I reached into my bag and pulled out the burner phone I'd told Enrique to call me on.

I pushed the button. "What?" I said.

"Brooke?"

"Yes, it's me, Ricky," I said. I had no inclination to be nice to anyone. Any milk of human kindness I'd had was gone. "What do you know?"

"I got it," he said. "The asshole was going to hock it."

"Oh Christ," I said. "Look, the police still think I had something to do with it. If I'm not off the hook soon, I'm going to tell them who it was."

"I can go to the police right now," he said. "I will tell them you had nothing to do with it."

"Too little, too late," I said. I rubbed my face. Although maybe him going to the police was the best thing to do. I didn't know anymore. "Where are you? I need to pick up the bracelet and get it back to its rightful owner."

He gave me the address of some restaurant downtown.

"I'll be there as soon as I can," I said. "Don't leave the parking lot."

He told me what his car looked like, and then I hung up.

"Mark, I need to go into the city," I said.

He nodded. I told him the address and the name of the restaurant. He knew the place.

"You okay?" I asked.

He shrugged. "You?"

I blinked and looked straight ahead, trying to figure out where we were.

"Do you know where we are?" I asked.

"Of course I do," he said.

"You always know where you are," I said. "I admire that. I don't know where I am. I always feel like I'm lost. That's not even a metaphor. Although maybe metaphorically—"

"Brooke," he said.

"Babbling brook," I mumbled.

"What?"

"That's what my dad used to call me," I said, "because I talked a lot. At least my parents thought so. But since they barely said a word between them, I guess I would seem like a chatterbox. He was wrong, you know. Ryan Bryan asshole. I didn't drink. I don't care what anyone says. I didn't drink when I was pregnant. I mean, probably wine at dinner until I found out."

"It's okay," he said.

"Don't try to reassure me," I said. "There's no need. Can you believe the nerve of him?"

I did not cause my baby's death. I knew that. I didn't start drinking until after Alberto died. I mean, wasn't that *why* I drank?

"I know I stopped drinking when I found out I was pregnant," I said. I was four months pregnant before I knew. My periods had always been irregular, so it hadn't occurred to me, especially since I had always used protection with Ryan, and Hayword and I hadn't had sex for months.

Maybe Ryan and I had had wine when we went out. I closed my eyes and leaned against the headrest. But we hadn't really gone out. I had gone to Ryan's apartment, which wasn't far from the studio. We'd eat, drink some wine, and make love. Sometimes we watched old movies together, drank some wine, and made love.

I didn't remember ever being drunk with him. Intoxicated on love—or at least, on sex. But on booze? No. I didn't like to drink.

I had felt guilty then. I had believed in fidelity. Before Ryan, I thought Hayword and I would live together in happy monogamy for the rest of our lives. Only I had gotten bored with the Hollywood life, was definitely bored taking care of the house and the kids, and I was pissed at Hayword for not making all my dreams come true.

Even though I was a feminist. Even though I stood on my own two feet, as it were, and I took care of myself. Even though I did not expect my husband to satisfy my every need and desire, I expected my husband to satisfy my every need and desire. When I wasn't happy, I blamed him.

Who else could I blame? Not the kids. Not the dog. Certainly not me or the gaping hole in my soul.

Hey, that rhymed.

Gaping hole in my soul.

Perhaps I should write a hit song around that one line.

Gaping hole in my soul.

Summed up my life.

How quickly I fell back into the pity party for myself.

I chuckled.

"What's so funny?" Mark asked.

I opened my eyes and looked over at him. "Me," I said. "I was suddenly that drunk again, blaming everyone and everything for my problems. I guess I still have some unresolved feelings regarding Mr. Nichols."

Mark laughed. "You think?"

"Gawd," I said, "this town is just too fucking small."

"I hear ya," he said. "What are we doing anyway?"

"Getting back the stolen goods," I said. "You're about to become an accomplice. You up for it?"

"Been waiting my whole life for it."

Soon enough—since I'm skipping by all the boring stuck in traffic crap—we were in some parking structure next to some restaurant called Charley's Steakhouse or Charley's Blue Plate Special. I didn't know. I didn't care. Mark wanted to come with me, but I said no. I got out of the truck and looked around until I saw Enrique's car. It didn't take much doing. He was standing by his open door, waving wildly, and yelling, "Over here! Over here!"

So much for discretion.

I got into Enrique's dumpy little car. It smelled like stale clothes and rotten coffee. Or stale coffee and rotten clothes.

Enrique wasted no time. He pulled out the bracelet, which was wrapped in a white kerchief, and handed it to me. I opened the cloth on my palm. So this was what a ten thousand dollar diamond bracelet looked like.

"Doesn't look like that much, does it?" he said.

"No, not really," I said. "Could be glass for all I know. Did your friend know how much it's worth?"

"Naw," he said. "I didn't tell him because I was afraid I'd never get it back."

"Smart," I said.

"I know you think what I did was stupid," Enrique said, "but

I've been desperate. I thought I was being clever. It never occurred to me anyone could get hurt. I am sorry."

"Should have probably run it by your AA group," I said. "They would have stopped you. Although I guess it's good you didn't. You didn't tell anyone, did you?"

I had never been part of a criminal conspiracy before. I didn't really know what to do and what not to do. How do people cover their tracks anyway?

"Naw, I didn't tell anyone," he said. "I don't think my friend—John Doe—did either. He doesn't have any friends anyway. I wiped off the prints. Should be good to go."

"Okay," I said. "I'm going to take it back to Juliet's."

"Thanks, Brooke," he said.

"Forget you ever saw me," I said.

I wrapped up the bracelet and stuffed it in my jacket pocket, and then I got out of Ricky's car and ran to Mark's pickup.

"Got the goods, baby?" Mark said.

"Funny guy," I said. "Yes. Now let's go to Juliet's."

"What's your plan?"

"I need to leave the bracelet in the restaurant somewhere," I said, "and make sure someone finds it who will give it to Donna and not steal it."

"How are you going to do that?" Mark asked. "You'll have to be there when someone finds it, right? So that you know it's found and no one stole it."

"Yes," I said.

"But *you* can't find it because they'll figure you just stole it and brought it back," he said.

"Oh crap," I said. "I had not thought about that."

"Why don't you go there now and tell Donna—is that the owner's name?—that you lost an earring last time you were there and look around for it. Something like that. Meanwhile, I'll put the bracelet somewhere. Maybe over by that potted plant near the buffet area. I'll wander away, and you can enlist Donna to help you find the earring. You can point her in the buffet direction while you look somewhere else. And then she'll find it."

"That's good," I said. "Do you have a criminal past I don't now about?"

"You're my criminal past, baby," he said, "and my criminal present."

"Stop that!" I said. "You sound weird when you do gangster."

"Why?"

"Because you sound too good at it," I said. "Remember, I've never liked bad boys."

"That's because you're the bad boy in relationships," he said.

"Got that right, motherfucka! Drive on, Macbeth!"

Okay. So we got there, and right away I could see that I was never going to be a great criminal either. I was nearly as dumb as Ricky. Juliet's is a restaurant: It's busy at dinner time. It was packed to the gills. One good thing, Mark had no trouble slipping by me to go plant the bracelet since no one was paying any attention to us. I finally caught Donna's eye, and she came over to me.

"Hello, darling!" she said. "How are you after the trauma drama this morning? And the news coverage. Wow! First you're a hero and then you're a thief. I could not stand being famous."

"I'm not famous," I said.

"You are now, honey," she said. She actually slapped me on the back. "And so is Juliet's. We haven't had a Wednesday night like this in—well, in ever. Thank you, stupid actors!" She clapped her hands together and laughed.

"So you believe they were actors, too?"

"Of course," she said. "For one thing, you said it, and I believe you. For another, real thieves would have taken the jewelry. So they pocketed one bracelet." She shrugged. "No big deal. They're out of work actors. They needed work, obviously, so they probably needed cash."

"About that," I said, "the reason the police think I had something to do with it is because of that missing bracelet. Is it possible the actor thieves left it here, dropped it or something? Did you look all over the restaurant for it?"

"Good lord, no," she said. "It didn't occur to me. Shall we look for it now?"

My. This was going to be a lot easier than I thought. Thank you, Universe. Make me a hero in the morning, a pariah in the afternoon, and a baby killer by evening: But make it all right before bedtime. My kind of day.

"Lead on," I said.

I followed Donna around the busy restaurant. She stopped to say hello to a lot of people, and I stood next to her, mute, feeling kind of silly—and nervous. At one point I caught Mark's gaze, and he nodded. I almost laughed out loud. What was this foolishness we were doing?

"This is Brooke McMurphy," Donna was saying before I had a chance to run. "She's the one who saved us all from those bad actors." She laughed. "I suppose they weren't *bad* actors since we believed they were robbers. But she got them out of the restaurant before anything went awry."

The people at the table nodded and smiled.

"Oh yes," one of them said. "I heard the police think you helped them rob the place." The group laughed. That made me look at them—really look at them. They seemed strange. Actually the entire restaurant felt strange.

"Must be that weird full moon," someone else at the table said.

"Or maybe we're all turning into zombies like the ones in your movies," another said. A woman? I tried to look at her, but

I felt overstimulated. I couldn't concentrate. This was a familiar feeling. One of those feelings that drove me to drink.

Or so that was my excuse.

"Not zombie movies plural," someone else said. "Only one, and it was quite nuanced and funny. You should see *Love and Other Insanities*. Wonderful, too."

I looked at this person. A woman. She had long white hair and blue eyes. She looked vaguely familiar, but I didn't know why. She wore a blue sweater with a blue and green dragon arching up across it. The woman and I looked into each other's eyes, and I knew that she knew I was just about to go over some edge that would have been unimaginable just a few short hours ago.

"Thank you for those hours of entertainment," the woman said.

"That's kind of you to say," I said. "Thank you." And then to Donna, I said, "May we continue?"

As we walked around the restaurant, Donna looked behind potted plants and under tables, causing her patrons to laugh. Everyone was in such a freaking good mood.

Must be the food.

Or the moon.

Donna headed toward the buffet. Thank god. She bent over at the tall potted plant. She didn't come up right away. When she did, she was clutching something in her hand. She grabbed my hand and pulled me along until we were in the kitchen—where the kitchen staff didn't even look up at us.

"You won't believe it," Donna said. "Look!" She opened her right hand. She had found it—just where Mark had left it.

"So they really weren't thieves!" she said. "Wow. This is beautiful. Would you like to hold it?"

"No!" I said. "The police are already suspicious of me. I can't have my fingerprints on it."

"I hear ya," she said. "In fact, why don't you leave? I mean,

I'm the one who found it. I'll call them straightaway and you don't have to have anything to do with it."

"I like the way you think," I said. I gave her a quick hug—I wasn't sure why she was being so nice to me—and then I hurried out of the restaurant.

Mark was standing by the pickup. I grinned. "Hello, Clyde."

He laughed. "Come on, Bonnie," he said. "Let's make our getaway."

"I'm with ya, baby," I said. And off we went.

SEVEN

In the morning, I awakened to sunshine—which wasn't exactly unusual in Southern California—but it was still glorious. I awakened to sunshine and quiet. Mark's side of the bed was empty. I had turned off my cellphone and unplugged the landline last night. No one could get a hold of me. I luxuriated in the blissful silence. Except for the seagulls. I could hear them. I smiled and buried my head in the pillow for a few more minutes.

I should get up. Do some writing. Greet the day.

Then I remembered yesterday. Remembered the "robbery," remembered recognizing Enrique, and then the events of the entire day came spilling out—like a sped up film. The climax came when Ryan Nichols suggested Alberto had died because I drank during my pregnancy.

Ugh.

Crap.

I had to figure out a way to get out of going to the party tonight.

I didn't know what I dreaded more: telling Fern I didn't want to go or actually going to the party.

Fucking Ryan Nichols. How life changed on a freaking dime.

I didn't want to think about *him*. Where was my man?

"Mark!" I called.

He didn't answer. Probably downstairs in the restaurant. I sighed. Wished I hadn't slept in. Would really love one of Mark's breakfasts.

I got up, slipped on a robe, and then opened the door that led down to the restaurant. We had agreed that we'd always leave the door locked so people couldn't mistakenly wander upstairs, but since the restaurant wasn't actually open, we weren't strict about it. I guessed Mark hadn't given it a second thought this morning.

I hurried down the stairs and went into the empty dining room.

"Mark!" I called.

No answer. I heard a radio playing in the kitchen, so I headed in that direction. I glanced out the window. What a great view his customers would have of the Pacific Ocean. And right now a flock of birds was circling the beach. I squinted. Couldn't tell what kind they were, but it was a huge flock. A few people on the beach had stopped and were pointing at the birds. The humans looked like stick figures in a diorama of the ocean beach. Strangely enough the birds looked as big as the people. Must have been my perspective, or something.

I hoped Daphne du Maurier's story "The Birds" wasn't about to come to life. I laughed. What a silly thought. Maybe the birds were circling because they didn't want to land on the radioactive beach with the radioactive ocean water.

I sighed. I really hoped that wasn't the case. I could ask David—he'd know. Poor stressed-out kid.

I pushed open the swinging kitchen door and found Sherry and Mark leaning over something on a side countertop. They were so close they were almost touching.

Sherry looked over at me and quickly moved away from Mark.

I felt momentary butterflies in my stomach.

Mark looked up at me. "Good morning, sleepy head." He came right over to me and kissed me. Didn't hesitate. Didn't look at Sherry. Wasn't a guilty bone in his body.

I looked at Sherry. Squinted at her. Narrowed my vision. Tried to ascertain what was up with her.

I didn't trust her or like her and I didn't know why.

But then, I didn't trust anyone, really. Except David. But he was a kid. I wouldn't burden him with the burden of me only trusting him.

Maybe Joanie, too.

Hayword to a certain extent.

Okay, Mark. About some things.

Lordy. Maybe I was more trusting than I thought.

Good grief.

But right that moment, I did not trust Sherry Burns.

"What are you two so intent on?" I asked.

"I'm looking over where the tables are," he said. "I'm still not certain it's working. I'm worried the wait staff won't be able to get around each table."

"Are you still doing a practice run on Saturday?" I asked.

"Sure," he said.

"I guess you'll find out then," I said. "In the meanwhile, have you had breakfast yet?"

Mark laughed. "What you really mean is will I make you breakfast?"

"That sounds great," I said. "I'll take the house specialty." I grinned.

"Actually Giovanni is fixing something so the electricity is off," he said. "Sherry, you need me here?"

"No," she said. "In fact, I don't think you need me here either. We're ahead of schedule. You're going to the farmer's market on Saturday and Sunday, right? So we're good to go." She smiled. "And Brooke, I didn't see anything about you on the news this morning." She looked at me as if she wanted to say more or hear more. Like she wanted to be my confidante. For a moment, I felt sorry for her. I was not the easiest person to get to know, especially when I had no desire to get to know the other person.

"Good to hear," I said. I was tempted to take Mark's hand, but I realized that gesture was too akin to a dog pissing on its territory so I refrained. Instead, I said, "Nice to see you again, Sherry." Then I left the kitchen.

I heard Mark say something to her—I don't know what—and then he was close behind me, grabbing my ass. I laughed, and we ran across the restaurant and up the stairs. Once we were in my apartment and the door was closed and locked, Mark said, "Sherry's nervous around you. Can't you give her a break?"

"Why is she nervous?" I said. "You two seemed pretty darn cozy when I came in. She looked a little guilty."

Mark laughed as he went into the kitchen. "She wasn't guilty. She was probably scared when she saw you. You are formidable."

"Good," I said. I got up on a stool at the bar between the kitchen and the living room. This apartment was a lot like my writing studio. I liked the coziness of both. "I hope she's scared of me. Then she'll keep her mitts off what's mine."

"What's that mean?" Mark asked. "What is yours? This building?"

"You know exactly what I mean," I said.

He frowned. "Are you telling me you're jealous of her? That doesn't seem like you."

"It doesn't, does it?" I said. "I'm feeling strange. Must be what happened yesterday."

"Have you been thinking about what Ryan said to you?" He cracked an egg into a bowl. Then another.

"Oh, Christ, no," I said. "I'm trying not to think about it."

"What about the police?" he asked. He whipped the eggs with a fork. "Are you off the hook?"

Ugh.

He looked over at me. "I bet you'd like me to stop interrogating you?"

"Yes, please." I smiled. "I'd really just like to go back to bed."

"Wish I could," he said. He poured the eggs into a pan. "I've got so much to do today. Ian has a soccer game tonight. Do you remember I'm staying at my house tonight because Ian is staying?"

"Yep," I said. "I remember. I'll probably stay at my studio after David's science report tomorrow. I need to get the script done by Saturday, so that'll force me to work."

He laughed. "Will that work?"

I shrugged. "I don't know." I grinned wanly. "I could be in denial. It's not like millions of dollars are riding on this or anything."

"It'll give you something to do on Saturday," he said. He spooned some takeout Chinese food onto the omelette. Smelled delicious.

"I really don't want you around for the dry run," Mark said. "It would make me too nervous."

"Hah!" I said. "I can't imagine you nervous."

He glanced over at me and then folded the omelette.

"Are you excited?" I asked. "Your dream is about to come true."

He slipped the omelette out of the pan and onto a plate and

then brought the plate over to me. The omelette smelled lovely. Like soy sauce and ginger. I took a bite. Mmmmm.

"Wow," I said. "Will you marry me?"

I said it without thinking. But then a silence throbbed between us. I looked at Mark, who was watching me eat.

"Just kidding," I said. "You know, the whole bigamy thing. This is delicious. So, about your dream coming true?" I grinned. I did not want to talk about our relationship now. Geez, Louise.

"Sure," he said. He turned away from me and went back to the stove.

Talk about avoiding a question.

"Mark, come on," I said. "Be excited. I'm excited for you."

"And that's what counts," he said.

That almost sounded snarky. Mark didn't do snark. I felt another twinge, or something, like when I saw him standing so close to Sherry.

This was odd.

I should ask him about it. I should reassure him. Or do something human.

But I didn't.

"I better check my messages to see if the shit has stopped hitting the fan," I said.

I checked my voice mail on my landline. Three messages. First one: "Uh, this is Detective Baxter," he said. "I've called your lawyer, or the studio lawyer—whoever he is—but I wanted you to know we're dropping this. For now." I heard him sigh or breathe hard. Like he wanted to say something else.

I deleted the message.

Fern was up next: "Mom, you better not be using the robbery to get out of the party. I'm counting on you."

"Gee, thanks, daughter." I erased her messages, too.

Joanie: "Answer your damn phone, asshole."

I laughed and erased her message, too.

Sally had left two messages on my cell phone, telling me she thought all was well now. The big mucky mucks had calmed down. Now I just needed to get a final script to them and all would be well.

"Yeah, yeah," I said to no one. "I'll get you the fucking script." I just needed some time to sit down and think about zombies.

One message and a text from Irving Jackson. He repeated that he needed to talk to me. What the fuck did he want?

One message from Hayword, wondering how I was doing.

I called Hayword first.

"Hey, Brooke," he said. "Are you okay?"

"Yes," I said. "I'm so sorry I didn't call you back last night."

"I assumed you either killed Nichols or you didn't," he said. "And since you weren't on the news again, I figured you hadn't. In fact, I haven't seen anything about you on the news. Your 15 minutes are up."

"Thank god," I said. "David okay? I actually forgot to call him last night."

"Yeah," he said. "I told him you had called and were going to be incommunicado for a bit. He accepted that. Plus he got a text from you, so that was good. Having him become a teenager has been so much easier than when Fern became . . . well, any age."

I laughed. "Yes. You're meeting me at the school tomorrow, right? For the science project?"

"Sure," he said. "So do you want to talk about what happened last night?"

I shook my head. But I didn't say anything. I walked over to the window. It looked like the flock of birds that had been circling earlier had landed on the beach. Thousands of them. The beach was black with them. I squinted. The people on the beach seemed to be hurrying away from them, but they walked stiffly, almost like the zombies in my movie. I chuckled.

"What?" Hayword said.

"There are these birds on the beach," I said. "And the people are acting peculiar."

"I heard some strange things have been going on today," he said. "They're blaming it on a new wave of radiation from Japan. But I think that's highly unlikely. Some dolphins beached themselves down in Santa Monica, but they won't let people help them. It's as if they're refusing aid. Coyotes are doing something somewhere. I bet we'll find out they're all hoaxes."

"Maybe," I said, "but I'm seeing the birds." I moved the phone away from my mouth and called out, "Mark, come look at this."

Mark left the kitchen and came over to stand by me.

"So what happened when you saw Ryan?" Hayword asked.

I walked away from Mark. He glanced at me. I looked down at the phone.

"He implied Alberto had died because of my drinking," I said to Hayword. "But I pointed out I hadn't been a drinker until after he left me."

"What a fucking bastard." Hayword sounded pissed.

"I know. He's gone all this time and then shows up to blame me."

Mark looked at me again and then went back to the kitchen. Or somewhere. I didn't see. I didn't pay attention.

"I didn't drink back then," I said. "Right?"

"Even if you did," Hayword said, "that doesn't mean you caused it."

I nodded. Then I realized he hadn't agreed with me. Agreed that I didn't drink.

"Hayword," I said. "Did I drink or not?"

He made a noise. Then he said, "Do you want a real answer or do you just want me to make you feel better?"

"I want to feel better!" I said. "What do you think I've been trying to do for the last two years? No, longer than that. I've been trying to feel better for over a decade, give or take."

"I know, honey," Hayword said.

"Don't call me that," I said. I felt furious and weepy all at the same time. My knees wobbled.

"You'd been unhappy for a while," he said. "So you drank. And yes, when you were with Ryan, you drank."

"But I stopped when I knew I was pregnant," I said. "Come on."

"Sure," he said. "Sure. I'm sure you did. Of course. You were four months gone before you knew."

The implication being that Alberto stewed in my alcohol-filled womb for four months.

"No one says that anymore," I said. "Four months gone. I wasn't gone. I was pregnant."

"Well—"

"Hayword," I warned.

"Okay, look," he said. "Come home. You can spend the night, and we can talk."

"I can't have a sleepover with you," I said. "I don't think that would be kosher given I'm living with another man, and you must be dating someone."

"No," he said. "I'm not. I'm waiting for you to come to your senses and come home." He laughed, and I laughed with him. But I couldn't tell if he was joking or not. I glanced behind me, toward the kitchen, but Mark wasn't there. He was looking out the windows again.

"I'll meet you at the party tonight," Hayword said, "and then we can go home together afterward. Mark can come, too."

I laughed. Somehow the turn this conversation had taken was cheering me up. Was my husband actually flirting with me?

"That is not going to happen," I said. "For one thing, Mark is not coming to the party. For another, that would just be weird. I might come back to the studio, though, since I have to be in the area for David's science project tomorrow."

"Okay," Hayword said. "But I'll be at the party tonight if you want to talk."

"I think Fern wants me to talk to some young writers," I said, "encourage them or some nonsense. It would be better if I told them to run for the hills."

We said our goodbyes, and then I went to stand by the window with Mark. The birds covered the sand like a tattered black beach blanket. The humans had all scurried away.

"What kind of birds are they?" I asked.

"Black birds," Mark said.

"Funny."

"I'm serious," he said. "It looks like they're different kinds of black birds. Those walking over there look like crows. Over here are starlings, I think. Maybe those are cowbirds. The ones closer to us are grackles."

"You have amazing eyesight," I said.

He lifted up his right hand and showed me the binoculars. I laughed.

"What are they doing?"

"Just hanging out, as far as I can tell," he said. "Looking out at the water. Some of them are picking at the sand."

"As long as they don't block the driveway so I can't go to this stupid party," I said as I moved away from him and the window. Apparently I had decided it was easier to go to the party than tell my daughter I didn't want to go.

"I was thinking a similar thing," he said, looking back at me. "As long as they don't interfere with the opening on Sunday." He faced the window again. "I guess that's what we all do. We're all NIMBYs. What if there is something catastrophic going on, and we're just fiddling while Rome burns?"

"Of course something catastrophic is going on," I said. "Haven't you been paying attention to the weather? To the oceans? Christ. We've all been fiddling."

Mark turned around and leaned back against the window. "Shouldn't we do something?"

"Yes! Of course!" I said. "But I haven't a clue what to do. So I'm taking my fiddle, and I'm going to the party. You wanna come?"

"I thought you told Hayword I wasn't going," he said.

"You never want to go to these things," I said.

"That's true," he said. "But if you asked me, if you really wanted me to go, I'd do it."

I rolled my eyes and sighed. "Mark, what the fuck? I'm not going to make you go someplace *I* don't even want to be. One of the reasons Hayword and I split was because I couldn't stand going to these bullshit things."

"Yet here you are going," he said, "and meeting Hayword there."

"I told you it was Fern," I said. "She begged me. The robbery thing traumatized her. The non-robbery thing. Why are you giving me a hard time about this?"

"I'm not," he said. He rubbed his face. He suddenly looked tired. "I'm just juggling a lot, I guess, and you know, you've got a history with Hayword. It would be so easy to fall back into familiar routines."

"Familiar routines? The last familiar routines I had with Hayword was living with him while fucking you."

He shrugged. "And fucking him."

This conversation was making my teeth hurt. I didn't understand it.

"Do you get the urge to go back to your wife?" I asked. "You had familiar routines with her."

"We've been apart for a long time," he said. "So, no, I don't get that urge. I want to see my son more, and I could do that if I were with her. But beyond that, no. But you work with Hayword. You guys talk to each other like you're still married."

"Because we are."

"Exactly," he said.

We stared at one another.

"I—I'm just not sure," he said. "I'm not sure that you're actually committed to us. Or if we were just easy after you got out of rehab."

"We live together," I said. "Your restaurant is practically in my house. That sounds like commitment to me."

"We don't live together," he said. "Some weeks we barely see one another. We've got three different residences! I want a life together. I want to cuddle with you every morning as we wake up together and every night before we fall to sleep. I want to read the Sunday newspaper in bed with you. I want us to plan our days together, our vacations, our lives together."

"No one reads the newspaper anymore," I said.

Mark just looked at me.

"I'm sorry," I said. "Inappropriate time to joke. I am absolutely committed to you. Come on, Mark."

"Brooke, you don't talk to me," he said. "Not about anything deep and real."

"You sound like a girl," I said.

"God damn it," he said. "Quit trying to make this into a joke. I'm trying to speak to you. To tell you what's in my heart and you're making a fucking joke out of it. You're starting to treat me just like you treated Hayword. Maybe not starting to. Maybe you always have. I'm not a spear-carrier in your life, Brooke. I've got my own life. You're either in it with me or you're not."

"I don't treat you like a spear-carrier," I said. "I'm not going to kill you off in the next scene."

He shook his head. "I just told you how I feel."

I nodded. "Okay. Okay. I—"

"I don't want to hear about you dealing with another crisis," he said. "Don't use that as an excuse. We'll talk about this after a, b, or c happens. That's what you always say. And then there's another drama."

Ouch. That stung. Was he implying I was a drama queen?

"It's not all about you, Brooke," he said. "It's not always all about you. Or your family."

"If this is about me not asking you to come to the party—"

"No, god damn it," he said. "You're still not listening. Just think about what I said. You don't have to have an answer. You don't have to defend yourself or your position. Just think about it. We'll talk next week."

"Next week?" I said. "Won't I see you before then?"

"Sure," he said. "We'll run into each other before then."

I made a noise. "Don't pout," I said.

"I'm not pouting!" he said. "We've got a busy few days coming up." He glanced out the window. "Besides, if the birds and other animals start coming after us, who knows what will happen?"

I went to Mark and put my arms around his waist and kissed his mouth. "But I want you with me during the animal attacks. Won't it prove my commitment if we're together when we're torn to bits by wild animals?"

"Not if they're black birds," he said. "We'd probably be pecked to death. Far less dramatic."

"Says you. Don't you remember *The Birds*? Gave me nightmares for weeks."

He put his arms around me, and we embraced, heart to heart.

"It's been a weird couple of days," I said.

"Understatement."

"Maybe the worst part of it is over," I said.

"Naw, the full moon is actually today," he said, "so my guess is the bird shit is really going to hit the fan today."

I moved out of the hug and looked at his face. "You don't believe that do you?"

He laughed. "Of course not. Unless it turns out to be true."

I pushed him away. "I've gotta go to work," I said. "If I don't get this screenplay done, more than shit is going to hit the fan."

EIGHT

I tried to write. Sat on my bed with my laptop in front of me, overheating on top of the bedspread. I had tried writing at my desk in the guest room, but I kept looking out the window and watching the flock of black birds. After a while, they flew up, divided themselves into other flocks, and flew away.

I had read reports on the interwebs from all over our area of birds and animals "acting strangely." On TV talking heads speculated that an earthquake was coming. Others blamed it on the moon or radiation. The strange was mostly animals gathering together. Coyotes and bobcats. Crows and cowbirds (although that wasn't particularly strange.) Dogs and cats.

"Dogs and cats living together!" I said as I scrolled through the articles. It all seemed pretty vague to me—and a stupid distraction when I should be working.

Nevertheless, I managed to piss away the day without talking to another human being—besides Mark when he came in the room to kiss me goodbye before he left for the day. I texted

125

David, asked him about his day. Texted Joanie. Sally. Fern. But I didn't talk to anyone. Didn't speak out loud.

I didn't try to locate Ryan Nichols. Didn't try to find out what he'd been doing for the last decade. Didn't try to get his phone number.

Even though I was tempted.

I was.

I didn't understand it either. I was furious with him. I still couldn't believe what he had said to me. I still felt mildly sick to my stomach that maybe I had remembered everything wrong. Maybe I had been drinking when I was pregnant—before I knew.

Even with all of that, I was tempted to find out more about Ryan. Tempted to find out how to contact him.

So that I could contact him.

Not to scream at him.

Although I might.

Not to tell him I hated him.

No.

Maybe I would scream at him. Maybe I would slug him. But part of me wanted to touch him. Part of me wanted to know what it would be like to touch him one more time. Would I feel that sexual electricity again? Would he feel familiar? Would it be like touching Alberto again? Would there be some kind of connection, some kind of sense memory of Alberto once I touched Ryan again?

I knew this sounded ridiculous. I didn't understand it. But there it was.

I hadn't had a drink in two years, so I could certainly resist trying to get in touch with my old love.

It was a strange few hours of resisting and trying to be creative. I didn't write a word. But I did resist searching for Ryan.

I felt strange. As if I wasn't all there. Or almost lonely. Yet I wasn't willing to do anything about the loneliness—if that was what it was—like actually talk to another human being.

When it was time, I ate something and then got dressed and headed for downtown.

Miraculously, traffic was light, and I watched the full moon rise above the city. It was so lovely I felt like howling, and I wished someone was with me to see it. Someone else in this city of many millions must be looking at the moon, too. Maybe even someone I loved.

And probably lots of people who annoyed the hell out of me.

The party was bigger than I had anticipated—too many people, big venue, lots of food, and a loud band—and I felt a twinge of shyness as I walked into the ballroom. Wished I had let Hayword take me, wished I had coerced Mark into coming with me, wished I'd come with Joanie. Something. But I didn't dwell on it. I sucked in my stomach, put on what I hoped was a bright smile, and off I went.

I made a beeline for Sally St. James. She smiled when she saw me, and we gave each other air kisses just to amuse ourselves.

"So glad you agreed to come," Sally said. "A friendly face, finally."

I kept my arm around her waist as we looked out at the spiffily dressed crowd. I smiled at this or that person, waved at one or two.

"You're the boss," I said. "Isn't everyone a friendly face?"

She laughed and made a noise. "I don't trust anyone. Do you? Your daughter. She's loyal. She's a good worker. But the rest? Come on. The bigwigs have been on my case. Didn't like the numbers from last quarter."

"I thought you had the owners—investors?—in your back pocket," I said. "Must be more than just a number thing. I thought AFT was all about the love of filmmaking."

"Easy for billionaires to say," Sally said. "But even billionaires worry about money. In fact, maybe they worry more than millionaires. I think someone has been badmouthing me. It's not you, is it?"

I dropped my arm, looked at her, and rolled my eyes. "Yes, Sally. I regularly hang with these unknown billionaires."

"I introduce you to them all the time," she said. "Why can't you remember them?"

"They have no interest in me," I said. "In fact, weren't they embarrassed that a zombie movie made them so much money? I think they'd just as soon I went away."

"Not true," she said. "We're counting on part two. How's that coming?"

I smiled and looked away from her.

"Brooke, I've got to have that in hand like yesterday," she said.

"I know," I said, "but haven't you heard about all the animals acting strangely, and then there's the radiation. And a green moon."

"What the fuck are you talking about?"

"The robbery and all this other weird stuff has thrown me off my stride," I said. "I'll get the script to you very, very soon. I promise. Have I ever let you down?"

"Sure," she said, "when you stopped fucking me. That left me very down, so to speak. Don't you ever miss the old days?"

"You mean when I was drunk and depressed and fucking everyone in sight?"

"Sometimes I miss a woman going down on me," she said. "I miss the curves. The juiciness." She sighed. "On the other hand, my husband can fuck like a banshee, and he never asks me what I'm thinking."

"How does a banshee fuck?" I asked. "I mean, aren't they dead Irish women wailing over dead people?"

"Way to kill the mood, Mac," she said. "Just saying if you ever want to have a quickie in my office, I'm up for it."

"I think this constitutes sexual harassment," I said.

"Oh good," she said. "Maybe they'll fire me then. Brooke, I haven't told you everything. I didn't want to worry you. Or I didn't want to talk about it." She lowered her voice as she smiled at this or that person walking by us. "AFT is in big trouble. They don't want to dump *Beauty and the Zombie*. I was wrong about that. There have been some financial . . . irregularities. The studio might be going belly up. They might have to cancel Hayword's movie—unless *Beauty and the Zombie Part Two* starts on time and the buzz is good. They think they can stall the creditors and maybe even the feds for 24 months, give or take."

"The feds?" I said. "What's going on? Is this you? Did you do something?"

"No!" She smiled and waved at someone across the room. "No. I'm not really sure who did what. They don't trust me. I don't know how much longer I'll be studio head. A lot is hanging on this little zombie movie, Brooke. The fate of the world as it were. At least our little world."

"Christ, Brooke. That's a lot of pressure."

"But you're almost done, right? You'll have it to me by Saturday?"

Hadn't written a word, beyond the initial treatment.

Fuck me.

"Sure," I said. "It's almost done. You'll love it."

Man, I suddenly wished I had a drink.

Buck up, Brooke baby. This is the adult world. Just do your job and everything will be all right.

Hah! What kind of bullshit advice was that? I really needed to get a better inner voice.

"By the way," I said, "did I mention that Irving Jackson has been trying to get a hold of me? Do you know what he wants?"

"That little weasel," she said. "I hired him, you know. I had faith in him, and now he's after my job. I bet you anything he's the one who's trying to take me down."

"What would he want with me?" I asked.

"Probably trying to figure out a way to fuck me up," Sally said. "He's not the man I thought he was. Be careful around him. In fact, I'd avoid him if I could. I'm trying to figure out a way to fire him."

"He's management," I said. "It's not like he has a union. Can't you just fire him?"

"You'd think," she said, "but some of the investors like him. I don't get it."

Just then we both saw Fern and waved at her. She looked all grown up in her black cocktail dress, holding a drink in her hand. Looked like hard liquor. Really wished the girl would stick to lemonade.

"Hello, Mom," she said. "Hi, Sally. Everything seems to be going well. Everyone is happy."

"That's great," Sally said. "Good job. Now just relax and have a good time. I better mingle."

Sally winked and then sashayed away; the crowd parted as she neared, like Moses approaching the Red Sea. I smiled. I did enjoy watching her walk.

I looked back at Fern. "Okay. Where are the writers you wanted me to meet?"

"They're not here yet," she said. "But Dad is on his way."

"He already knows how to write, dear," I said.

My daughter looked stressed, and her eyes were glittery. Drugs, alcohol, or both?

"What's going on with you?" I asked.

She shook her head, distracted. "Nothing," she said. "Nothing. Just trying to keep it all together. This party. You know. Let me go call. Go get a drink or something, Mom. I'll get back to you."

And then she hurried away.

Go get a drink? What was wrong with that girl? Was she purposely trying to turn me back into a drunk?

I saw Irving Jackson across the room, and I knew I should go over and see what the hell he wanted from me, but I decided I'd rather powder my nose. I headed for the bathrooms. What a relief it was to step out of the ballroom and into the relative quiet of the corridor.

A man in a suit was walking toward me. He smiled, was ready to talk to me, I could tell. Why didn't I know him? And then I knew him.

Christ almighty! What was *he* doing here? I hadn't seen him in 15 years, and now I saw him twice in two days?

"Ricky!" I said in a harsh whisper. "What are you doing here?" I looked around quickly.

"Hello, Brooke," he said loudly. "I haven't seen you in ages!" Then he whispered, "I was invited." We walked away from the bathrooms and stepped into an empty red and gold dining room that smelled like stale donuts.

"What do you mean you were invited?" I asked.

He nodded. "I've written a script," he said, "and AFT is interested in it. So they invited me to this."

"What?" I said.

Was he one of the writers my daughter had wanted me to meet?

"Ricky," I said, "my daughter Fern works for AFT. What if she recognizes your voice? You have to go! She was very traumatized by what happened yesterday."

"I'm glad you're here," Enrique said, ignoring what I'd just said. "Did everything work out with the bracelet?"

"Shhh!" I said. Why wasn't he understanding me? He needed to leave. "Yes, the bracelet is back with its owner, and the police seem to be satisfied, at least for now. You've got to get out of here!"

"This is a business obligation," he said. "I can't hide for the rest of my life. No one saw me at Juliet's. No one will recognize my voice. It was deeper. Harsher. That was my character. He was a little taller, too, I think, don't you?"

"Ricky!"

"I needed to tell you something."

"Good grief. The suspense is killing me. What now?"

"Manny wants money or he's going to go to the police," Enrique said. "I don't have anything to give him. He wants his due."

"His due?" I said. "I'll give him his due by going straight to the police and telling them everything."

This entire debacle had absolutely nothing to do with me, yet it had turned my life upside down. And to top it off, now some asshole I didn't know was fucking blackmailing me.

That was not going to happen.

"Where is this little motherfucker?" I asked. "I'd like to tell him no to his face."

"He's not here," Enrique said. "He's working tonight at Juliet's."

"Then let's go," I said. "I want this done and over with because I am done and over with it."

"Sure," Enrique said. "But now? I just got here and—"

I made a noise. "Enrique, this is not how I manage my life," I said. "I stay far from drama. I certainly stay far from any criminal element. If someone thinks they can blackmail me, then I need to put an end to that particular thought form. I don't care if you just got here or not. Why would this little flea believe he could blackmail me?"

"He figures you wouldn't want the police to know that

you knew me," he said. "And he knows everyone who was involved."

I shrugged. "So? Everyone involved is you, your friend, and Manny, the one who is trying to blackmail me. I don't care about any of you."

I was speaking too loudly. Even though the dining room was empty, someone might hear me. I had to calm down. For one thing, Fern had left the ballroom and was walking toward me. She was actually smiling, nervously. She waved. I waved back. Enrique waved, too.

"Stop that," I whispered. "She doesn't know she knows you. You had your mask on."

He didn't say anything.

Then Fern was there.

"Hello, Mom."

She put her hand out. I started to take her hand and I realized my daughter had never reached for me in her life.

"Hello, Enrique." She took Enrique's hand. They held tightly to each other's hands and looked at me.

My eyes widened.

And then they narrowed.

"So you knew about all of this?" I said to Fern. "You brought me to Juliet's so I could be a witness to this stupid robbery? For what purpose?"

"Mom, shhh," Fern said. "Your voice carries."

"My voice carries! Fern! What the fuck is going on?"

"It was supposed to be harmless," she said. "We were trying to figure out a way to get Enrique and . . . his friend noticed. Manny tried to get Mahoney to come to Juliet's. When that didn't work, I suggested you. You and Dad both have new movies. We thought if you could see Enrique in a new light, you might hire him. And he is a brilliant scriptwriter. You could read his script, give him some advice."

"Then why didn't you just fucking *ask* me?" I said. I had definitely raised my voice. "Enrique, you could have called me. I would have found you work."

"I didn't want charity," he said.

"So robbing me is better?"

"It wasn't—"

"It wouldn't have been charity," I interrupted him. "I thought you were a good actor. But trying to scare me into hiring you, that's just bizarre! And to get me implicated in a crime, what the hell were you thinking?"

"Don't yell at him," Fern said. "It was my idea."

"I'll yell at anyone I want to yell at," I said. "Fern, you have no idea the backlash I've gotten because of this. Yesterday—" I couldn't tell her about the blowout at the Not Okay Corral yesterday (aka the AA meeting). She didn't know about Ryan Nichols. She didn't know Hayword wasn't Alberto's biological dad. I wasn't up to that conversation.

"The details don't matter," I said. "Just know that yesterday was not good."

"I know," Fern said.

Enrique nodded. "It's my fault. I should have thought it through."

"Damn right it's your fault," I said. "You're old enough to be her father!"

"No," he said. They both shook their heads.

"No, he's younger than Dad," Fern said. "But none of that matters."

"And you, Fern," I said, "you're supposed to be some kind of genius. This was just plain stupid."

"Let's not call each other names," Fern said.

"Yes, let's," I said. "This was a stupid plan. You're quite the good little actor yourself, daughter o' mine. And now what? Are you behind this plan of Manny's to blackmail me?"

Fern looked at her shoes. Enrique stared up at the ceiling.

"Look at me!" I cried.

"No," Fern said. "We have nothing to do with it. We tried to talk him out of it."

"So when you say Manny knows *everyone* who was involved," I said, "he's talking about *you*, Fern, isn't he? He knows I'm your mother and Hayword is your father and that maybe we have some scratch we can spare?"

She nodded.

"I'm not paying him off," I said.

"Then I'll go to jail," Fern said. "Enrique will go to jail! I'll lose my job."

"Maybe you should lose your job," I said. "I think you all need to get your heads examined. I mean, why the hell didn't you just ask me for a job, Ricky?"

"You hate all the Hollywood schmoozing," Fern said. "And I knew you'd be pissed that we were dating."

I shook my head. "And I wouldn't be pissed that you tried to have your boyfriend rob me?"

"It wasn't a real robbery," Enrique said.

I shot him a look.

"I thought it was a novel way to audition," Fern said.

"Did you come up with this when you were drunk?" I asked.

"I was trying to be creative," Fern hissed. She looked like she was eleven years old again, hurt and angry all at the same time. "I know everyone sees me as this automaton without a creative bone in my body."

"Criminality is not creative," I said. "It's ludicrous." I shook my head. "But it's all water under the bridge. We need to shut this guy up."

Oh Lord. I was sounding like some criminal from a noir film.

"Is he an actor?" I asked.

Fern and Enrique nodded.

"What does he want more?" I asked. "A job or the cash?"

"But if there's a job," Fern said, "shouldn't it go to En-rique?"

"I think that ship has sailed," Enrique said.

"Yep," I said. "First smart thing you've said."

"Hey, leave him alone."

I put my hands up. "Don't either of you dare tell me what to do, say or feel. Because right now I could say things to both of you that none of us would ever forget. You have no idea the can of putrid devouring monstrous worms you have unleashed. Find out what this guy wants: a job or cash. And don't just come out and ask. Be subtle. And get me an audition tape. His audition tape. Have him meet me tomorrow in the village near our house, Fern. At The Coffee Shoppe at eight a.m. sharp. And text me his exact name and address."

"Why?" Fern asked.

"Because I said so." I grinned maniacally—I hoped. Then I said, "I've got a goddamn plan, man. Now, if there are no real writers to meet here, I am leaving. I came here as a favor to you, Fern. Because you asked. See what happens when you just ask instead of concocting some elaborate scheme. It's so simple."

"Asking you a favor is like torture," Fern said.

"Obviously, you have never been tortured," I said. "I would do anything for you. I wish you'd understand that. Maybe it's time you get help for your mommy issues, Fern. They're driving me fucking crazy, and I can only imagine what they're doing to you." I shook my head. "We'll all talk later, I'm sure."

I walked away from Fern and her paramour. I wondered how long they'd been sleeping together. No. I shook my head. I was not going there.

Suddenly, just before I left the nearly empty dining room, Irving Jackson was beside me.

"Hello, Irving," I said, trying to muster all the cheer I could. "I was just coming to look for you. I'm sorry I haven't returned your calls. Family and business stuff going on. How's everything?"

He smiled. "Everything is fine," he said. He put his hand on my elbow and deftly turned me around and steered me into the dining room. Enrique and Fern walked past us, and Irving nodded hello to them. He took me to a table and pulled out a chair for me.

"Irving, you seem so serious," I said. "What's going on?"

I sat in the chair, and he sat in one next to me. Sat a bit too close.

"I want you to help me push Sally St. James out of AFT," he said.

I laughed. "Okay. Right to the point. Didn't Sally hire you?"

"Yes," he said, "but now it's my time."

"Sally is one of my closest friends," I said. "I barely know you. Why on Earth would I help you do anything to hurt her?"

"Because I know what your daughter did," he said. "And my guess is you'd like to keep that quiet and keep her out of jail."

He looked straight at me and barely blinked.

I said, "What the hell are you talking about?"

"You know," he said.

So now Irving Jackson was blackmailing me over this stupid fake robbery incident? Christ. I should go to the police and tell them the whole thing: Couldn't be any worse than this bullshit.

"I don't know." I could play stupid as well as anyone. "What has she done? She's a grown woman, you know. Why aren't you blackmailing *her* over her supposed digression?"

"Because she has no power," he said. "You do." He shrugged. "Besides, she doesn't even know she told me. She was drunk.

She drinks too much, you know. Like mother, like daughter, I guess."

I wanted to throw something at him. Instead, I smiled. "I don't drink."

"Anymore," he said.

"What did she tell you in her drunken state?"

"About burning down the house," he said. "Your house."

You have *got* to be fucking kidding me.

I laughed. I almost said, "Oh that." Instead, I let myself take a breath. Then I said, "She was a child when the house burned down. In her grief over the death of her brother, she believed she was responsible for the fire."

He looked at me and then slowly shook his head. "No. She burned it down. She told me about how she lit some things on fire in a waste paper basket and put it near the dryer. Then the house burned down."

"She is mistaken about that," I said. "It was an electrical fire."

"I have a cop on the police force," he said.

"Of course."

"He works arson and I had him look into the fire," he said.

I felt a wave of anxiety.

"He did say they believed it was an electrical fire, but if they had new evidence they might change their ruling. There was a note in the file about a fire in a wastepaper basket. If they investigated and ruled it arson—arson by someone who lived in the house—my guess is you'd have to pay the insurance company back, with interest. Plus there's the whole jail thing. I can encourage him to open the file again or throw the whole thing out."

I didn't say anything. Even if they decided Fern was guilty, she'd been a child. They wouldn't send her to jail now. Plus, what about statute of limitations?

"There is no statute of limitations on arson in California,

by the way," Irving said, as though reading my mind. "I know I would do anything for my children, if I had any, so I'm guessing you would do anything to protect your children. After all, you've only got two left."

"If you want me to help you," I said, "you should probably shut the fuck up now. What do you want me to do?"

"Call Mr. Green and tell him you want Sally off your movie," he said.

"Who the fuck is Mr. Green?"

"He's the chairman of our board," he said. "Just tell him you're having trouble finishing the script because Sally is bothering you. Or something. You figure it out. Tell them you want me as your producer."

"Why?" I said. "I'm just the writer. You should talk to the director."

"I don't have anything on the director," he said. "Besides, you own a huge chunk of the movie. You've got the power."

"Then I'd be careful, Jackson," I said. "I could just as easily get you kicked out on your ass."

He smiled. "I don't think so. If I lose my job, I just go to my police friend, and then your daughter will be arrested. It's true she probably won't go to jail for long since she committed this offense when she was a child, but I'm betting she will do some jail time. She will lose her job certainly. And you'll lose your reputation."

I laughed. "I don't have a reputation to lose."

"You do, actually," he said. He paused. "Will you do as I ask? Will you call Chairman Green?"

I made a noise. "Why can't I just ask Sally if you can be my producer? She'd think it was strange, but she'd do it."

He shook his head. "No. I want to be studio head. I'm next in line."

"I don't think it works that way," I said. "I can't fuck over a friend. It's not right."

"It's Hollywood," he said.

I made a noise.

"There's more," he said. "Everyone in this town who has fucked you or been fucked by you is successful."

"What are you talking about?"

"Every director, every actor, every producer, writer. If you've had a relationship with them, they're doing well. No matter what I do, I don't seem to make it. So I want to make it with you."

"What? Are you kidding me? Is this a joke?"

He shook his head. "I'm dead serious. I want to come to your writing studio, your love nest—I've heard all about it. I want us to have sex. You won't be sorry. I am very good."

I stared at him. Had everyone drunk some kind of crazy ass juice in the last twenty-four hours?

"I am not going to have sex with you," I said. "Are you fucking crazy? I'm not going to screw Sally over. You can go fuck yourself."

"Your daughter is in big trouble," he said. "She drinks too much. She talks when she drinks and tells everyone your business. And her business. Probably AFT's business. That's going to get her fired if she isn't careful. She's going to tell someone else about the fire. You need to get her help. You need to keep her out of jail. I'm giving you the opportunity to do that. My police friend says he'll trash the file if I want." He shrugged. "Or he'll open it and investigate. I'll give him my statement about her confession. You help me get rid of Sally and you have sex with me in your studio, and I'll protect Fern. When Sally leaves, I'll make sure Fern keeps her job."

"I'm in a relationship," I said. "I can't have sex with you."

He smiled. "As I understand it, you're still married, and you live with a man who is not your husband. And before that, you pretty much fucked everyone in Hollywood."

"Not everyone."

"Everyone who is successful now," he said.

"What? You think my vagina is a success-maker or something?"

"Maybe. Women are mysterious beings."

"What about your wife?" I asked. "If we have sex, I could then blackmail you by saying I'd tell your wife."

"She wouldn't care," he said.

That's what married men usually said.

"More importantly," he said, "I wouldn't care."

I shook my head. "Okay. Okay. But I've got too much going on now. Give me until Monday."

"No," he said. "That'll give you time to figure out how to get out of it. Tomorrow night. I'll meet you at your place at seven. I'll bring the wine." He smiled. "Oops. Maybe it's time for you to start drinking again."

Then Irving Jackson got up and walked out of the dining room.

I sat there alone, just for a moment. I laughed. Then I rubbed my face and said out loud, "What the fuck just happened here?"

NINE

I had to leave this place. This was a crazy fucking city. This was exactly why I hated Hollywood. Or the Hollywood life. Or whatever you wanted to call it.

I had to find some sanity.

I left the dining room and hurried back toward the ballroom. Needed to tell Sally where I was going.

I stopped at the threshold. Tell Sally? Maybe that wasn't the best idea. I had to figure out what to do. I was supposed to stab her in the back so Irving Jackson could get ahead. And I was supposed to fuck him because he believed I had a magical vagina.

Only in Hollywood.

Only in fucking Hollywood.

All at once I saw Fern standing next to Enrique and Sally across the room speaking with Irving Jackson who sipped on a martini like it was someone's cock. And there was Hayword—Hayword looking around the room for someone. For me?

My stomach lurched when I saw him. I wanted to call out

to him. I wanted to beg him to save me from all of this bullshit. He knew about Ryan Nichols. He knew about Alberto. He knew it all. Except the part about his daughter confessing arson to a sociopath. And he didn't know about his daughter orchestrating the stupidest stunt in history for love because she couldn't ask her freaking mother for a favor.

I didn't have the stomach to bring him up to date.

I turned around and hurried out of the ballroom before Hayword could see me. Fortunately the valet was quick, and I was soon in my car heading for the beach. Mark wouldn't be there since he was staying in his house tonight—his turn with Ian. But I'd have peace and quiet. I'd have time to think about what to do next.

Have time to have a drink.

Yikes! Where had that come from?

I turned on the radio and headed home. I didn't like driving in the dark. Wasn't that a sign of getting old? Especially on these freeways where everyone was driving too fast, too fast, too fast.

Suddenly, about halfway home, the freeway was lit with red. Brakes screeched. Cars stopped. My side of the freeway became an instant parking lot. Cars on the other side whizzed by. I stopped, too, of course, thank god, and I didn't hear the sound of metal anywhere. No accident, maybe.

I saw people getting out of their cars and running forward.

"What the fuck?"

I put the driver's window down and leaned out. Couldn't see anything but people running. People ran past my car. Heard a few horns honking.

What were they running toward?

To save someone? To help someone? To gape at someone in distress? What was it?

I was tempted to get out, too, but my momma didn't raise

any idiots. I stayed in my car. A few minutes later people began running back, not as fast but as determined.

I shouted to someone passing, "What is it? What did you see?"

One woman just shook her head and kept running. But a man stopped and said, "It's a seal."

"A what? A seal? Like the seal of Solomon?"

"No, lady. Ain't no demons out and about. It's a frigging seal. Like from the ocean. It's there in the middle of the highway. Lucky no one hit it. Can't understand how no one hit it. But everyone is waiting. Waiting for the seal to keep going."

"Keep going? It's miles from the sea. Where on Earth could it be going?"

The man shrugged. "I don't know. But it's going somewhere." And off he ran.

I had to see this.

I got out of the car. Remembered to take the keys, remembered to lock it, but still, crazy ass me got out of the car and hurried forward. I waited for someone to stop me or call to me or call me names. Didn't happen. I counted the cars as I ran by, so I'd know where my car was when it was time to come back. One, two, three, four, five, six, seven, eight.

Then I was there, at the front of the row. Ahead was empty freeway for as far as I could see—which wasn't far because it was dark out. The front row of cars—four or five abreast—all had their lights on. I stood with half a dozen other people on the pavement. I didn't think I'd ever stood on the freeway before. It was strange. It felt otherworldly.

It felt end-of-worldly.

And there in the glare of headlights was a seal, looking preternaturally white in the artificial light. I blinked and saw spots—on the seal.

"It was moving quickly," someone said to me, as though

catching me up on the latest news, as if this had been going on for hours rather than minutes. "But it stopped."

"*She* stopped," someone else said. "It's a female. She was heading east. Her radar or whatever must be screwed up."

"I can relate," someone else said. Or was that me?

Then the seal did the strangest thing: She turned and looked directly at me. At me. She stared at me.

I looked at my human companions for the first time, and they looked back at me.

"She's looking at *you*," one of them whispered.

I looked back at the seal. I laughed, quietly. Couldn't be looking at me in particular. Must be the stress of the last day or more, me thinking she was looking at me. Maybe I was imagining *all* of this. It had been a rather odd twenty-four hours or more.

"Animals acting crazy last day or two," someone said.

I took a step closer to the seal. Don't know why. I wasn't particularly an animal lover. Didn't hate animals. But you know, they've got their tribes or flocks or whatever, and I've got mine.

The seal looked perplexed or frightened. Or lost. I heard her say, clear as day, "Where are you going? What are you doing?"

Okay. I didn't see her lips move or anything, but I heard the words. I glanced over at the woman next to me. "Did you hear that?" I asked.

"I sure did," she said. She looked over her shoulder and yelled, "Turn that radio down. We're trying to have a moment with the wild here."

Ohhh. It was the radio. I almost burst out laughing. Almost told the complete stranger next to me that I thought the seal was talking to me, because it would have been absolutely fitting: Where was I going? What was I doing?

For a moment there was silence. The cars were still racing

by on the other side, but here, all engines had stopped, and it was quiet.

"Honey," I said to the seal. "Darling wild thing, you are far from home. The ocean is thataway." I pointed west. "Is it the radiation? Is it pollution? Is there a big earthquake coming? Did you get in a fight with your mate? Or are you just trying to keep moving?"

The seal continued to stare at me until she burped or hiccoughed or whatever it was seals do, and she started moving across the pavement, awkwardly—probably painfully—undulating like a fish out of water. Or, actually, more like a seal out of water. Didn't she long for the ocean now that she was so far from it? Didn't she long for the freedom of the water?

Didn't she long for home?

I heard someone or something say, "You can't go home again."

I looked around, but no one was speaking.

"You go, girl!" I called out to the seal.

Yes, I fucking did. We all started clapping and hooting. Shouting, "We're rooting for you!" "Go home, ET!" "Send us a postcard." Probably scaring the shit out of her. Soon enough she was across the road. She disappeared into the darkness just like that, and I realized, "I'm standing on the freeway in front of a line of traffic that goes on forever. I'm gonna be dead if I don't get back to my car."

I heard engines start up. Sounded like a car race about to begin. I turned and ran back toward my car. Counting: one, two, three, four, five, six, seven, eight.

There it was. Unlocked it. Got in.

Start your engines, ladies and germs.

Off we all went again. Up to 70 mph in no time at all. As if it had never happened.

As if this incredible encounter had never happened.

How many things a day did we just take for granted? Driving these cars, for one thing. Talking to someone on a little box, for another. Or writing things on a little box and a second later, someone thousands of miles away could read what we'd written.

Those were just the technical amazements.

What about that wild creature on the freeway? How had she gotten there?

And why did she tell me I couldn't go home again?

I laughed and hit the steering wheel with the palms of my hand.

"Brooke, you crazy cunt, that seal was not talking to you."

Fucking stranger things had happened in my life. That was fer sure.

Well, maybe not.

Just like that, I was out of the blackmail funk, singing to some song as I headed home. I couldn't wait to take a shower, slip under the covers, and go to sleep. Wished Mark was going to be home.

Home? Home, home, home.

You can't go home again.

Soon enough, I drove up the private drive to my house. The porch light was on. Mark's truck was there. Yay! He must not be taking care of his son tonight as planned. I'd get to split the sheets with my sweetheart after all. I parked the car and then glanced at my phone. No messages from Mark. Wondered why he hadn't texted me he was going to be here instead of at his house as planned. Must have figured I wouldn't be home until very late.

I couldn't wait to tell him about the seal. I hurried up the back steps, opened the door, went into the laundry room and then stepped into the hallway that led to the bedrooms.

I heard voices.

Oh crap. Mark had company. I didn't really want to see anyone else. I would just sneak into the bedroom, text Mark I was there, and wait for the company to leave.

But I heard a woman laugh, and I froze.

It was more of giggle. The giggle of a woman who had either just been fucked or was about to be fucked.

I knew the sound well.

I heard water running. It was the shower. More voices again. A man. A woman. Murmurs.

Then the bathroom door opened, and Sherry stepped out. Completely naked. She didn't see me. She was so lost in what she was doing—or had been doing—that she didn't look around. She had no idea I was there. No idea. She was confident in her tight skin and unwrinkled face and her easiness in life as she fucked another woman's man that she did not, could not, see me.

"I need to get dressed, silly!" she said as she walked into my bedroom. "Before *she* gets back."

In that moment, I almost threw up, I almost killed them both, I almost went screaming through the house ready to destroy everything in my path.

Instead, I stepped back. Retraced my steps. Went through the laundry room. Stumbled down the steps and out to my car. Suddenly remembered Hayword fucking that blonde up against the copier or filing cabinets or whatever it had been after Alberto died. Thank god, I hadn't actually seen Sherry and Mark fucking one another.

I threw up. Splattered my lunch all over the pavement.

I got in the car and drove away. I was so shocked and angry and pissed and horrified, I could barely see. It was dark, it was dark. I couldn't keep driving. Where could I go? They had been fucking in my house. My own fucking house. How could Mark do this to me?

Fuck. I thought I knew him. I thought he was the stalwart man.

I started laughing. Could this night get worse? Fern and Enrique, then Irving Jackson, and now Sherry and Mark.

Mark was actually fucking that stupid airhead?

All right, all right, all right.

I should call my sponsor. Yes, that was it. Should call her.

Didn't want to.

I wanted revenge.

I was suddenly so angry I felt like the car could not contain me. I was on the freeway. Wasn't sure how I'd gotten there. Maybe I should go fuck Hayword now. That would teach Mark. Of course, when we'd first gotten together, Mark and I had sex for a year during which time I continued to fuck Hayword. He was used to that.

Besides, if I fucked Hayword, he would think I wanted him back.

Maybe I did.

Maybe I did want our old life back.

I didn't know. Didn't know.

Where *was* I going? What had I been doing for the last couple of years?

I had changed my entire life so that I could be sober. So I could be a good mother. A good person.

Yet everything was the same: except the details.

Except the fucking details. I wasn't drinking. But I was doing everything else to keep the rage down.

And why? Why? It hadn't done any good! Fern was fucking up her life, and she had fucked up mine by blabbing to Irving Jackson. Now Mark, my stalwart man, was cheating on me with the manager of his restaurant. The restaurant that was situated in my building. How messy was this going to be?

Christ. What now? What now?

Don't cry for me, Argentina.

I could go fuck Ryan Nichols. Yes, that was it. Lure him into my web again. Fuck him like crazy and then go tell him to fuck himself.

Good lord. Really needed a new set of curse words.

I shook my head. Okay. Okay. I'd go to my bungalow. The former love nest. I'd stay there the night. I needed to go to David's science experiment tomorrow morning. After I met with one of my blackmailers.

And then tomorrow night I had to meet Irving Jackson and let him fuck me.

No fucking way.

No cock-sucking way.

No damn way.

No darn way.

Hell no.

Maybe I should just stop cursing.

Heck no.

I giggled.

Man, I needed a fucking drink. Wanted a fucking drink.

Fuck, fuck, fuck.

I could not handle the next twenty-four hours without a drink.

I could not.

Handle.

The next.

Three minutes.

Without.

A.

Drink.

I got off the freeway and drove toward the village.

My head ached. My stomach hurt. My ears rang.

A coyote ran out in front of the car.

I braked, but he, she, it kept going. She had no messages for me.

I opened the window and howled. The coyote didn't even pause to listen.

Howling snob.

Wait. Coyotes yipped and wolves howled. Right? When I was growing up in the Midwest, we didn't have wolves or coyotes, so how the hell would I know?

Crazy talk, crazy thinking.

Just like that I was crazy again.

How easy they tumble.

Since the car was stopped, I pulled out my phone and called Joanie. She'd get drunk with me.

No, no. She'd help me get revenge. No drinking.

"Aren't you supposed to be at some swank par-tay that you should have invited me to?" she said when she answered the phone.

"Damn straight I should have invited you," I said. "Should have, could have, would have. I need your help."

"Who do I have to kill?"

"Um—" That was an idea. Naw. That would just land me in jail because I would fucking brag about it. "Can you get your hands on knock out drugs or date rape drugs or whatever they are? Something that I can give someone that won't kill him, but I will be able to fool him into thinking he had sex with me?"

"Do tell," Joanie said. She sounded far too interested.

"It's a long story," I said. "Upshot is that some asshole thinks my vagina is magic."

"From what I hear, it just might be," Joanie said. "If I was interested, I'd certainly be interested, if you know what I mean."

"Everyone on the planet knows what you mean," I said. "Probably the zombies from another planet in my movie know what you mean."

"I've known people who have been in your vagina," she said.

"I've heard it is nice, but I'm not sure anyone has ever classified it as magical."

"Joanie! Fucking focus!" I said. "This man is blackmailing me. He wants to hurt Fern."

"Nuff said. You nearby? I can meet you at the love nest in thirty."

"Writing studio," I said.

"I thought it was an art studio," she said, "aka love nest."

"Now that I'm not pretending to do art there," I said, "it's a writing studio."

"Where you actually write?"

"That's not the point," I said. "How about we call it the fucking bungalow. I'll meet you there in thirty minutes."

"We're calling it the 'fucking' bungalow? I thought you didn't do that anymore."

"Joanie!"

"See you then. Drugs in hand."

I called Irving Jackson. I made a face when I heard his voice. Made my fucking skin crawl.

"Can you be here in an hour?" I asked.

"Sure," he said. "What changed your mind?"

"I haven't changed my mind about anything," I said. "I just want to get it over with. Bring a bottle of wine."

"Got it. Glad to help the wicked."

Shut the fuck up, you moron. You threaten me, that's one thing. But you threatened my family. I. Will. Take. You. Down.

I ended the call before I said all of that to him. Because I was going to say it to him one way or another.

Now. What about Manny? Fern had texted me his full name and address.

I called our cop friend Philip.

"I need a favor," I told him.

"Of course," he said.

"I need to get some dirt on a John Manuel Reilly. He presently works at Juliet's. They call him Manny. I can give you his address."

"I can't, Brooke," Philip said. "I can't just violate someone's civil rights because you don't like him."

"I don't even know him," I said. "He's trying to blackmail me. He knows something about Fern, and if I don't give him money or maybe a part in a movie, he's going to the police."

"Blackmail is against the law," Philip said. "You should be going to the police about this."

"You are the police," I said. "Besides, if I went to the real police, or the other police, Fern could be in trouble."

"Legal trouble?" he asked.

"I think so."

"Don't tell me anything else," he said. "This is the last fucking time I'm doing this. For either of you. Last night Hayword got me to track down Ryan Nichols, some guy who worked in your first movie. I'm not the fucking phone book."

"Did you give him his address?"

"No," he said. "This Ryan guy must be in some guild or union. He can track him that way."

"Okay, last time I ask," I said. "Last time either of us asks."

"Give me this guy's address." He sounded disgusted.

I gave him the address.

"Can you get back to me before eight tomorrow morning?" I asked. "I'm meeting him at The Coffee Shoppe."

"Jesus H. Christ," Philip said.

"Please."

"Don't beg," he said. "It's so . . . not like you. Speaking of strange. Have you seen what's been going on with the animals? They're calling it the zombie animal apocalypse. I've heard your movie mentioned several times in relation to this."

What? "Why my movie?"

"Maybe because it was the most successful zombie movie of all time," he said. "You've surpassed *Night of the Living Dead* and *The Walking Dead.*"

"The animals who are being weird aren't dead," I said. "They're not coming back from the dead. They're just acting strangely. Actually saw a seal on the freeway tonight. No one hit it. It was odd."

I didn't mention that the seal had talked to me. Or that I *thought* it had talked to me.

"So they're alive," he said. *"The Living Dead?"*

"Isn't that what we all are?" I said. Then I laughed so I didn't sound melodramatic. "Thanks, Philip. I appreciate all you do for us. You want a part in my next movie?"

I knew he didn't want a part. He was the only person in this whole damn town who didn't want a part in a movie. Okay. Slight exaggeration. As far as I knew, Mark didn't want a part in a movie either.

My stomach lurched. *Mark.* Fuck. I had almost forgotten about all of that.

"Naw, not this time," Philip said. "Later." He was gone.

I called Hayword.

"You okay?" he asked. "I've been looking all over for you. They said you left suddenly."

"I'm fine," I said. "You know how much I love those gatherings. I'll tell you the rest later. Hayword, I was just talking to Philip. What the hell you doing looking for Ryan? What were you thinking?"

"I don't know," he said. "I wanted to tell him off. Tell him how he ruined our family and ruined you."

"First off," I said, "all those TV shows about someone ending up dead always start off like this. Some guy finding someone's address and then going to confront him. Never turns out well."

"It probably usually turns out well enough," Hayword said.

"I think those so-called news shows just retell the same murders over and over. Most of life does not end in murder or in the end of the world. You and David need to understand that."

"Off topic, Hayword!" I yelled. "And secondly, you wanted to tell Ryan he *ruined* our family. No way. I don't want him to think he was that fucking important."

"He *was* that fucking important!"

I rubbed my face. Oh god, oh god, oh god. Okay. If I can't drink, could I please have a hit of acid? Or maybe that had already happened. Maybe the past two days were a result of a hit of acid I hadn't known I'd taken.

"Man, I wish I did drugs," I said.

"Don't even joke about that," Hayword said.

"Who's joking?"

Dead silence.

I laughed. It was a hoarse strained laugh, but it was a laugh.

"All right," I said. "No joking. But you can't talk to Ryan, and you really can't tell him he ruined my life. He didn't ruin my life, Hayword. *I* fucking ruined our lives. And actually I didn't ruin our lives. We had Alberto. We got back on track after the affair."

"But you see me and that woman," Hayword said. "I know you still do. Every time we made love afterward, you saw me fucking her. You couldn't get it gone. If you and Ryan had never been together, I would have never cheated."

He was right. I had never been able to stop seeing him fucking the blonde. Seared into my memory. I thought memories were supposed to fade with time. Not that one.

"So you fucked her because I fucked Ryan?" I said. "I don't think so. All those years I was fucking everyone and their mother, you never cheated on me. So why her, why then?"

Were we really having this conversation now over the phone while I was in the car, stopped off the side of a dark road?

"I have no idea," he said. "I really don't know. I was angry, and I was grieving. You wouldn't talk to me. You wouldn't listen to me. And she was there."

Convenience. Was that why Mark had fucked Sherry? She was convenient?

Bleck.

"Is that what you told her?" I asked. "You said my wife won't listen to me?"

"No," he said. "I didn't tell her anything. I was so sad, Brooke. I loved that little boy, and yet, I didn't feel like I was entitled to my grief. Because he wasn't mine. I never felt like he was mine. You seemed to hate us all."

"I didn't hate you all!" I felt like I was going to throw up. Why were we having this conversation now? I wanted to scream.

"I had lost my son," I said. "I couldn't be there, for anyone. But I certainly didn't hate you or the kids."

"Before that," he said. "Before that, you had lost Ryan, and you blamed us all. Or that's what it felt like. He left you, so you left us."

"I don't know what the fuck you're talking about," I said.

"I know!" he said. "You always say that. None of us is able to have an opinion about any of this—about Alberto's death— because you're the mother, you're the one grieving."

"What do you mean 'none of us?'" I said. "David and Fern didn't know about Ryan."

"They knew Alberto was dead and you disappeared," he said. "Even before Alberto died, you disappeared."

"What are you saying? I wasn't there for you so you fucked someone? I wasn't there for Fern so she burned down the house? I wasn't there for David so he got neurotic? I wasn't there for Alberto so what? He died?"

"No," he said. "That's not what I mean."

Another coyote crossed the road in front of me. Or maybe it was the first one coming back. It stood in my light beams and watched me. Then she sat on her haunches, easy with herself, and looked casually from side to side. Peering into the darkness, I supposed.

I took a deep breath. "You know, Hayword. I can feel myself becoming really pissed—and I was already pretty pissed. I've got a lot of balls I'm juggling right now."

That didn't sound quite right.

"Can we have this heart-to-heart later?" I asked. I didn't really care if he agreed or not because I was not going to keep talking about it.

Silence.

A sigh.

"We all have a right to our grief," Hayword said. "Even Ryan."

I screamed. I let out the loudest scream I could manage, and it came bouncing back into my own ears. I dropped the phone and raised my hands. I could hear Hayword's squeaky voice calling to me. I leaned down, picked up the phone, and ended the call. And then I said, "Shut up, you motherfucking cuntsucking asshole."

I leaned back in my seat.

Then I picked up the phone and texted Hayword, "I dropped the phone. My apologies. Text me Ryan's number and address if you found it. I'll go tell him he's entitled to his fucking grief."

I looked at my watch. I had time to stop at The Coffee Shoppe and get a drink. A drink of coffee. Tea. Whatever. I had time for a pause before I either killed Irving Jackson or made incriminating photos of him that I could use against him forever. Not that I wanted to do that. But I wanted him out of my life. Two hours ago I hadn't even known he was in my life, except peripherally.

I looked ahead. The coyote was gone. Just like that. Hadn't she a message for me, too?

I drove into the village and parked in front of The Coffee Shoppe. The neon OPEN sign glowed unnaturally in the foggy night. Five minutes ago, it had been a clear and beautiful night. Now fog clouded everything.

I got out of the car and went into The Coffee Shoppe. Glanced around. Two other people were there. One with her back to me. The other person was a twenty-something with ear-buds on while she read a book. She glanced up at me, but I could tell she didn't see me. She turned the book over and set it down while she took a sip of coffee. *Call of the Wild.* Really? Someone was reading Jack London on this foggy night? Fitting, I supposed.

"It was a dark and stormy night," I murmured.

I went to the counter and ordered a coffee. The barista was young, tattooed, with a pierced nose, pierced ears, and a pierced belly button. Yep, I could see the pierced belly button. I hadn't noticed her in here before.

"You from Portland?" I asked.

She grinned as she handed me the coffee and I gave her money. "Yeah, what gave it away? My dashing good looks?"

"Of course," I said. "That and the salmon swimming up your arm."

"We're all swimming upstream, sister," she said as she handed me my change.

I nodded, took the money, and sat at the nearest table. Something weird about The Coffee Shoppe tonight. I had been here hundreds of times. Always seemed perfectly normal. Now I felt like I was in a George Romero movie. I looked around again. Everything was in color, not in black and white. We weren't in *Night of the Living Dead*. I closed my eyes and tried to breathe deeply. It was difficult. My stomach was in a knot. A million knots. How could my life have unraveled so quickly in such a short time?

"Hello, there." The voice was calm, quiet, gentle. I opened my eyes, and the woman from Juliet's was there: the friendly one with long white hair, blue eyes, and dragon sweater. Only she wasn't wearing the sweater tonight. She carried a bag on her shoulder and held a book in her left hand, using her middle fingers as a bookmark. I couldn't see the title, but the cover looked red.

"Hello," I said. I started to stand, but she waved me off.

"Don't get up," she said. "I'm just leaving. But I wanted to formally introduce myself. I'm Gabriella. I live around here. Just so you don't think I'm stalking you or anything."

"Now I do," I said. I smiled. I remembered how calm and pleasant she'd been at the restaurant. How familiar she'd seemed. Maybe I had seen her here before and had forgotten.

"Are you all right?" she asked.

"Why? Do I not look all right?"

She smiled. "You look a little bit shaky, actually," she said.

"It's been a strange couple of days," I said, "and it's about to get stranger."

She nodded. "With the robbery and all," she said. "I bet. And the world has been a bit strange these last couple of days. Forcing us all to walk on the wild side a bit, I suppose."

I motioned to the chair across from me. She said, "Just for a bit. I don't want to bother you."

"What do you mean: forcing us to walk on the wild side?"

"Don't you ever feel like that?" she said. "As though we walk through the world believing we're not a part of it. Believing we don't live and die. That we are tame beings instead of wild beings. That's what makes us sick: believing we are tame. Striving to be tame."

"But being wild is chaotic," I said. "It's dangerous. We've created civilization, so we don't have to live like animals."

"Of course we live like animals!" she said. She laughed. "We *are* animals. As animals, we create art and beauty and buildings and structure. We listen to the cosmos and create music. We listen to the earth and we tell stories. It's like your movie."

"*Love and Other Insanities?*"

She smiled. I swear her eyes were twinkling.

"No, love," she said. "*Beauty and the Zombie*. They were the living dead until she dug her toes into the earth and let the sun bath her in its light. It was the connection between the light and the dark, the earthly with the heavenly. It was really quite spiritual. They became human again when they became human again."

I laughed. "No one has ever claimed *Beauty and the Zombie* is a spiritual movie."

"An earthly spiritual movie, of course. They got down and dirty while bathing in the light. They became *earth*lings, truly, while also accepting their heavenly nature, as it were."

"I don't believe in heaven," I said. "But today, I believe in hell."

"It doesn't matter what you believe," she said. "Heaven is just a word to convey a concept. Don't get so caught up in semantics.

It's one word that probably came from another word that meant something else. Everything is always changing meaning, isn't it?"

She said all of this so gently, without any judgment, it seemed.

"Everything isn't semantics," I said. "Some things are real. Some things are horrible."

"It's true," Gabriella said. "I saw this interview with a woman who was the sole survivor of a plane crash not too long ago. The plane crashed in the jungle. Statistically she was sitting in the least safe place. Yet she was the only one who survived the initial crash. You know why?"

I shook my head.

"She was the only one not wearing a seatbelt. When the plane disintegrated, she fell free. So there she was, after the crash, in this jungle, surrounded by the dead, including her fiancé, and she said she accepted the situation straight away. She didn't think why me? She accepted it and tried to figure out what was next. And she noticed the beauty all around her. She noticed how beautiful the jungle was. She didn't focus on the death and destruction—she didn't deny it either. She accepted it, and she accepted the beauty of the jungle. And she survived."

I squinted. Why was the woman telling me all this?

"No matter how hard we try," she said, "we can't be safe. Sometimes trying hard makes us unsafe. Sometimes we need to get a new perspective."

I sighed. Perspective? I couldn't see it. I really was getting blackmailed by two different people. My husband and lover had cheated on me. My son had actually died. *That* was my perspective.

"I just saw a seal on the freeway," I said, apropos of something. Or nothing. "She was traveling away from the ocean. She wasn't walking on the wild side. Or hearing the call of the wild. She was scooting across a highway. What the hell was that about?”

“I have no idea,” Gabriella said. “She must have heard the call of something.”

Why was I asking her? Just because her name was Gabriella didn’t mean she had the ear of God.

Not that I believed in God.

I did believe I was having a strange night, and I needed to get going. I had to pick up knockout drugs from a girlfriend so I could blackmail my blackmailer.

“I can see you need to go,” Gabriella said. “I hope I haven’t taken up too much of your time.”

“It was nice running into you,” I said as we both got up. Amazing how we could still maintain our civility even in times when the shit was hitting the fan.

“Just remember,” she said, “things are not always what they seem.”

“You got that right,” I said.

We shook hands, which seemed strange, and then she was out the door. I soon followed, but I didn’t see her anywhere. She had disappeared into the fog. In the distance, I could hear a coyote yipping.

I got into the car, then checked my phone messages. One from Jackson: He was stuck in traffic and would be a little late. One from Joanie: She was at my bungalow. One from Hayword: Where the hell was I? One from Mark. I stared at his name, stared and breathed, stared and breathed. But I didn’t look at his message. Didn’t want to hear or read anything he had to say. Nothing from Phil Case telling me all I needed to know about Manny, the other guy trying to blackmail me.

I drove slowly through the fog to my bungalow. Felt like I was driving through the end of the world. By the time I got there,

Joanie was leaning against her car in my driveway, looking like some tarted-up ghost in the fog, her ruby red lipstick shiny in my headlights, her short blue dress sparkling prettily, ready to dance to whatever tune the universe was playing. She had no idea what it was like to be discreet, apparently. We were about to commit a freaking crime. I hadn't wanted any of the neighbors to see her at my house. Of course, in this weather, no one could see anything. I nodded to her as I got out of the car, and we hurried into my darkened house. I switched on the light over the kitchen sink. We stood close to each other while she showed me the pills on her palm.

"This one will just knock him out," she said. "This one is like a memory loss pill. It will eventually knock him out, but you can have fun with him if you like, and he'll never remember the next day."

"I don't want to have *fun* with him," I said. "You mean fuck him? Good gawd. No! I mean, I thought about it. Because that's what he wanted and it might solve the immediate problem. But I'm not a drunk anymore. I can't do shit like that. At least I can't do shit like that and forget about it."

Joanie laughed. "Fortunately, I can still do embarrassing shit and forget about it."

"What embarrassing shit do you do?" I asked.

"Fuck my husband," she said. She threw her head back and cackled. Then she said, "Oh, and this pill is if you just want to get high yourself."

I looked at her. What was wrong with the people in my life? First Fern, then Irving Jackson, and now Joanie? Everyone wanted me to drink and drug again?

She returned the pills to a plastic baggie and gave the baggie to me.

"Let me know if you need any help later," she said, "like moving the dead body. I've done it before. I can do it again."

"Funny lady," I said.

"I'm not joking."

"If I could get away with it," I said, "I would consider it."

She shook her head. "No, you wouldn't. I would. But not you. I'll hang out at The Coffee Shoppe for the next hour or so, just in case you need me."

We hugged each other, and then she was gone. I took the baggie into my bedroom and hid it under one of the pillows on the bed. Then I went into the living room and sat on the edge of the couch, waiting. I could hear the kitchen clock tick, tick, ticking. I could hear my heartbeat. My breath. My everything.

I did not like it.

This stillness.

This waiting.

Waiting for death?

I felt that undeniable urge. No. No. It was deniable. I could deny it.

I was not going to drink.

Was. Not. Going. To. Drink.

Unless Irving Jackson brought wine. Then I might drink. Come on. Wine was not actually drinking, was it now? It was just wine. *Christ*. Yes, speaking of Christ, he drank wine. In fact, didn't he turn water into wine? Must have thought there was something divine about it.

Finally, I heard a knock at the door.

"I love the smell of napalm in the morning," I murmured as I got up to answer the door. It was time to tank this motherfucker.

I opened the door and smiled.

Irving Jackson stood on my threshold, dressed in a cream-colored suit, like some kind of natty Grim Reaper. Or Darth Vader in normal drag. He grinned, and I could see the whites of his pearlies. He looked like the proverbial cat and I was the canary he was about to eat.

Well. Not if I could help it.

"Come on in, Irving," I said.

"It's so dark," he said.

"Oh, yes, sorry," I said. "I just got here. Let me lighten it up." I turned on a couple of the lamps in the living room.

"Much better," he said. "Very cozy."

I smiled. How dare he comment on what my house looked like. As if he had a right to an opinion about anything of mine.

He held out a bottle of wine to me. I took it and went into the kitchen.

"Make yourself at home," I said. I opened a drawer and pulled out a corkscrew. I hesitated. If I smelled the wine, I was afraid I might gulp the entire bottle down. I bit my lip.

Wine would make these next moments easier, wouldn't it?

I got a wine glass from the cupboard and carried the bottle and the corkscrew into the living room. Irving was sitting in my chair, the one where I usually sat to figure out what came next in whatever narrative I was spinning at the time. I didn't want him there.

"Come sit on the couch," I said. "There's not room for me in that chair."

He looked surprised, but he smiled and got up and went to the couch. I put the glass on the end table and handed him the bottle and corkscrew.

"Could you open this for me?" I asked.

He didn't ask me why. He just did it. I sat on the couch next to him, but I leaned away as the cork came out. I could still smell it a bit. Loved the sound: gulp, gulp, gulp as he poured the wine into his glass. He set the bottle on the end table.

"You're not having any?" he asked.

"You know I don't drink, Irving," I said. "So, listen, I've started composing the email in my head to Mr. Green, and I've already left him a voice mail, asking for a meeting on Monday. I have some ideas on how to get Sally out."

"Excellent," he said.

His excellent sounded so diabolical that I almost laughed.

"And the other thing?" he asked.

The other thing being sex.

I nodded. "Yes, the other thing," I said. "Let me go put on something less comfortable but more arousing." I smiled as I rose from the couch.

"I like what you have on," he said. He reached for my hand, and I let him have it. Actually wished my hand would drop off my arm once he had it in his grasp.

"Trust me," I said. "You'll like this. Besides, you wanted the full Brooke McMurphy treatment. So I'm gonna give it to you."

I leaned over and picked up the bottle of wine. "Maybe I'll just have a nip."

"That's my girl," he said.

Oh my gawd. Did he just say "that's my girl?" Really, I should just fucking kill him.

"I ain't anyone's girl," I said through gritted teeth. "Even when I was a girl, I was nobody's girl. Don't fucking forget that." I smiled.

"Whatever gets you through the night," he said. "I'll be here, waiting."

I took the bottle into the bedroom, closed the door behind me, and sat on the bed. I brought the wine bottle up to my mouth, and I breathed in deeply. I smelled fruit. Sourness. I almost coughed. Then I looked at the label.

"Cheap bastard," I whispered.

I reached under the pillow, grabbed the plastic bag of pills, and opened it. "Okay. This pill to get high. This one to make him pass out. This one to get him to do whatever I wanted and then pass out. Yep. That's the one."

I took the pill out, got up and went to the dresser. I set the pill on the plastic and then—as quietly as I could— pounded the bottom of the wine bottle onto the pill to crush it to powder.

I looked at the wine bottle, took another sniff. Maybe I could just have a swallow. I felt so thirsty I almost ached. I knew just a gulp would help. It would slake my thirst, as it were. Satisfy my longing. Fill the void.

Fill the fucking abyss.

Maybe I could just sit here and drink half of the bottle. Hell with a gulp or a swallow. The whole thing.

I had every reason to drink it, didn't I? No one understood the pressure I was under. No one understood what it was like to be me. To feel like me. First, my daughter was so afraid of me that she had staged a mock robbery to get me to notice her boyfriend. Then I was at once hailed and then pilloried in the press. No big deal, that. It passed quickly but not before my ex-lover discovered his child was dead because of the news reports about me and my personal life. I got to curse him in front of the world, and now I was probably banned from every AA group from here to Mexico and back up to Canada. And some punk kid was trying to blackmail me into giving him cash or a job or he'd tell the world that Fern had been involved in the faux robbery. Not to mention the asshole sitting in my living room waiting for me to come and fuck him. On top of it all, the love of my life Mark Pantano was fucking some bimbo who could barely walk and talk at the same time.

I turned the bottle around and around in my hand.

The love of my life.

Didn't I used to think Ryan Nichols was the love of my life? Hadn't I lain in bed at night, next to Hayword, thinking that I had never loved anyone as much as I loved Ryan. When I found out I was pregnant, I was horrified, terrified, and happier than I'd been when I was pregnant with Fern or David.

I loved David and Fern when they were born, but I hadn't liked being pregnant with them. I was afraid I'd be a bad mother.

Lo and behold, I had been right about that. A good mother didn't drink herself into a stupor because things went wrong.

Although the thing that went wrong was huge.

Except, according to Ryan, according to Hayword, I was drinking before Alberto died.

I shook my head.

Why would I have been drinking then?

I'd been sad.

Why?

Ah, yes, the abyss in my soul.

Why should I be different from everyone else in the world?

Naw. That was too facile. Not everyone felt that way.

But they had to. Weren't we the first to know what was happening all over the planet? In an instant. Weren't we the first to witness the destruction of our world? Because of us, the seas were rising, the climate was fucked, the oceans were filled with trash and radioactive whatever, and on good days, people could leave their homes and walk the streets of Beijing wearing masks as they made their way through the polluted air. The polluted air that made its way to our shores in the good ole U. S. of A.

All of that should be a fucking crime.

I heard last week the air in Paris was more polluted than the air in China.

Let's have a contest to see who has the worse air.

The Parisians had fought the Nazis only to die from polluted air?

What the fuck?

I had birthed three children into this world.

No wonder I drank.

Used to drink.

Thinking about this was not helpful. What the fuck was I supposed to do? We were living in whackadoodle times. I could only observe it. Write about it? Drown my sorrows?

Yes, that was the answer. Drown my sorrows.

In lovely alcohol.

The crazy ones were the ones who saw the world as it really was. Were the ones who saw it and faced it straight.

What had Gabriella told me tonight? About the sole survivor of a plane crash. She had survived because she faced the truth. She faced reality.

And then she saw beauty.

She didn't pretend the horror wasn't there.

She didn't sink into delusion.

I felt like I was going to throw up again.

I faced reality. Every day. *I did. I did.*

So where was the fucking beauty?

I glanced at the clock. Shit. I'd been in here for twenty minutes. Jackson must have thought I'd fallen asleep.

I opened the door a crack and shouted out, "I'll be right there. Had a little woman thing going on!"

He didn't answer. Good. Maybe he had gotten drunk and passed out on one glass of wine. That would be all right with me.

I closed the door again. I took the wine bottle into the bathroom and poured most of it out. I went back into the bedroom and swept up the crushed pill into my palm. Then I carefully brushed the powder into the wine bottle.

I took the remaining pills into the bathroom and dropped them into the toilet and flushed them away.

I wiped the powder off the rim of the wine bottle.

I stopped. Wait.

What the hell was I doing?

This didn't make any sense. I rubbed my face.

What *was* I doing? I couldn't fix this. If Fern had burned down the house, maybe she needed to face the consequences. Maybe I should just tell the police everything about the fake robbery. Maybe I should just stop trying to fix and control everything. Maybe I should trust someone to . . . to what? To tell them what I was really feeling?

I shook my head.

Maybe, maybe, maybe.

Wished someone loved me enough to make this all go away.

I laughed. Or whimpered. Such a child's wish.

Was I actually really in that thing called reality looking for the love of my life. Still?

Ryan Nichols hadn't been the love of my life. Mark wasn't the love of my life either. I leaned my head back. Neither was Hayword.

The real love of my life had been Alberto.

My little dead boy.

I had been bereft when Ryan left me. Felt like a rose crushed under his heels. Ground into the earth. All the color gone. All the meaning gone. I had felt like a teenager again then. Awful, awful, awful. Hayword had waited for me to come back to him. And Fern and David. All of them wanted me to be home again, home in myself.

But I had left home long ago.

You can't go home again.

You have to be in your body when you're giving birth. You have to be. Unless you're drugged out of your mind, I suppose. But I wasn't drugged. I didn't drink a drop once I knew I was pregnant. When I went into labor, I said no to every drug they offered. Alberto was the easiest birth of any of the three kids. When they put him in my arms, when they laid him on my chest, I fell in love. Instantly. I knew he was the reason I was put on this earth. And I didn't even believe in that kind of thing. Any pain I had felt about Ryan leaving me, any pain from the birth itself, any pain I had felt my entire life was meaningless because my life now had meaning. Because I had my baby boy.

Alberto was the love of my life.

Yes.

I wanted to wail.

But I needed to go drug that motherfucker sitting in my living room. Get him in my bed. Get him stripped. Get him in compromising positions and take photographs. Use the photographs to blackmail him. Shame him. Show them to his wife or Mr. Green. Tell everyone he had been blackmailing me.

No.

"This is stupid," I said. "Stupidest thing I have ever done."

It was a scheme a drunk would have concocted. I was still thinking like a drunk, acting like a drunk.

Everything is not as it seems.

"No fuck."

I picked up the bottle, strode across the bedroom, and opened the door.

"Jackson," I said as I stepped into the hall and headed to the living room. "This is all complete horse shit."

Irving was sitting on my couch, naked except for a black garter, black fishnet stockings, and a pair of black stilettos. And he was asleep.

"Were you wearing those under your clothes?" I asked.

He didn't say anything.

"Jackson? Your bare ass is on my couch. I'm gonna have to burn that couch now, man. Such an asshole. You blackmail me and then you don't have the decency to stay awake."

He didn't move. I stood just a few feet from him.

"Irving!" I yelled. I didn't want to get any closer. It was bad enough seeing him naked and flaccid from across the room. Didn't want him to wake up and get an erection.

"Jackson! Wake up. I'm not doing this. I'm not writing to Mr. Green. I'm not fucking you. Well, pretending to fuck you actually. I was never going to do that. Jesus H. Christ. Wake up!"

Crap.

I went over to him, hesitated, and then shook his arm.

Something not right here.

I turned on the lamp closest to him.

His eyes were slightly open. He was vaguely blue and cool to the touch.

"Fuck, fuck, fuck."

He was dead. Dead, dead, dead. Dead as a doornail. Dead as an almost naked asshole fucking up my life even in death.

I knew he was dead, but I checked his pulse at his cold neck and his wrist.

Crap. He must have died as soon as I went into the bedroom. No sense doing mouth to mouth on him now.

Was there?

"Christ, Christ, Christ." I got my phone and called Joanie. "Get your ass up here!"

I threw the phone down, and then I grabbed a pillow and put it on the floor beneath Jackson. I went to his feet and pulled on them gently—"Ugh!"—until his limp, heavy body slipped off of the couch and onto the floor. I thought his head would hit the pillow—that's why I put it there—but his ass hit it and dragged it with him so his head bounced on the carpeted floor. If he wasn't already dead, he now had a cracked skull.

I quickly positioned him so he was flat on the floor. Then I did my resuscitation ABC's: checked his airway, checked his breathing, and checked his circulation by trying to find his pulse again.

Dead, dead, dead. Breathed two long breaths into him, then I did fifteen compressions.

Wasn't I supposed to call the ambulance first, before I did this?

But he'd clearly been dead for a while.

Could you bring someone back from the dead after twenty minutes?

You couldn't. And I couldn't have them find him in my house dressed only in fishnet stockings.

How the hell had he died? Had there been something in the wine? They'd think I killed him.

I checked his pulse again. I tried compressions three more times. About that time Joanie showed up.

I let her in.

"Oh my," she said as she surveyed the scene.

"I tried mouth to mouth," I said.

"Ew," she said. "Don't ever kiss me again then. You've been making out with a dead guy. I've seen dead and this guy is long past dead. One of the pills kill him outright or did you give them all to him?"

"No!" I said. "I didn't give him anything. I went into the bedroom and kind of got waylaid as I went down memory lane. Half 'n hour later I came out and he was like this."

"Call the paramedics," she said. "They won't be able to revive him, but they'll haul his sorry ass out of here."

"Not like this," I said. "I gotta get him dressed. It's quicker if we both do it."

She nodded. "Okay, well, we're even then. You helped me when I was naked with my toe up the faucet. I'll help you dress a dead guy."

And then we just did it. We pulled off his fishnets.

"I didn't know they still made these," I said.

Joanie said as we took off his stilettos, "Where you been? The Junk Shop has them right in the village."

I grabbed the garter, stilettos, and fishnets and ran into the bedroom and put them in my dirty clothes basket. Then I ran back into the living room and helped Joanie put on Jackson's pants—sans underwear because he didn't have any.

"Man, he is really a dead weight," Joanie said.

We put on his shirt next. We left off his jacket. I unbuttoned his shirt after we buttoned it.

"What?" Joanie asked.

"I want it to look like I tried to resuscitate," I said. "Which I did."

Joanie put her hands over his eyes and closed them.

"Why the hell didn't you do that five minutes ago?" I asked.

She shrugged.

I picked up the phone again, called 911, told them someone was dead at my house. After I hung up, I washed out Irving's wine glass and put it away. I poured the rest of the wine down the drain, rinsed the bottle, and scrubbed the sink. Then I stuffed Jackson's girdle, hose, and stilettos into a paper sack along with the bottle and the empty pill baggie. I took it all out to Joanie. "Just put the clothes in your closet, as if they were yours, if that's okay. You can throw them out later."

"Sure," she said. "I love fishnet stockings. The shoes might be a little big for me."

"Get out," I said. "I'll call you later and let you know."

She nodded.

"Thanks, Joanie."

"This will be okay," she said. "You didn't do anything wrong."

"I know," I said. "But it feels weird. I'm not sorry he's dead.

I'm just sorry he's dead in my living room. I had just decided I wasn't going to lie or bullshit about anything, and now this."

"Ah, the Universe provides," Joanie said.

"I can't tell the paramedics he was here blackmailing me to have sex with him. Christ."

"He was here for a business meeting," Joanie said. "Period."

"Are you still here?" I said. "Go, go."

She left, and I was alone with a dead guy.

ELEVEN

Then I remembered the drug dust on my dresser top. I ran into my bathroom, grabbed a wet washcloth, then wiped down the dresser, rinsed off the cloth and hung it in my bathroom.

"You didn't do anything wrong," I told myself. "You didn't do anything wrong."

My clothes! If I was going to pretend this had just been a business meeting—which is what I was going to do—I probably shouldn't be dressed in party clothes.

I quickly stripped off my dress, threw it into the closet, then pulled on jeans and a shirt. I wiped off the little bit of make-up I had on and then looked in the mirror. I was white as a sheet. A white sheet. I pinched my cheeks.

I went back into the living room and glanced around. Everything looked normal. Except for the dead guy.

Heard sirens. Suddenly I flashed right back to the night Alberto died. Flashed on finding Alberto in his crib. Blue. Cold. And then the sound of sirens. I had continued hearing the sirens even after the paramedics came into the house, even after they gently pulled Hayword away from Alberto, where he had been performing baby CPR. He'd known how to do it. I hadn't. I hadn't known what to do.

Although later, later, after everyone was gone and I was alone in the house—even though the rest of my family was still there— later, I took a drink. Many drinks. Just to block out the sound of the sirens from my ears.

Now I felt like I was going to throw up for the second time that day.

Instead, I opened the door.

Things got a little fuzzy after that. Or foggy. Busy? The paramedics did their thing. Asked me questions: Had he taken any drugs, drunk any alcohol, complained of anything?

"I don't know," I said. "It was a business meeting. He might have taken something before he got here, but he seemed fine." I was tempted to tell them the whole long made up story: We'd been at an industry party together, and he was nervous about *Beauty and the Zombie Part Two*, so we decided to work on the script for a bit tonight.

But I didn't say any of that.

The guy was dead. Declared. The police arrived. Different police than I'd talked to yesterday, of course. Different jurisdiction. I wasn't a criminal, but I was an alcoholic, so I was—by nature— good at lying. Lying is the second language of addicts, after all. If anyone doubted my version of anything, I couldn't tell.

Before long, they were all gone. Dead guy. Medics. Police. They had said they'd notify the family. Said something about an autopsy.

Gone.

I stood in the middle of my living room.

I wanted to burn down the house.

"Bleck."

Was it too late to have someone come in and clean? No bodily fluids or anything. Just . . . ickiness.

I texted Miranda, my cleaning guru. Begged her to come first thing in the morning.

Crap. Tomorrow morning. I had to go to David's science project presentation in the morning.

I went into my bedroom and phoned Joanie.

"Thanks," I said. "I'll call you tomorrow."

"They know what killed him?" she asked.

"No, heard someone mention maybe a heart attack. They have to do an autopsy."

Then I called Sally St. James.

"You still at the party?" I asked.

"No," she said. "I'm home fucking my husband. You wanna join us?"

I wasn't in the mood.

"Irving Jackson is dead," I told her.

"Really? How do you know?"

"He died at my house," I said. "At the bungalow."

"Your love nest?" She sounded surprised and angry.

"That's not what was going on," I said.

"What other reason would that slimeball have for being there?"

"I'll tell you about it later," I said. "But he's dead. I don't know what killed him. They've taken him to the hospital, and they're going to notify his family."

"Brooke, what the hell is going on?"

"Can we talk tomorrow?" I asked. "You wouldn't believe the day I've had."

"Sounds like Irving had quite a day, too," Sally said. "I'm sorry he's dead, but I can't say that I'm sad to have that thorn out of my side. Is there anything I need to know about this before I call our media department?"

"No," I said.

"They're gonna want to know why he was at your house," she said.

"He was helping me with *Beauty and the Zombie Part Two*," I said.

"He was not," Sally said.

"Wasn't he AFT's creative director or some such?" I asked. "He was helping me be creative."

"What the fuck, Brooke?"

"Sally, you've just got to trust me," I said. "The line can be 'while working on a script with screenwriter Brooke McMurphy, creative executive Irving Jackson passed away.' Blah, blah, blah."

"All right," she said. "I do trust you. Talk to you tomorrow then. By the way, you okay?"

"Sure," I said. "Why not? I've been fake robbed, blackmailed three times now, caught my lover fucking around on me, cursed my baby's father, and now had a guy die in my living room all in less than 48 hours. Good times all around."

"What? Mark?"

"I'll talk to you tomorrow, Sally."

"You want me to come over?"

I thought about it.

"No," I said. "I don't think so."

"The script still on schedule?" she asked.

"Jesus, Sally."

"I'm sorry," she said. "I don't care about me, not really." Bullshit.

"But your whole family is wrapped up in this company."

"Not David," I said. "Maybe he'll save us all. Man, I am tired."

"Get me that script and all will be well in the world."

"Guess the mourning period is over?"

"Why would I mourn Irving Jackson?" she said. "He was not a good guy."

"No shit," I said.

"Talk to you later," Sally said.

Then I was in silence again.

I looked at my list of texts. Mark had texted three times. Was he feeling guilty or had he figured out I'd been at the house? I sighed. I didn't have the energy to deal with that drama yet. Fern had texted, too. Nope, didn't have the energy for that drama either. Phil Case left a voice mail. "Call me."

I called Phil.

"What the fuck, Brooke?" he said. "One of the guys in your neck of the woods said they found a dead man in your house. Are you a one woman crime wave?"

"Hey, I wasn't the fake robber yesterday," I said, "and Irving Jackson just died. I didn't do anything to him."

"What happened?"

"He came over to my place, and he died. I was in the other room when he died. I was gone for a bit, and when I returned, he was very dead."

"You were gone for a while?"

"We had gone to an industry party, separately," I said. "The studio is nervous about my new film. I haven't finished the script, and it's supposed to be done in the next couple of days. They're ready to shoot. Jackson wanted to help me with the script."

"At your house late at night?" he said. "I remember what you used to use that place for."

I was silent for a moment. Then I said, "What do you mean?"

"Come on," Philip said. "I'm one of Hayword's best friends. He knew what you were doing. I knew what you were doing. The entire fucking world knew what you were doing. I thought you'd given that up once you got sober."

Who the fuck was he to ask me these questions?

I took a deep breath. I still had to protect my family. Had to protect myself.

"Phil, I promise you that nothing like that was going on," I said. "But more importantly—since having sex isn't against the law—nothing illegal was going on. Unless dying is illegal. Now, did you find out anything about John Manuel Reilly?"

Phil made a noise. Trying to convey disgust, perhaps. Then he said, "He's got an outstanding warrant in Ohio."

"For what? Anything I can blackmail him with?"

"As I mentioned in a previous conversation, blackmail is illegal. But no, the warrant is for parking tickets. His parents live in Ohio. If he goes home he could go to jail, though. He got these tickets in a town where the fine keeps multiplying and they put people in jail until they pay it. He's racked up eight thousand dollars in fines. Hasn't been home in three years as far as I could tell. Been trying to get his SAG card for a while. Hasn't been able to get a gig, and even if he got one, he couldn't afford the initial dues. Doesn't seem like a bad guy, just kind of an ordinary loser. Does that help?"

"Not sure," I said. "Thanks. Man, I swear. I don't think I know what I'm doing. I forgot Alberto's birthday, Philip. Forgot it. Once I remembered I'd forgotten it, everything has gone to shit."

"I forget my kids' birth dates all the time," he said. "My wife always has to remind me."

"Seems like I should remember my dead child's birthday," I said. "Seems like a good mother would remember that kind of thing."

Oops. I hadn't meant to say that last part out loud.

Philip didn't say anything.

"I know you don't like me," I said. "I know you think I ruined Hayword's life. That I'm a bitch and a slut. And a drunk who is only temporarily reformed. I know that. In spite of all that, you try to help me whenever I ask, and on behalf of my family, I appreciate that."

I heard him sigh. "Brooke, I don't hate you. I don't think you ruined Hayword's life, and I certainly don't believe any of those other things about you. In fact, I think you're one of the bravest people I've ever known. Now, if you need help kicking this Manny kid's ass, let me know. I'll be there."

"Thanks, Phil."

The house throbbed with quiet. And the ghost of Irving Jackson past?

I phoned Hayword.

"Can I spend the night?" I asked.

"At home?" he asked.

"Yeah, at your house."

"At *our* house?"

"Whatever," I said. "May I spend the night?"

"Um, sure. Come on over. Where are you?"

"The bungalow. Hayword?"

"Yeah?"

"Can I sleep in our bed? With you? No sex. Just you and me in bed together."

"You mean like when we were married?"

"Funny guy," I said. "And we're still married."

"Might confuse David," he said.

"Let's not tell him."

A few minutes later, I walked into my old house. I felt such relief as I went through the front door. I stood in the kitchen for a moment, breathing deeply some smell I couldn't quite place, until I realized I was smelling oranges: an orange about to cross over into rottenness.

I went up the stairs, taking two steps at a time. I started to announce, "I'm home!" But I realized that would definitely send mixed messages.

"Hey, you guys!" I called. "You forgot to change the locks. I was able to get in."

David was out of his room and at the stairs before I got all the way up. He grinned.

"Hiya sailor," I said. We gave each other a big hug. He was nearly taller than me. I frowned. When the hell had that happened?

"Why are you here?" he asked.

Hayword came out of our old room. He was grinning, too, like a child on Christmas morning. Perhaps sleeping in the same bed was not a good idea, no matter how needy I was.

"I came to see my best buds," I said. I put my arm around David's waist. "How's the science project coming?"

"All finished," David said.

"You wanna tell us about it?" I asked.

He smiled and shook his head. "Nope. Just wait until tomorrow. You'll be so surprised."

I glanced at Hayword. He shrugged.

"David," I said, "I'm spending the night. I might be in your father's room for a while."

"You mean your room?" David said.

"What?" I asked.

"Your room," David said. "That room is *your* room. *Yours*. The two of you. It's your room."

"Technically it's not *my* room anymore," I said. "It's your father's room."

David shook his head. "No. It's *yours*."

I felt like my head was going to explode. Why was he insisting on this now? I hadn't lived here for nearly two years.

"We don't need to have this discussion now," I said. "I—we didn't want you to be confused. I need to talk to your father about some things, so we might be in his room—our room—tonight.

But it doesn't mean anything. We're not having sex. It's nothing like that."

"Why not?" he said. "Why not have sex? You're married. Mark doesn't have anything to say about that. So, you know, he's in the wrong here because you're already married."

Hayword and I looked at one another.

"It's difficult to argue with that," Hayword said.

"You're not helping," I said. "Maybe this was a bad idea. I just had a terrible day, and I wanted to be with family. I didn't want to be alone."

"Where is Mark?" David asked. He almost sounded angry. I thought he liked Mark.

"It's his night to be with his son," I said. I wasn't going to tell David the rest of the story. That could come later.

"Anyway, are you cool with your dad and me hanging out for a while, and I may spend the night? It doesn't mean we're back together or anything."

"No shit, Mom."

I stepped back from him. "Whoa! Where'd that come from?"

"Sorry," he said sheepishly. "I didn't mean to channel Fern."

"Good," I said, "cuz I couldn't deal with more than one of her."

"Go ahead and stay," David said as he turned and walked away from us. "Have sex if you want. Just don't be loud. I'm already screwed up enough as it is."

"But you're our normal kid," I called. "The one and only normal one. Our hopes and dreams are pinned entirely on you."

"Then you're screwed," he said.

I ran after him and tickled him. He laughed. I tickled him all the way to his bedroom. Then I hugged him again, kissed him, and left his room.

"Close the door on your way out so I'm not privy to your marital perversions," he said.

I closed the door. "Privy, eh? Where did he come from?"

Hayword held his hand out to me. I took it. "Okay. Let's get this pajama party started. Ice cream or coconut fake ice cream?"

"Hell," I said. "Let's just eat anything and everything with sugar in it."

"Deal," he said.

We went downstairs. I sat on a stool at the island while Hayword pulled out chocolate and vanilla ice cream and vanilla fudge almond Coconut Bliss from the freezer. He found fresh strawberries, too, and soon piled ice cream, Coconut Bliss, strawberries, chocolate syrup, and bananas into two bowls. We took our goodies into the living room and curled up on the couch together.

I looked around and couldn't believe that less than an hour ago, give or take, I'd been taking fishnet stockings off a dead man and then dressing him again. Made me shudder.

"Hayword," I said. "Can I tell you what's been going on without you freaking out?"

"Way to start a conversation, Brooke," I said. "But yes, you can tell me anything. I've been seeing a therapist, you know. Learning how to be a grown up. It's art therapy, but she calls it something else. Learning to be a grown up by painting like a child. I hadn't realized how strange I had gotten. How wrapped up in this life of ours. This life of mine. It was so important for me to be noticed. To be successful. Everything else just paled. Even you and the kids. I couldn't hear you when you said this wasn't the life you wanted. I couldn't hear it because it was as if you were speaking another language. I thought this was paradise. Or thought I would be happy once I achieved my goals. I don't know. I can't really describe it. I'm just sorry I wasn't what you needed. I'm sorry I was a bundle of nerves—a tender bundle of nerves you had to watch over. Or whatever it was you did."

"Hayword, I was fucking drunk," I said. "I didn't watch over anything."

"Yes, you did, Brooke," he said. "You watched over all of us."

"Not all of us," I said. "One of us died." I shook my head. "God. When will that go away? Not Alberto. I don't want him to go away. But I'd like the hurt to go away."

"Maybe it will never go away," he said. "Maybe it's a kind of sacred wound. When we decide to love, it's incredibly brave, because it's all temporary. We're all temporary. Maybe love is temporary. And so we are opening ourselves up to being wounded. Once we love and then we lose love, we should get a purple heart, or something, to let everyone know we were brave enough to love. I mean, how cool is that?"

"That's very cool," I said. "Wow, Hayword. Did you think of that yourself?"

"Sure," he said. He put a spoonful of chocolate into his mouth. A bit dribbled onto his chin. "I've had a lot of nights alone to think about our lives."

I reached over and wiped the chocolate off his chin with my forefinger and then sucked the chocolate off my finger.

"That robbery yesterday," I said, "or the fake robbery. Enrique deChamp was one of the fake robbers. It turns out Fern planned it all as a way to get me to notice Enrique, so I would put him in the next *Beauty and the Zombie* film—even though I'm not the fucking director, even though I don't make those kinds of decisions. She couldn't just ask me. She had to concoct this elaborate scheme."

Then I told him the rest of it. All of it. The various blackmails, the seal on the highway, all about finding Mark with that bimbo woman, about Irving Jackson and my magic vagina, talking to

Phil Case, Joanie bringing the pills, me almost drugging Jackson, finding Jackson dead and then dressing him. The paramedics.

Hayword didn't say anything. Although he did stop eating his ice cream about the time I mentioned fishnet stockings.

"Oh, and you already know about me seeing Ryan Nichols yesterday. And the worst part, the worst part of it all—besides contemplating how fucked up our daughter must be—is realizing I forgot Alberto's birthday."

"Man, I'm sorry," he said. "What a fucking day." He set his bowl down. He reached for me and pulled me up onto his lap. He wrapped his arms around me, and I wrapped my arms around him. I curled up on his lap, just like I used to when we were younger, when we were new together, when I actually went to him for comfort and solace. In the before time. Before Hollywood, before kids, before Ryan. Before we . . .

Before we what?

Didn't matter. I closed my eyes and held him. Breathed deeply his familiar smell. For the moment at least, I was home.

Before I knew it, I fell asleep.

TWELVE

I awakened to laughter. David and Hayword were giggling about something. Just like old times. Was I dreaming? I opened my eyes to sunshine, and I felt a wave of relief and happiness. I was with my family again, in my house, and all was well, all was well, all was as it . . . had never been in this house.

"Hop on the reality train, sister," I mumbled to myself. I had been an unhappy drunk in this house. I had been a lousy wife and a lousy mother in this house.

I pushed the quilt off of me and sat up. I was on the couch in the living room. Must have slept through the night here. That was not how I had planned on spending the evening, but it was probably for the best. Who knew what would have happened if Hayword and I *had* gotten into bed together. Old habits died hard.

"I hear moaning," Hayword called from the kitchen. "The dragon awakes."

"Not the dragon," I said. "The dragonslayer."

Hayword brought me a cup of coffee. David followed him into the living room. I took the cup from Hayword gratefully.

"Dragonslayer?" David said. "What did the dragon ever do to you?"

"This particular dragon tried to screw with my kids," I said.

David raised his eyebrows. I took a sip of the coffee and waved a hand in front of me.

"Pay no attention to me," I said. "I'm just babbling."

"I'll take David to school," Hayword said, "and I'll meet you at his presentation at ten? Your other thing is at eight?"

I nodded. "How are you doing, sweetheart?" I asked David.

"Great!" he said. "I'm ready to give this presentation. It will blow your mind. Come on, Dad. I don't want to be late."

David kissed the top of my head. "See you later, Mom."

Hayword leaned down and kissed me on the forehead. "You okay?" he asked.

"Did it all really happen?" I asked.

"It was on the news," Hayword said, "so I told David about it. About Jackson being at your house for a business meeting."

"I never liked that guy," David said.

"I didn't know you had met him," I said.

"A couple times," he said. "He was always asking me questions. I never thought he really wanted the answers. He was pretending to be a nice guy when he so clearly was not."

"You're right," I said. "He was not a nice guy. I never knew that before. I just thought he was, well, kind of a nothing."

"Really?" David said. "You think of people that way?"

"Um, well, I hadn't realized that until this moment." I looked up at my son. I felt like I had a hangover. "I will try to do better."

David and Hayword left, and I was alone in my old house.

I felt like a stranger in a strange land. And a familiar in a familiar land. Whose familiar was I?

I was tempted to go online and see what they were saying about Irving Jackson's death. Hoping they didn't mention he died at my house. Hoped they didn't mention the fake robbery again. But I didn't do it, and I didn't wander around my old home like some kind of ghost come to wail over a former life.

No matter what had happened last night, I still had some little weasel I had to deal with this morning.

I checked my phone. Four texts from Mark. I hesitated and then I read the latest one. "Where are you? I called to say good-night and never heard from you. Love." Second one: "Miss you. Wish you were here. Love." First one: "Ian and I went to Wally World. Ate too much cotton candy. I'll let you guess which one. Love." I smiled. And then I remembered what I had seen. Remembered the naked woman talking about me, in my house, after fucking my man.

In my freaking house.

I would lay waste to her later. She was so fired. And Mark? What was I going to do with him? He was opening a restaurant in my building in two days. I could sell him the building. Move back here. Live in the bungalow.

The bungalow where Irving Jackson had died dressed in fishnets and a garter. Was I ever going to get that image out of my brain? The feeling of my lips pressed against his dead lips as I tried to bring him back from the dead?

I went upstairs to my old bedroom. The bed was made. Either Hayword hadn't slept in the bed last night or else he had actually made the bed. He was a fairly neat man, actually. I was the one who didn't give a shit about things like made or unmade beds. I couldn't remember if I'd always been that way. I mean, I must have taught my children how to live in the world, how to make their beds, put away their toys, set the table, things like that.

Hadn't I?

I sat on the edge of the bed. How many nights had I slept in this bed? How many times had I made love to Hayword in it? No one else but Hayword. I'd never brought another man to our bed—or another woman, for that matter. I wondered if he'd had sex with anyone else in it, since I had left.

I made a noise and got up. This was stupid.

I went to the closet and slid open the door. My side of it was still empty. He hadn't even pushed his clothes over to fill it. I looked up on the shelf. I'd left behind some boxes of stuff. And one precious item.

I dragged the chair from the dressing table over to the closet and stood on it. Then I reached to the back of the shelf until my fingers touched metal. I put my hands around what I knew to be a small urn, and I pulled it down off the shelf.

Alberto's ashes.

In the beginning, Hayword and I had planned on going out to sea and scattering Alberto's ashes in the Pacific. But we didn't do that. Then we thought about taking his ashes all over the world with us. Until I realized that was macabre. And stupid. Alberto was not in his ashes. I couldn't press the urn against my chest and feel his little heartbeat one last time. I had tried that with his little body after he died.

I had tried.

Now I pressed the urn against my chest anyway. I closed my eyes.

I tried to remember what it felt like to hold Alberto. Tried to remember that smell. The glorious smell of his newness. His Alberto-ness. He had been the happiest being on the planet Earth. Always felt like a kind of betrayal to him that I could not be happy after he died. Not that I ever really tried. Except lately. Yes, lately I had been trying.

I looked down at the urn. We should really do something with his ashes. Maybe next year.

I got back up on the chair and pushed the urn to the back of the closet again.

Enough of this. Wasn't my home no more, no more.

Time to go.

I went downstairs, finished my coffee, grabbed an apple from the table, and left the building.

I didn't look back.

I drove down the hill and into the village. Parked the car in front of The Coffee Shoppe. Wasn't sure what I was going to do or say.

The fog had lifted, and it was a sunny cool day. Everything seemed so different from last night. Chirpy, almost. I felt a spring in my step. Heard a crow cawing from somewhere. When I looked around for her, all I saw was blue sky. Suddenly I had an idea. I pulled my phone out, turned on the record function, and slipped it into my pocket.

Then I opened the door to The Coffee Shoppe. A bell tinkled as the door moved outward. I hadn't noticed that before.

Inside, The Coffee Shoppe seemed normal and perky, as usual. The weirdness from last night was gone, and Portland with the tattoos was nowhere in sight. I glanced around and immediately saw a young man with blond hair and black roots sitting in a corner. Must be Manny. He looked completely out of place here. Couldn't quite put my finger on why.

Maybe because he was a criminal and the other customers were not.

I sauntered over to the table, stopped, and looked down at him. "Gonna fake rob anyone today, Manny?"

He smiled. As if he were charmed by me.

I wasn't trying to charm him.

He held out his hand to me. "Nice to finally meet you, Ms. McMurphy. But I didn't fake rob anyone. I wasn't even there."

"Save it," I said. I sat across from him without shaking his hand.

"You want me to get you a coffee?" he asked.

"What? So you can charge me for it? No. Let's get down to business here."

He shrugged. "Okay. Things haven't been going well for me."

I thought, "Probably because you're a dick," but I didn't say anything.

"I'm always on the lookout for opportunity," he said, "and this opportunity just landed in my lap."

He had pretty blue eyes, but his mouth was a little crooked. His hair was dirty. He should really do something about those black roots. He could very easily play a scuzzball on screen.

"What opportunity?"

"You know," he said, "finding out it was your daughter who helped plan this thing."

"What thing?" I asked. I leaned back. I'd just play dumb.

"The fake robbery," he said. "We never guessed people would get so upset about it all."

"You thought people would enjoy getting robbed?"

"It wasn't a real robbery," he said, "although now I can see that they wouldn't have known that until it was all over. So I understand. But I've got rent to pay like anyone else, and I need a job."

"Go work at McDonald's," I said.

"Like that will pay my rent," he said. "Come on. You and your old man must be flush."

I made a face. Who talked like they were in some noir film?

"I figured you'd pay me ten thousand to keep my mouth shut," he said. "Otherwise I'd go to the police."

"You were involved just as much as anyone else," I said.

"They'd cut me a deal," he said. He shrugged. "On all the police shows I've seen, that's what they do."

I stared at him. He was looking at his fingers. He didn't understand how ridiculous he sounded.

"If I gave you ten thousand dollars to keep quiet," I said, "if I gave in to your blackmail, who's to say you wouldn't just come back for more?"

He looked at me. "Who's to say? But if you don't, I will go to the police."

I heard the bell at the door tinkle or twinkle. What was the word? I had a headache. Needed a fucking drink. I suddenly felt like a songbird in a cage. And this kid wanted to keep me in one.

A shadow fell across me. I looked up. Hayword stood on one side of me, Phil Case stood on the other. Neither said a word. They just looked tough. My own personal Wookiees.

Perfect timing. I knew exactly what to do.

I turned back to Manny and smiled.

I reached into my pocket and pulled out my phone and put it on the table. "This is Brooke McMurphy signing off." I pushed stop and then put the phone back into my pocket.

"This is how it's going to go, John Manuel Reilly," I said. "I just recorded you trying to blackmail me. That's a crime. The police know all about the fake robbery and they know about everyone's involvement. This is Detective Philip Case." I held my hand up in Phil's direction. Phil took out his badge and flashed it. Still didn't say a word, just held out the badge for a long time, long enough for Manny to see it was real. "And this gentleman is Mr. Smith. He's a hit man for Louie Berlugetti. Gangsta supreme. Mr. Berlugetti is a private man. Keeps his business neat and tidy. He is a personal friend of mine. Half of Hollywood is mobbed up, you know, and the other half is going down on the half that is mobbed up. It's a nasty business. You've stepped right into it." I stood up, and then I leaned over, resting my hands on the table. "Here's the thing, you little shit ass motherfucker, you've tried to fuck with my family. You've tried to fuck with my children. I make a mamma grizzly bear look like a soccer mom. The last man who tried to fuck with my family ended up dead. You hear about Irving Jackson? Yes, that guy. You aren't getting a fucking dime from me. Ever." I felt rage surging through my body. Pent-up rage. Pent-up anger and frustration. Hadn't realized I had so much fucking anger and grief. If this boy said one wrong word to me, I was certain I would club him to death.

I took in a breath, and then I said, "If you go quietly, I won't tell my friend Louie about you. Detective Case here will pretend he never heard of you. Go back to Ohio for a while—you'll find Mr. Berlugetti paid off your tickets at my bequest. You can come back here one day if you like, maybe even work in the movie business if you've got any talent. If you've got any talent for keeping your mouth shut and keeping away from me and my family. You got that?"

He looked like he had shit his pants.

He nodded.

"Good," I said. "We'll be watching you."

I turned around and walked across the restaurant. I heard Phil and Hayword following me. The door tinkled as I opened it. I went to my car and leaned against it.

I was shaking with anger. I tried to breathe it out, breathe it down and out.

"Who the fuck is Louie Berlugetti?" Phil asked me.

"I made him up," I said. "Sounds like a gangster, doesn't he?"

He laughed and then put his hand across his mouth to keep from laughing.

"That was perfect, guys," I said. "Thank you so much."

Phil shrugged. "Blame Hayword. He called me last night and we concocted this. Couldn't let the dame have all the fun."

Hayword and I laughed.

"If he truly goes to the cops," Phil said, "I don't know if I can do anything."

Hayword came and stood next to me. He put his arm around my waist and I leaned into him. Let Manny see that I was on good terms with Berlugetti's hit man.

"Thank you for everything," I said to Phil.

He shrugged. "What are friends for? And remember, I don't want any details." He leaned over and kissed my cheek. Then he walked away.

"You want a ride up to the school?" I asked Hayword as we moved away from one another.

"Sure," he said. "So you see me as a hit man, eh?" He grinned. "That's kind of sexy."

I got into the driver's seat, and he slid into the passenger's seat.

"Why would you think being a murderous thug was sexy?" I asked.

"Blame it on TV."

I pulled out my phone. "Better call Fern and let her know."

Hayword's phone rang as I called Fern.

"Mom?" she answered.

"I think we took care of it," I said. "Just stay away from Manny. If he asks any questions about me, play up the murderous rageful aspect of my personality."

"Done," she said.

I heard Hayword saying something like, "I'll ask, but I don't think she wants to talk to you."

"Fern, we're going to have to talk about all of this," I said. "I have a lot to tell you."

"Okay," she said. She did not sound okay. I ended the call.

Then I phoned my business manager. I instructed her to pay off some parking tickets in Ohio, anonymously, so that Manny would think the gangster did it. I texted her Manny's name and the name of his town.

"Who were you talking to?" I asked Hayword as I started up the car.

"Mark," he said.

"Mark who?" Really, for a second I didn't know who the hell he was talking about. He gave me a look. "Oh. He called *you*?"

"He said he's been calling you and texting you," Hayword said. "He was worried. I told him you were at our house last night."

"Good," I said. "I hope you told him we fucked each other's brains out."

Hayword didn't say anything.

"Sorry," I said.

I drove us out of the village and up the canyon road to David's school.

"I would have," Hayword said.

"Would have what?"

"Fucked your brains out," he said.

I laughed. One thing about Hayword, he could almost always make me laugh.

"In fact, I'd be willing to try right here and now."

"Thanks for the offer," I said, "but we've got a science experiment to watch."

Hayword and I got to the gym a few minutes before David was due to give his presentation. Each kid had fifteen minutes for his or her experiment, and god bless the school, they didn't make the parents sit through every student's experiment. All of the kids in David's class had their booths set up in various places throughout the gym.

David grinned and waved as we walked toward him. I refrained from hugging and kissing him, but he gave us each a big hug.

Then we heard a bell ring, which startled me. In the corner of my vision, I thought I saw kids moving away from their booths, but I didn't pay much attention.

"Hello everyone," David said. He cleared his throat and smiled nervously. "Today my experiment involves gases." His voice shook slightly. "We are surrounded by gases. If it weren't for gases, we would die. The atmosphere we breathe is 78 percent nitrogen, 21 percent oxygen, .9 perfect argon, and .03 carbon dioxide. Each one of these is clear and odorless. We breathe other things all day, too, and they affect us in different ways. Some things we breathe in we can smell. Like flowers, for instance."

He was smiling and pointing to things on a large screen next to him as he occasionally moved something on his laptop. He was showing us a bouquet of roses now. "Scent is the first sense activated when we're born." A baby was on screen. "Some scents make us feel good." He pointed to the baby. "Some don't." The screen flashed a photo of garbage.

"Some gases we smell," he said. "Some we don't, and yet they affect us." He picked up a jar from his table, took off the lid, then set the jar, open, on the table.

"For instance, the gas in this jar will fill the gym in seconds," he said. "It's gas produced from an odorless flower in the Amazon. The scent from this flower is a renowned love potion. When people breathe in the molecules from this plant, they often feel quite loving, and they're able to express their true feelings to one another."

Parents looked around the room at one another. I noticed the other kids were all standing by the gym doors, like guardians. I vaguely wondered what was up with that. David was watching us—the adults. He had a twinkle in his eyes. I was glad he was spreading love. I saw people hugging one another. I looked at

Hayword and rolled my eyes. He laughed and grabbed my hand and pulled me to him. He whispered in my ear, "He's doing this to get us back together. I bet that's why he wanted to make sure we came together."

I nodded, and we moved slightly apart.

"It would be all right with me," Hayword said quietly. "I wish you would come home."

"Hayword," I said. "It's not like I've been on vacation. I've moved out. I've moved on."

"But we really never tried a normal life," he said. "With you sober. Just home with us. As a family. Maybe it would be great. I mean, last night felt so normal."

"We never wanted normal," I said.

"Then right," Hayword said. "It felt right."

That was true. When I was in trouble, last night when I felt alone and friendless, I headed back home. I headed to my family.

I looked at Hayword. I did love him. I loved being in the same house as David. But I didn't want that life. Didn't want that vacuous life. I wasn't that person anymore. I hoped. I was someone now, wasn't I? I mean, I wasn't just a big abyss of grief and nothingness.

"I'm glad you're all enjoying the Amazon Love Plant," David said. He put the cap back on the jar.

"Awwww," several people said.

Then we all clapped.

"Thank you," David said. "You could see how even though you didn't smell anything, your mood changed, didn't it? You felt more affection."

I shrugged and then nodded. I supposed he was right. He began wiggling the top off another jar.

"Now what's in here is a thousand times more powerful," he said, "and will move across the gym in seconds."

I heard the gym doors open. Then heard them close. I glanced over. The kids were gone. Heard another strange sound. Like something dragging across metal.

The top came off the jar. David set the lid aside.

"Inside this job is a particular type of ionizing radiation in a gaseous form. It's like the radiation from the Japanese power plant. Only this is more concentrated. It can disable in minutes. But it's been designed to affect only some people. It's a manufactured nuclear weapon. One of the other kids here got it for me—from his dad."

Suddenly the air seemed to go out of the room.

What had my son just said?

The eyes on the principal widened. Several parents raced for the gym doors.

"They're locked!" one of the parents shouted as she reached the door. "They've put chains across them."

What the fuck? I looked over at David. He was still smiling, like some maniac from a bad TV show.

"We've locked all exits," David said. "You shouldn't worry, though. This weapon only affects some people. The symptoms are a racing heart. Next is itchy skin. Then throat tightening. And trouble breathing."

I saw one man start to scratch his neck. Then he stopped and looked horrified.

"Are you one of those lucky people who won't be affected?" David looked around the room. His gaze stopped on us, for just a moment, and then he continued glancing around.

One woman began to weep. Another man kept scratching behind his ear. The rest seemed to be waiting, paralyzed with fear? Why did no one reach for a cell phone?

Wait.

I knew my son.

He was not a monster.

Was he?

"David," the principal said. "You must stop this."

David nodded. He put the lid back on the "nuclear potion."

"It's too late!" someone said. "Look, I've got the rash!"

David then took the lid off of the Amazon Love Potion. "Here, this will counteract the radiation."

I could hear the chains sliding off of the doors. Then the doors opened, and the kids came back into the gym.

"No, go back," one of the parents shouted. "It's contaminated."

"Yes, it is," one of the students said. A girl. Tracy someone. "It's all contaminated."

The other fifteen students or so came and stood around David.

"This was a community experiment," David said, "designed by all of us."

One of the boys—Jeremy Fox—picked up the love potion bottle.

"There was no love potion," Jeremy said, "although some of you were effected."

Another one of the girls—KateLynn Morris—picked up the radiation bottle. "There was no radiation in this bottle," she said. "If there had been, we all would have been doomed because radiation does not discriminate. It cannot. Everyone is affected by radiation. Right now radiation contaminates our ocean. Radiation contaminates our air."

"Air pollution doesn't discriminate either," Betsy Day spoke up. "We are all affected by what is going on in the world today."

"And we feel as though you, our parents and teachers, are fiddling while Rome is burning," David said. "We want you to do *something*. We want you to stop the radiation and the pollution and all the crazy stuff that's going on."

The gymnasium was spooky silent.

Dead quiet.

The kids stared at us.

I thought of that woman who had survived the plane crash. She hadn't worn a seat belt. She acknowledged the truth. Acknowledged the horror. And saw the beauty anyway.

I said, "How?"

The kids all looked at me. For a second I felt like they were those children from *Village of the Damned*.

"How what?" one of them asked.

"How do we stop it? How do we fix it?" I asked.

The kids glanced at one another. Then David looked at me and said, "We don't know. That's why we did this. We want you to figure it out."

I shrugged. "Obviously we haven't figured it out. The thing is, some of us are still trying to figure it out. Some of us aren't. We each have different abilities to respond, depending upon our circumstances in life, depending upon who we are, how we're feeling, etc. Responsibility. Our generation tried to change the system, and then we tried to live with the system. Didn't work. We're living in whackadoodle times, kids. We can't escape that fact. So what do we do? We look around. We face the truth and figure out how we can respond. As we respond, we also enjoy the beauty around us. I mean, really, what else can you do? If you wait for someone else to fix it, you're fucked. If you try to ignore it, you're fucked—or you're a drunk. Figure out how you want to respond, then respond, and enjoy yourself as best you can. You bitch-slapped us here today. You got us to think in a surprising and wonderful way—and a dangerous way, I might add. You're lucky no one collapsed with a heart attack."

"That could still happen!" one of the parents shouted.

Nervous laughter all around.

The principal said, "I should suspend you all, and if your

parents want me to do that, I will. If not, we will have a conversation with the entire class about ethics. I want each of you to write a detailed essay about this experiment and how it has affected you—and what you're going to do to change the world. Now say goodbye to your parents and let's get back to work."

"Wow, Mom," David said. "It was like you were Mom again."

"You mean because I could put more than two sentences together?" I said.

"No, because you knew what to say," he said. He smiled. "What'd you think?"

"Very effective," I said. "You are a bad, bad boy."

David stood between us with one arm around my waist and one around his father's.

"So did you two decide to get back together," he said, "so we could live happily ever after?"

"Is that why you did this?" Hayword asked.

"I did it so they'd kick me out of school," he said, "but then everyone else wanted to do it with me, so odds were they weren't going to kick us all out. Are you coming home, Mom?"

"If you're asking me if I'm moving back to your house," I said, "no."

At least I didn't think so. Right this moment, I felt like I could go back. It would be okay, right? I could undo some of the damage I had done all those years I was drinking.

"Why the hell do you want to get kicked out of school?" I asked. "I thought you loved school."

David rolled his eyes. "Mom. I am always the outsider. I hate school. Or I did. Planning this faux killing spree really bonded us."

"Do not call it that when you talk to the principal," Hayword said. "Really, David, this could have gone really wrong."

"But it didn't," David said. "It didn't." He grinned. "It will not show up on my disaster app."

I laughed. I couldn't help it. My boy had been nervous about one catastrophe after another for almost as long as I could remember.

"Please think about coming home," David said. "I miss you. Dad misses you. If we had a dog, the dog would miss you. Can we get a dog?" He grinned.

I sighed and looked at Hayword. He shrugged and shook his head, trying to tell me he hadn't put David up to it.

"I better go," I said. "I have to finish the script. The fate of the world hangs on it."

"The fate of the world?" Hayword said. I could see the anxiety in his eyes. His insecurity was always just below the surface.

"Just a figure of speech. I'll talk to you both later."

I kissed David on the cheek and gave Hayword a quick peck on the lips. We were both surprised by it. I laughed, uncomfortably.

"Habit," I said.

"Don't try to break that one," Hayword said.

I backed away, and then I left the love-potioned radioactive gym and headed out to my car.

THIRTEEN

The day seemed brimming with spring. The sound of birds came from everywhere. Hopefully they weren't gathering in the trees à la *The Birds* to swoop down and peck my eyes out.

I breathed deeply. Okay. Now I needed to call Sally and then Mark. I'd have to deal with the whole thing with Mark before I started writing the script. The script, the script. How was I going to write that stupid script?

I jogged across the road toward my car.

Then I saw Mark leaning against my car, his arms crossed. He smiled when he saw me.

I felt butterflies in my stomach. He was so beautiful.

"There you are!" he said, dropping his arms, coming toward me. "I've been worried sick."

"What are you doing here?" I asked. I tried to get to the driver's side of my car, but Mark was standing in my way.

"What? Brooke, look at me. What's going on? I've phoned

you, texted you, called your husband, for god's sake, and he said you wouldn't talk to me. Why?"

"Get the fuck out of my way," I said.

Startled, Mark moved, and I opened the car door.

"Why don't you ask your naked fuck bunny Sherry," I said. I slid into the car seat and started to close the door, but Mark held it open.

"What the hell are you talking about?"

"Don't play innocent with me," I said. "I got home from the party early last night and there was Sherry, walking around in my house, naked, after taking a shower, trying to hurry and get out before I returned and caught you two together."

"What? Sherry was in our house naked?"

"Let me close this fucking door," I said, trying to jerk it out of his hand.

"No!" he said. "Get out here and tell me what the fuck is going on."

Disgusted I got out of the car.

"I went home," I said. "My home, by the way, not *our* home. Left the party early. I saw your truck, and I was so excited that I'd get to see you, surprise you. So I went in the back. There Sherry was, naked, talking to you about getting dressed before the bitch got home. The bitch being me. I always knew she was after you— or after something of mine. Worthless piece of trash."

"That wasn't *me*!" Mark said. "I lent Giovanni my truck because his broke down. That SOB. I'm gonna kill him. How dare he do this to my sister."

"What are you talking about?" I said.

"What are *you* talking about?" he said. "You thought I was cheating on you? You believed that and you didn't have the courtesy of asking me?" He was pissed. I hadn't seen him pissed before.

"You were naked!" I said. "I—I couldn't ask you. I couldn't

confront you. I'd seen Hayword fucking someone, and I never got over it. I couldn't go through that again!"

"It never occurred to you that it wasn't me?"

I looked at him. I was so relieved it hadn't been him that I wanted to fling myself into his arms. I wanted to forget the entire thing. Let's fire Sherry and move on.

"No," I said softly, "it never occurred to me. My daughter had told me she'd seen you and Sherry together and you looked really cozy together."

"I was with Ian last night," Mark said. "Just as I said I would be. Giovanni's car died, and he needed to finish up some things at the restaurant, so I told him to take my truck. Brooke, I would never cheat on you. It's not in my nature."

He looked so desperately hurt and angry all at the same time.

"I know it's not," I said.

Then why had I so readily believed it? What was wrong with me?

"And you went home," he said. "You went back to Hayword."

"No," I said. "I went to the bungalow because Irving Jackson told me if I didn't have sex with him he was going to tell the police that Fern burned down our house in Brentwood."

"What?" Mark said.

I shook my head. "No, no. That can all wait. Mark, I'm so sorry. I don't know what to say. It was such an awful day yesterday. You wouldn't believe what happened. When I came home and saw Sherry and heard them—and thought it was you—I just . . . I have no explanation. I felt like the whole world had crashed and burned."

"Did you have sex with him?"

"Who?"

"Irving Jackson, whoever the fuck he is."

"No." I shivered. "No."

"But you invited him to the bungalow," he said.

I sighed. "It's such a long story. I was planning on blackmailing him. Not sure how." I rubbed my face. "It was a stupid plan, and if I had told someone besides Joanie about it ahead of time, I might not have gone through with it. In fact, I wasn't going to go through with it, but when I came to tell him, I found him dead."

"What?"

"I told you. It's long and complicated. My guess is he died of a heart attack or a stroke or something. I'm really hoping that's what it was. I don't think I'd like to be involved in a murder investigation."

"I really don't know what to say," Mark said.

"Can I hug you?" I asked.

Mark shook his head. "No. I don't think so. I don't know what I'm feeling. You dumped me, just like that, right out of your life. Making it clear that our home is not our home but it is your home." He put a hand up. "I need to go fire Sherry and Giovanni and tell my sister. I will talk to Sherry and Giovanni first, to see if they are actually having an affair."

"Come on, Mark," I said. "If you came home and saw Hayword naked, for instance, and heard someone else in the shower and my car was there. Wouldn't you assume it was me? Would you actually wait and try to talk to me?"

"Yes, I would. Jesus, Brooke."

"I told you she was fucking bad news," I said. "Please get all the locks changed in the house ASAP."

"Yes, your majesty," Mark said. "Let me get that done for you right away."

"For us," I said.

He shook his head. "Naw. Ain't my house."

"Mark," I said. "Please have some understanding. It's been crazy."

"That's what you *always* say," Mark said. He shook his head. "Of course no one else matters when things are crazy for *you*."

"That's not fair!" I said. "I've been putting out fires to protect my family. It's not about me! I know you've got the restaurant opening. I know that's stressful. But you seem to be handling it."

"I'm glad you're okay," he said. "Now I guess I'll go figure out the rest of it. I'll talk to you later."

"Um, can you get someone to come and clean the house?" I asked. "I want everything Sherry touched scrubbed or thrown out. I don't think my cleaning lady from here will go that far."

Mark nodded.

"I'll see you tonight?" I asked. "Oh wait. I can't. I need to finish up this script. And you didn't want me around for the soft opening."

"I'll stay at my place," he said. "Maybe I should postpone the opening."

"What? Why? You've been looking forward to this!"

He looked at me. "No, I haven't. I don't give a shit about any of this. I did this for you, Brooke. I did it because it was clear you're not comfortable being in a relationship with a mere plumber. But a Hollywood chef? Yeah, you can handle that."

"You are out of your fucking mind," I said. "I don't care about Hollywood. I don't care about appearances. I only care about your happiness."

Mark laughed. "Yeah, right."

"Everything okay?" Hayword was walking toward us.

"Of course she runs to you as soon as anything goes wrong," Mark said.

"What are you talking about?" Hayword asked.

"She sees Ryan at an AA meeting and she calls you," Mark said. "She thinks I'm cheating and she goes straight to you."

"She didn't," Hayword said.

"It's like you're still fucking married," Mark said. "Oh wait! You still are! *I* am the interloper."

"Mark—" I started.

"I've been a part of this weird triangle for three years," he said. "That is three years too long. I've had enough. You two figure out your shit. I'm outta here."

He started to walk away.

"Goddamn it, Mark," I said. "This isn't you! You're just upset."

He stopped and laughed—it was more of a snort—really. "I'm *just* upset. You bet I am. How would you know if this was the real me or not? Do you have any idea who I am? Or Hayword? How about your kids? We've all got our roles in your life, right? And they're all about not rocking the boat and doing exactly what you'd like us to do. We're not fucking spear-carriers in your life, Brooke. When you're not around, we don't just disappear from the world and we turn on again, like little dolls, when you want us."

"Are you spear-carriers or dolls?" I said. "You're mixing metaphors here, Pantano."

"Brooke—" Hayword.

"Perfect," Mark said. "That's fucking perfect."

This time he kept walking to his car. Then he drove off.

I turned and looked at Hayword. "What was that?"

"He has a point," Hayword said. "I hate to admit it. I mean, I'd love to say screw him, come home with me and life will be great, but he's got a point."

"I don't understand this," I said. "I did not cause this! I didn't do anything wrong. Except maybe I should have double-checked to see who Sherry was fucking. Apparently it wasn't Mark."

"I gathered that," Hayword said. "And again, darn. Although I hope you detect the sarcasm. I need to get to work. Give me a ride down the hill?"

"I thought you liked Mark," I said.

"Brooke, you don't seem to understand that other people in the world—besides you—are going through difficult and confusing times."

"No shit, Sherlock," I said. "Come on. I'll take you to your car. Then I need to write another hit movie. That'll make everyone happy. That'll save our particular world."

"Why do you keep saying that?" Hayword asked. "Is there something going on at AFT?"

"You mean besides one of the execs dying in my house after he tried to blackmail me? No, nothing else."

Hayword and I didn't say much to each other as I drove him down to his car.

Before he got out of the car, he said, "I'm glad our child didn't actually dose us with fatal radiation. Always a good day when that happens."

I nodded. "Yes, always a good day then."

He was gone, and I headed to the bungalow. I hesitated before I opened the front door. I shouldn't have. Miranda had come and gone, and she'd done a fabulous job. She not only cleaned houses: She *cleaned* houses. Did feng shui. Performed cleansing ceremonies. Etcetera. When I walked through the door, I felt no death hangover. No visions of Irving Jackson danced through my head. She'd left a vase filled with yellow sunflowers on the table. Sunlight streamed through the picture windows that looked out over the backyard.

"Thank you, Miranda," I said. She was going to get a big bonus for this.

I closed the door behind me. I needed to eat something and then start writing. I went to the fridge. Miranda had stocked the fridge, too, with all my favorites. How had she known? Organic fair trade chocolate bombs from Vita's, along with various salads and hors d'oeuvre. A mushroom quiche. Chilled Martinelli's organic sparkling apple cider.

Wait a minute. That quiche plate was from my house at the beach. Miranda hadn't filled the fridge. Mark must have been here.

I closed the fridge and walked over to the table. A small card rested against the flowers. I opened it.

"Good luck. I know you can do it. Picked the flowers myself. Your neighbor is pretty pissed at me. Reheat quiche at 375 for 15 or eat at room temp. Love, Mark."

I pulled out my phone and texted Mark. "Thx for flowers & food. For everything. Let me know if I can help w/ restaurant. Or anything."

I slid the quiche in the oven and then put my laptop on the coffee table in front of the couch. I read over my treatment.

"Ugh," I said when I'd finished it. If it had been on a piece of paper, I would have balled it up and thrown it across the room. As it was, it was light and dark on my computer screen.

"This script has to save the world." I shrugged. "Let's not be a drama queen, Brooke. It's only a movie."

In the last movie, scientist Colleen Kelly falls in love with the zombie alien leader, Thomas. She convinces the world that the aliens aren't bad—they just have a wasting disease. Turns out the zombie aliens, including Thomas, are trying to wipe out the human race. Colleen goes on the run from the zombies and humans with her friend Marissa. They try to develop a cure but fail.

One day, figuring it's their last day, they stand barefoot on the earth as the sun comes up. Some kind of chemical combination occurs between the sunlight and the earth that cures them, and the world is saved. Thomas is put behind bars with the other zombie aliens. Colleen declares she never loved Thomas while he whispers that he really loves her. The last shot of the movie is of Colleen standing on a hilltop—and she is very pregnant and very afraid.

"Okay," I said. "Now what?"

I started typing. "Black screen. We hear Colleen screaming in terror. At first we think she's being hurt, but then the camera fades in to a hospital room where Colleen is giving birth to a beautiful baby boy. He looks completely human except when he opens his eyes: They are all shiny blue. Colleen names him Adam."

"No, too corny," I said, as I deleted the name.

"Colleen names him Aiden. The boy grows quickly. He ages a year for every month. He's very bright. He learns to read within days of his birth. Very soon he's doing math and physics. By the time he is eighteen months old, he is an adult working by his mother's side. The world is still devastated from the zombie invasion, and the humans are trying to put their world back together. Meanwhile the humans don't know what to do about the zombies who have survived and are imprisoned. In some countries, they have been put to death. Not all zombie aliens participated in the invasion and not all of them knew about the plot to kill off the human race. Should those aliens be put to death, too?

"Other zombie-human babies have been born, with varying abilities. Some are strong. Some are extraordinarily smart. They are ostracized, and legislation is introduced in the United States to incarcerate them all. Colleen works to prevent this from happening. Meanwhile, Aiden tells her he is homesick and wishes to return to the alien world—the alien world he has never seen. He becomes so depressed that Colleen takes him to prison to visit Thomas. She doesn't want to see Thomas, but she doesn't want to leave her son alone with him.

"Thomas seems the same as the last time Colleen saw him. He tells his son that he can't return to the home world because it is no longer livable. They destroyed their world and then came here to make it their home, but they were wrong. What they had done was very wrong and now they needed to repair any damage done to Earth. He hoped his son would work with Colleen to heal the damage.

"Colleen believes Thomas is bullshitting, but she's grateful for the speech. Before they leave, Thomas gives his son a ring with a swan carved in bone on it—a blue green swan. 'To remind you of me,' he says, 'and to remind you that everything wasn't terrible about me. Your mother loved me once enough to give me this ring—this ring that belonged to her father. She told me their crest was a swan. She told me the swan is a fearsome guardian.' Colleen is touched Thomas remembers her words. Aiden puts on the ring."

I stopped typing. "Crap. What next?" I needed an action scene now. I looked outside. The morning light spotlit a dog lying on the grass in my backyard. I squinted. No, not a dog. I got up and went to the window.

It was a bobcat. It turned and looked at me, saw me, and then looked away. What an exquisite-looking animal. Its pointed ears reminded me of something out of a fairy tale.

"You're welcome to stay," I whispered. I had never seen a wild animal like this near any of my houses.

I went back to the couch and stepped back into my imaginary world.

"Colleen and Aiden go back to their lives in the lab. Overnight, it seems, the animals begin to act strangely. First the domestic animals attack their owners, in some cases killing and eating them. When doctors examine the animals, they discover they have the animal version of the zombie disease. Soon enough it spreads to the wild animals. The world is once again thrown into chaos.

"The governments believe the zombie-human children are responsible for this new variant of the old disease. These children—who have all now grown quickly into adulthood—are ordered into camps. Aiden becomes convinced he can come up with a cure for the animals—and maybe even a cure for his own people. 'They aren't really evil,' he declares to his mother. 'It's just the disease.'

"Aiden goes on the run with his girlfriend, the zombie-human Molly. She is also a scientist. Soon the full forces of the government are focused on finding Aiden and Molly. Thomas sends a message to Colleen that he must see her. Reluctantly she goes to the prison again.

"He's bribed the guard to allow him to talk to Colleen privately. He tells her he is in telepathic communication with Aiden and has been since he was born. He knows where he is and can help her find him before the government does, and he has a cure for the animal plague. The same thing happened on their planet, and they discovered the cure too late. But it's in a ship that's hidden from the humans. Only he—Thomas—can retrieve it.

"Colleen doesn't know what to do. It's probably a trick. He might get to the ship and use the weapons on it to destroy the Earth or signal to any zombie aliens that are off-world. But she's desperate. The world is in such chaos, and her son is in danger. She agrees to help Thomas escape from prison."

I stopped typing. "How the hell are they going to escape from Alcatraz?" My fingers tapped the keys lightly as I tried to think of a way. Then I start typing.

"The government has used some zombies in experiments. Colleen arranges it so that Thomas is temporarily released into her custody on the ruse that she will experiment on him. Getting him off of Alcatraz is full of suspense. They're almost caught several times, but finally they are off the island, and now they, too, are on the run. Thomas takes her to the ship and arranges— telepathically—for Aiden to meet them. Of course they have to battle their way through crazy domestic and wild animals to get to the ship which is buried in the desert.

"Once in the ship, Colleen is certain Thomas will betray her. He powers up the ship and discovers that the information on the cure is gone. Colleen wonders if it was ever there. Suddenly three alien ships appear in the sky above them. Thomas swears he didn't call them. Just then Aiden arrives with Molly. They claim they have the cure. The army shows up then, too, demanding they all surrender. The alien ships begin firing on the army. Thomas tells Molly, Colleen, and Aiden to run. But first Thomas tells Colleen he loves her, and they kiss. He tells her that he believes these are the last of the alien ships. If he can get rid of them, Earth will be free. Colleen wants to stay, but Aiden drags his mother away. Once the three of them are off the ship, Thomas brings the ship's power online all the way and he fires on the zombie ships all at once, blowing them to bits.

"Just as Colleen and Aiden are about to go back to the ship and get Thomas, the ship rises up into the air. When it is high above them, the ship explodes. Colleen is bereft, but she sees the army has turned their attention to them. They demand that the three of them put up their hands and surrender. Aiden starts to walk toward one of the soldiers, holding something in his hand, 'We've found the cure. We've got to get it out right away.' A single shot rings out, and Aiden falls to the ground. Colleen runs to his side. 'It's up to you now, Mom,' he says. 'You've got to save the world.'

"Aiden dies, and Colleen screams. 'He was trying to save us!' she cries. 'Save us!' Months later, we see Colleen standing by Aiden's grave. Molly is next to her for a few moments, but then she kisses her and walks away. 'Well, baby boy,' Colleen says, 'the cure worked. Things are settling back to normal, whatever that is. They've released the zombie-human children from incarceration. Although you aren't really children. I'm not sure what to call you. Your father saved us, and he is now regarded as a hero.' She shrugs. 'Of sorts. Now, I better leave and get back to work.'

"She turns and walks away, but the camera continues to frame the grave. A few moments after Colleen walks away, a hand and arm burst from the ground at Aiden's grave. On one of the fingers of that hand is the swan ring. Hold for several beats. Fade to black.

"The End."

I laughed and pumped my fist into the air. "Yes!" I sighed. "Now for the script."

I ate part of the quiche, and then I started typing.

"So glad Colleen is gonna get her baby boy back," I whispered.

That's what I loved about fiction.

FOURTEEN

Once I got going on any writing project, I was a dynamo. I could write faster than anyone I knew, and what I wrote was good. Screenwriting is dialogue, basically. I mean, sure, you've got to think about shots and place and things like that, but it's really all character, from my viewpoint, and what they say to one another. And what they don't say. Those silent moments. The pauses. Sometimes it feels like the pauses are everything. Although in a movie like this, the pauses were certainly short and sweet.

Anyway, I wrote quickly. I didn't think about anything else as I wrote. I was in the world of chaos and zombies, and horror—and I was in the world where Colleen Kelly gets to work beside her baby boy. Where she gets to love him and try to save him. In the end, he dies, but he is saved, too. Perhaps. I suppose another screenwriter could be fooling with the audience. But I wasn't fooling. I could already imagine what happens next. As he bursts through the earth and calls out for his momma.

As I wrote, I saw several deer come into my yard, and another bobcat. Lots of birds. None of them were zombie animals. No one was attacking any humans. They weren't attacking one another either. I got up now and again and watched them.

I called Sally when I broke for dinner or lunch or whatever it was.

"Irving died of a heart attack," Sally said. "As far as they can tell. They'll do a tox screen, but they're pretty sure."

"Thank god," I said.

"His wife called," Sally said. "Wanted to know if you and Irving were sleeping together. I said as far as I knew you couldn't stand the man."

"You said that to his widow?" I said.

"She didn't seem that upset," Sally said. "She said she found something of yours in his belongings. She wanted your address for the messenger. I gave it to her. Hope that's okay."

"How do you know she's not some nut case come to kill me for being with her husband?"

"I thought you weren't *with* him," she said.

"I wasn't. But he was blackmailing me. He wanted me to help overthrow you, and he wanted me to have sex with him."

"Ew! And you agreed?"

"I pretended to agree," I said. "He died before my stupid plan could come to fruition. I found him dead dressed only in a garter, fishnet stockings, and stilettos."

"Double ew. How am I going to get that picture out of my head? Thank you very much. Would you have gone through with it? What was he blackmailing you with?"

"Not gonna tell you that over open airways," I said. "But no, I wouldn't have gone through with it. Now I need to finish this script."

"I'll see you Sunday," she said.

"Sunday?"

"Mark's opening," Sally said. "Sheesh."

"Oh, yeah."

"Email me the script as soon as you have it."

I called Joanie, too. Thanked her. Told her she could trash Jackson's um, clothes. "He died of a heart attack," I said.

"Oh good," she said. "So no murder investigation? Those are no fun."

"You've been involved in a murder investigation before?" I asked.

"Sure," she said. "What do you think happened to my first husband?"

"He was murdered?"

"No, but I had to go through a bit of white-knuckle interrogation before they figured that out," she said. "Taught me not to marry someone quite so old next time. His kids didn't want me to get anything. Even accused me of sexing him to death, if you know what I mean."

I groaned.

"My advice, don't ever let anyone die while you're having sex with them," she said. "It's not very sexy, no matter what the movies say."

I laughed. "Oh my god, Joanie. I want to hear that story but not now. I've got to finish work. Love you."

I ended the phone call and went back to the couch. Being friends with Joanie was like peeling an onion. There was always something underneath and it made you cry. Or laugh.

She was a good friend, though, and I was lucky she was on my side.

Just then I heard a knock at the door. I got up, looked through the keyhole, and then opened the door.

Mark stood on my steps with a manila envelope in his hands.

"This was on the top step," he said, holding it out to me. He looked uncomfortable, nervous.

I took the envelope. "Wonder why they didn't ring the bell," I said. "Come on in."

I set the envelope on the coffee table and sat on the couch.

"Can I get you anything?" I asked. "Please sit. Thanks again for the quiche and the other goodies. I've been snacking on them all day. The script is going well. Even faster than usual."

My stomach was doing flip-flops. Mark looked so delicious standing there in a T-shirt and jeans. I wanted to rip off his clothes and take him to bed.

Or at the very least, I wanted to put my arms around him.

"I'm sorry I was so pissed," he said. "I was worried about you all night. That got my adrenaline pumping. And then to have you treat me like I was nothing to you—that was tough."

"I'm sorry," I said. Felt weird sitting while he stood. "Hayword said you had a point about the way I treat people."

"Hayword says it so you listen?"

"What? No! You're both saying similar things, so I'm trying to understand. I will figure it out. Eventually. I need to finish the script, and then we'll figure everything out."

"You always say that," Mark said. "There's always something going on and after that something is finished, you say, we'll figure things out. But then something else comes up. That's what alcoholics say. They'll stop drinking when things settle down. Or people who smoke. Whatever. It's an excuse."

Mark sat in the chair opposite the couch.

I sat cross-legged on the couch.

"You're right," I said. "It is an excuse. It's because I don't really know how to have deeply personal intimate relationships. Haven't you figured that out? I don't want to talk about our future or even our now because then I have to think about it. Hayword wants me to come home. David wants me to come home. You want me to be with you. I'm satisfied loving you all."

"And having us all do exactly what you want," Mark said.

"Yes, I guess. Is that so odd? Don't you want me to do what you want? I mean, you want me to divorce Hayword and be with you. Marry you."

"But I'm not threatening to leave you if you don't do those things."

"Sure you are," I said. "You said this morning that you were gone until we figured it out."

He shrugged. "Okay. So you may have a point. But I'm not trying to control you. I just want to know where I am in all of this. We seem to be ships passing in the night lately."

"I thought I had made my decision!" I said. "I moved out, didn't I? I moved away. I live with you. You're opening a restaurant in my house."

"You made it abundantly clear that it's *your* house," he said, "not *our* home."

"I was just pissed."

"It's not an equal relationship," he said. "It never has been. I want it to be. Otherwise, it's not healthy for me. I almost took a drink today. I try to live my life so that doesn't happen. Look, if you don't trust me, I don't think we can stay together. If your heart is at home with Hayword and David, then you need to do that. Just tell me. Talk to me about it. I'm a big boy. I want us to be together, but if we're not, I won't die. It won't be the end of me."

"Really?" I said. "But I want you to feel like it would be the end of you. I want you to love me that desperately."

"That only happens in the movies," he said, "and to teenagers. I have a child, I have responsibilities. If you break my heart, I will mend and move on. I mean, you thought I was cheating on you. Did you curl up into a ball and die?"

"No," I said. "But I did throw up. That counts."

He laughed. He glanced outside. It was twilight now, but I

could see the animals moving around, like strange little shadows—ghosts of what they had been.

"What is going on? Are those people?" Mark asked.

"People?" I said. "No! They're animals. They've been there all day."

We went to stand at the window together.

"I feel like something big is going to happen," Mark said. "Something is about to snap or break."

"Me, too," I said. "Just so many weird things. The animals, the blackmail, Ryan. You. So I'm keeping busy trying to save my family."

Mark nodded. He put his arm around my waist, and I leaned against him.

"Ian is going up to Oregon with his mom for a week," he said. "I'm glad. I felt relief when she called and asked if it was okay. I just took them to the airport. And I'm postponing the opening of the restaurant."

"No!" I said. "But you have all that food. What a waste."

He shook his head. "No. It'll be okay. It's better to figure out what's going on here, between us, and with your family and mine. Better to get that figured out. I talked to Giovanni. He finally admitted it was him with Sherry in our—in your house. I told my sister. She was devastated. And yes, I fired Sherry and had the locks changed. Remind me to give you the keys before I leave."

"Are you staying?" I said. "I mean, at the house. You seemed so finished with me this morning."

"I was hurt and pissed, Brooke," he said. "What did you expect? I still want some definition. Can't you come to me when something's going on, not to Hayword?"

"No, not always," I said. "We share children. What was going on with Irving Jackson had to do with Fern. I would have told you, but I thought you and Sherry were . . . together. Anyway. Can we start the day over? Or the last 48 hours? If you're not having the soft opening tomorrow, do you want to stay here with me?"

He shook his head. "No. You've got a script to finish by tomorrow. I've got people to call. But Sunday, you and I are sitting down for a talk. Until then, why don't you and your family come for a late lunch tomorrow, after you're done working? We can celebrate you finishing the script, and we'll eat some of the food. I'll make it a feast."

"Really?" I asked. "Hayword, too?"

"Yes, of course," he said. "I mean, he's your husband." He gave me a look. I put my arms around him and hugged him.

"I love you," I said.

He didn't say anything. He put his arms around me, and we held each other. Until I sighed. Until I relaxed. Hadn't realized how tense I'd been.

When we finally let each other go, I went to the table and picked up the envelope and opened it. Inside was a file folder from the LA Police Department. I opened it. One sheet of paper, essentially. About our house fire. Investigators determined it was an electrical fire. They had found some evidence of fire in a trash can, but the fire hadn't gone outside of the can. Case closed. Just like Phil Case had told us. I had seen a form like this before—when we had to settle an insurance claim.

"What is it?" Mark asked.

"I'm not sure," I said. I turned the folder over and found a large post-it note. I read it out loud. "My husband was a prick. Said he was using this to blackmail you. Now it's all yours."

I handed the folder to Mark.

"There's nothing here," Mark said. "There's nothing he could have used against you."

I nodded. "I need to show this to Fern. She has to understand she didn't burn the house down. Maybe that will give her some peace."

Mark nodded. "Okay. Tomorrow at two. Text me how many will be there. Now I've got stuff to do."

He kissed me on the lips. I pulled him close to me and continued the kiss.

He pulled away and looked at me. "Sherry? Really? She reads *Hollywood Gossip* throughout the day and then tells me about it."

"You hired her," I said.

Then he was gone. I texted my family. "Be at the restaurant at 2:00 tomorrow or be square. It's a celebration."

I smiled as I sent the invite. Maybe everything was going to be all right after all.

I wrote for several more hours. Then I slept for a few more.

Dreamed Alberto was Aiden standing on the shoreline looking out at the Pacific Ocean. His hand was raised in a fist above his head. I could see the swan ring. "Momma," he whispered. "Run!" Then a wave the size of the world rolled over both of us. I awakened gasping for breath.

"What the fuck was that?"

I made myself coffee, ate some quiche and chocolate, and then peered out into the darkness. Couldn't tell if the animals were still there or not.

I kept writing.

And writing.

And writing.

Until Aiden's fist came bursting up through the earth.

Then I laughed.

Never had written anything this quickly in my life. Wouldn't tell anyone that—besides my family and Mark. Let the world believe I toiled over it forever.

I attached the treatment and the script to an email to Sally with this message: "I haven't proofed it yet, but here it is."

I clicked on send.

"May it save the world!"

I looked out the window. The animals were gone—except for one. The bobcat was now sitting on my back porch.

I opened the door and looked out at her. "Do you have any messages for me?" I asked.

The bobcat stared at me. Perhaps she was asking, "Do you have any messages for *me*?"

"Run," I said.

FIFTEEN

Soon enough, I was on my way back to the beach and the restaurant. I had butterflies in my stomach. I couldn't remember any time we'd all been together. Maybe never? Wasn't sure it was a good idea, but we were doing it. Everyone had said yes. Even Fern—although she was bringing her boyfriend. Her *old* boyfriend, Enrique, who was partially responsible for all the turmoil I'd been going through for the last few days. Ah well. Be flexible, eh?

It was another beautiful warm sunny day. Hayword's SUV was already at the restaurant when I arrived. And Fern's car. Mark's truck. I opened the restaurant door almost reluctantly. I heard voices—laughter. Then I saw them all standing around a food-laden table. They turned and looked at me. Everyone smiled. Except Fern. Her face didn't move. Couldn't tell if that was good or bad. David was the first to come over to me.

"So you made the world better for zombies today," he said as he hugged me.

"Yep, I did."

I put my arms around him and gave him a bear hug. He was so grown-up, especially for a 14-year-old.

He took my hand, and we walked over to the rest of the group. Mark kissed me on the cheek.

"Heard you had a little trouble here," Fern said. She even hugged me.

"That's an understatement," I said. "Where's Ricky?"

"Something came up," she said, "but he sends his regards."

Hayword came over and kissed me on the cheek. I kissed him back and let go of David's hand to squeeze Hayword's. I didn't want him to feel like a third wheel. Or fifth wheel. Whatever it was.

"Wow, Mark," I said. "This is gorgeous. What a feast! I'm so sorry you didn't get to open today."

He shrugged. "Maybe it all happened for a reason. That's what some people would say."

I looked at him. "Would you say that?"

He smiled. "Probably not. But maybe. Let's just say it's all for the best. Now let's eat."

It was a round table so we didn't have to think about who sat at the head of it. My kids sat on either side of me which left Mark and Hayword sitting next to one another.

We ate omelettes, quiches, homemade sausages, crepes stuffed with fresh fruit, scrambled tofu, baked potatoes, hash brown potatoes, hash brown sweet potatoes, all kinds of salads and side dishes. Mark got up and opened one of the big windows so we could hear the seagulls and smell the ocean. David talked about his experiment at school, and Fern listened, dumbfounded. Mark seemed a bit surprised, too.

"Lucky they didn't haul you off to jail," Fern said.

"Me? I heard about you staging a robbery at Juliet's," he said.

"What?" Fern said. "Who told him?"

Hayword shrugged. "Your mother and I have decided it's best not to keep secrets. Anymore."

"Really? I don't remember that," I said. "Must have been something I agreed to in my sleep. Mark, this is all so delicious."

"It's really good," Fern said. "I didn't know you were such a good cook."

I laughed. "Why did you think he was opening a restaurant then?"

"Because you wanted him to," Fern said.

I frowned. "Really?"

"Sure," Fern said. "You seem to have this ability to get the men in your life to do whatever you want. How do you manage that? You treat them like shit, and then they still follow you around like lap dogs."

"Fern," Hayword said. "She never treated me badly. And I'm no one's lap dog."

Mark didn't say anything. He just shook his head.

"Are we going to spoil Mark's wonderful meal by arguing?" I asked.

"I wasn't arguing," Fern said. "I was actually curious. How do you get men to love you when you aren't very nice to them?"

"Wow," I said. "First, I don't believe I am unkind to anyone. I love and I am loved back. I'm quite fortunate. But I've had my heart broken." I look over at Hayword, trying to ask him silently if it would be all right now to share this secret. He nodded. I glanced at Mark. He knew what I was up to, too. "For instance, Alberto's father broke my heart. Crushed me. I thought I'd die. But I didn't. Life went on."

Fern and David looked at Hayword and then back at me.

"You cheated on Dad before Alberto died?" Fern asked. "How could you do that?"

"Our marriage really isn't any of your business," Hayword said. "Or our sex lives before, during, or after our marriage. That's between us. What your mother is trying to tell you is that she's had her heart broken, too. We all have. Your mom has always been honest with me."

"Even while she was sleeping with someone else?" Fern asked.

He nodded. "And my behavior wasn't always exemplary."

"It could never equal what she's done," Fern said.

"I think you should start giving your mother a break," Hayword said. "Yes, she drank. Yes, we had some hard times, but she was a good mother."

"She was a fucking drunk," Fern said.

"I don't want to listen to this," David said.

I put my hand over his. "Fern is entitled to her opinion."

"She is," Hayword said, "but she needs to hear the whole truth. About how you got drunk, Fern, and told Irving Jackson that you'd burned down our house. He used that information to get a police file, and he told your mother that he would expose your secret to the world unless she helped him get rid of Sally. He was trying to force your mother to have sex with him."

Fern looked at me. "So that's why he was at the bungalow? Did you kill him?"

"No!" I said. "I wouldn't do that for you or myself or anyone else. Christ. I was trying to figure a way out, and lo and behold, he died. Instant karma? His wife sent me the file he was holding over my head, the one from the police."

Fern stared straight ahead.

"Fern," I said. "Listen to me, Fern."

"What?"

"There was nothing in it," I said. "Dad had Phil Case look into it. There's nothing to it. There was an electrical fire. It was just a weird coincidence that you'd started a fire in a wastebasket. That fire went out. Coincidences happen all the time. And this was one. The house burned down because of electricity. You didn't do it. You may have wished it, but you didn't do it. You have got to let go of this. You aren't an arsonist. You didn't cause your brother to die. None of what happened to this family was your fault. Or David's fault. Or Alberto's. Maybe it was no one's fault. Maybe it's just life. You can put the blame on us." I put my hand over hers, and she didn't pull away. "You can blame me. But stop blaming yourself. Let this go. Let yourself be happy."

"You didn't burn the house down," Hayword said. "You didn't cause Alberto's death. It wasn't your fault Mom drank or that we split up."

Fern moved her hand away to wipe the tears off her face. She began to sob quietly.

I reached into my purse at my feet and pulled out the folded paper from the case file. I unfolded the paper on the table and pointed to "case closed."

"Maybe the spirit of fire heard my prayers," Fern said. "Maybe that's what caused the fire."

"Then the spirit of fire shouldn't be answering children's destructive prayers," I said. "Even if that were true in any world or any dimension, it still wouldn't be your fault. We can't be blamed for what we wish. Good grief. How many politicians would be dead if wishes like that came true?"

Fern looked over at me. Her face was streaked with tears and mascara.

"Why do you wear makeup?" I asked. "You're so beautiful."

"Shut up," she said, wiping her face with her napkin. "Do you ever wonder what it all means?"

I shook my head. "No, never. That way lies madness, darlin'. Complete and utter madness."

"I don't believe you," Fern said. "I see it in your eyes."

"What?" I asked.

"Substance," she said. "You've got substance. Depth. I look in the mirror and see only hollow places."

I shook my head. "Darlin,' we've all got hollow places. Why do you think I drank? We just all try to do the best we can. Try not to hurt other people. Try to be kind and do good work."

"Really?" Fern said. "Is that what you do?"

I laughed. "Yes, baby girl. Believe it or not, that's what I try to do. I'm sorry if it doesn't seem that way. I apologize to all of you if it doesn't seem that way. I think after Alberto died I was so afraid of another loss that I just tried to control everything and everyone. Including you all." I looked around the table. "I'm sorry. I know you've got your own feelings and foibles and wishes and they don't always coincide with mine. I understand that intellectually, and I'll try to live by it more literally."

"Mom, I'm sorry Irving did that to you," Fern said. "I'm sorry about the fake robbery."

"You don't know all of it," David said. "When she found him dead, he was only wearing a garter, fishnet stockings, and stiletto heels."

Fern's eyes widened—as did mine, I'm sure.

"Hayword! You told our son that?" I cried.

"Fishnet stockings?" Mark said.

"Joanie told me," David said. "She'll tell me anything. I just offer her chocolate and champagne."

"Oh my word," I said. "Now you're going to be scarred for life."

David shook his head. "Why? I've heard worse. At least you weren't . . . you know, with him."

I laughed. Mark sputtered on some cider he'd just sipped.

I held up my glass filled with apple cider. "Here's to not having sex with a naked dead guy dressed in fishnet stockings."

"I am not toasting to that," Hayword said. "How about here's to honesty."

I shrugged. "Mine was more imaginative." We held up our glasses and clinked them together. Then we drank.

"Mom, look," Fern said. She pointed out the window.

The tide was out, and the beach was covered in white birds: large and small, just as it had been covered the other day with black birds. We all got up and went to the window.

"The big birds are swans," David said.

Mark came up behind me and put his hands on my shoulders.

"Wow," Hayword said. "I wonder where they've all come from."

"Brooke had all kinds of animals at her house yesterday," Mark said.

I nodded. "Bobcats. Deer. Raccoons. Birds."

David said, "There were elk and coyotes at our house last night."

"What do you think is going on?" Fern asked.

"I have no idea," I said.

"Look, one of the swans!" Fern said, suddenly excited. "It's blue and green. Like the swan pin." She tapped the swan pin she was still wearing with the fingers of her right hand.

I squinted. She pointed out the window again, trying to help me see it. Yes. There. It did look like a blue and green swan. Which was impossible.

I had to get closer.

"Must be full moon," Hayword said. "That's a pretty low tide."

"Yesterday, I think," Mark said.

As a group, we hurried outside, went down the steps to the yard and then more stairs that led to the beach, and then down an incline until we were on the sand. The wet sand seemed to stretch to forever. The birds did not move and the swans made a kind of clicking noise as we walked. Other human beachcombers stood amongst the birds, too, looking dazed.

David, Mark, and Hayword stopped amidst the birds as Fern and I went forward, looking for the blue green swan.

"There," Fern said, pointing again.

We hurried forward. The sand was wet beneath our feet, and we sank a bit. For a moment, we hesitated. The swan was so beautiful. A real life blue and green swan.

Only, no such thing existed.

I blinked and realized the swan was caught in something. Fern glanced at me. She saw it now, too.

As we neared the blue and green swan, she didn't move. She was stuck inside some kind of blue green plastic. It was around her neck and digging into her skin. The rest was draped over her beautiful white body. The plastic was bloody where it choked her neck. Her beak was open as she gasped for breath.

"Oh my god," Fern said. She dropped to her knees beside the animal. "Mom, we've got to help her."

"Shhh," I said soothingly, to the bird. "It's okay, it's okay. We want to help you."

The swan moved nervously. I glanced behind me. Hayword, David, and Mark were coming nearer. I held up my hand to them, and they stopped.

"Do any of you have a pocket knife?" I asked.

"I do." Mark.

Mark pulled out a Swiss army knife. "It's got a knife and scissors," he said. I went and got it from him, then went back to the swan. I looked at the plastic. I couldn't figure out how it had gotten over her head.

"Shhh," I said. "Fern, try to keep her calm. Talk to her. Maybe pet her, if that's what she wants."

"How will I know what she wants?" Fern asked.

"Ask her," I said, "and see what you hear."

Yeah, I don't know where that came from, but Fern whispered to the swan. Then she pulled a kerchief from her back pocket and slowly and gently wrapped it around the swan's head, covering her eyes. I motioned the men over to us.

"Quietly," I said, "and quickly. Hold her down and still."

Fern cooed to the swan. The men fell on the bird, gently, almost tenderly, and she didn't move. I used the scissors to cut into the plastic. I heard the humans breathing around me, felt the heartbeat of the swans—of all the swans. The beach was so still. The ocean was such a long way off. At first the plastic wouldn't move, wouldn't give, but then it did, and I was able to cut enough away to slip it over the swan's head. Which I did, carefully, slowly.

"Take off the blindfold," I said. I stepped back. Fern slipped off the kerchief and then stepped back. I nodded to the guys. "Let her go." As one, the men stepped away.

The swan tottered a bit. Then she almost shuddered. She flapped her wings. She looked at us and seemed to bow, to acknowledge our existence. I laughed and looked at my daughter. She was smiling, too. Mark glanced at me and smiled and nodded.

The beach breathed again. And then as though they had all gotten a message from God or the Queen Swan or the Wind, every single bird on the beach lifted into the air. As if they had come to this beach and this time and place just for us to save this one bird. For a moment, the sky was a beautiful moving white quilt. I put my arms across Fern's shoulders as we watched. The birds circled us and then flew east.

"Go east, young woman."

Suddenly I remembered my dream from early this morning—where Alberto had screamed, "Run." I looked out across the beach. Where was the ocean?

This tide was too low even for full moon low tide.

"Run!" I cried to my family as I grabbed Fern's hand. "We've got to run!"

SIXTEEN

I'm not sure exactly what happened next, or in what order, but we ran. Not an easy thing to do as we climbed a small hill and then two sets of stairs.

"Grab as much non-perishable food as you can," I shouted when we got to the restaurant.

"What's going on?" Mark asked as the kids and Hayword began filling bags with food.

"David," I said, "have you heard about any earthquakes?" I looked at Mark. "He's got a disaster app on his phone."

"No," David said.

We got the food and a case of bottled water and headed for the SUV, after Mark locked the door.

"We're all going together?" Mark asked.

"Yes," I said. "Get in."

Then Hayword drove us away from the sea.

"The wild animals were at my house," I said. "I bet that means it must be safe there."

"Even safer up at the big house," Hayword said.

I didn't look back at the ocean or my house. Fern and David looked at the sky and watched the swans heading east.

"Mom, tsunamis come after an earthquake," David said. "Not before."

"I had a dream last night," I said. "Alberto told me to run. So I'm running. And the seal told me to go east."

"The seal?" Fern asked.

"Long story," I said.

Strangely enough, we didn't run into any traffic. At least nothing to speak of. The kids barely said a word. Mark and Hayword sat in the front together, figuring out the best way to go. I didn't care, as long as we were all together. David kept looking on his phone to see if anything had happened. I got a text from Sally telling me they loved the script and they'd go ahead with it as soon as possible.

We stopped at my bungalow. I packed a bag while the others filled any empty containers they could find with water. I packed extra clothes for Fern. Mark and Hayword turned off the gas. We locked the doors, and then Hayword drove us up the hill to our house.

We got out of the car and looked around.

It was a perfect beautiful blue day. Nothing going on.

Hadn't it been a perfect beautiful blue day when Alberto died?

Or had it been night?

I phoned Joanie. "I think something is going to happen," I said. "You alone?"

"Yes," she said. "Hubby is out of town."

"Come on over," I said.

We went through the house and filled up more bottles and containers with water. Hayword made certain the generator was working and ready to go. The kids filled up the bathtubs with water. I could hear them splashing each other and laughing as I went into Hayword's bedroom. I pushed the chair over to the closet, stood on it, and got Alberto's ashes.

I hopped off the chair. I heard Joanie downstairs. "This is awkward," she said. "Husband and lover. Or is it civilized?"

"We've just been waiting for you to make it a foursome," Hayword said.

I laughed.

Then I felt dizzy. I looked over at the window. The curtains were moving.

I wasn't dizzy.

"Run!" I screamed, holding the urn close to me.

Fern and David came out of the bathroom as the ground swayed, as the house swayed. We ran together down the stairs, barely able to keep ourselves upright, and then we were outside with Mark, Joanie, and Hayword, standing away from the house, between it and the pool house. Hayword took a hold of the kids, and Mark reached for me. I set the urn on the ground and reached for Joanie. The six of us held onto each other as the ground beneath us shook, as it undulated. The air seemed filled with static. Or electricity. I felt tense, as though white noise was roaring in the background, only I couldn't hear any. I looked up. The trees around us swayed. Only the sun seemed still. Birds flew up from the trees, soundlessly, and then disappeared into the blue.

"It's lasting so long," Fern said.

I heard windows breaking. I closed my eyes. I could almost imagine I was riding a surfboard. I kicked off my shoes and felt the cool earth beneath my soles. Could almost feel the waves beneath my feet. Or was that the tectonic plates? I smiled. Didn't matter. I was riding the waves. I moved away from my family and held out my arms, balanced myself on the earth.

"Come on, darlin's," I said. "Feel the ground!"

And just like that, they all took off their shoes. David fell to the ground as it continued to move like a live thing beneath us. He got back up. We all heard a tree crack and then fall in the woods behind the house.

"We're surfing the earthquake," I said. "Riders in the storm."

"Mixed metaphor, love," Hayword said.

I laughed. Mark went along with it, too. Surfing the Earth.

Joanie watched us and shook her head. But she was barefoot.

"I was never a very good surfer," she said.

"Mom," David said. "The urn fell over."

I looked behind me. Hayword leaned over and picked up the urn. The cap had come off.

"Part of it spilled," Hayword said.

And then, just like that, the quake stopped.

Fern ran over to her father and took the urn from him. Then she began running around the yard with the urn. As she ran she slowly tipped it over and the ashes spilled out in a line behind her.

"Goodbye, Alberto," she called. "We love you!"

We watched her run and run, long after the urn was empty. I hadn't seen her look that free since she was a girl, since before Alberto died. Then she stopped and grinned.

We all clapped. Spontaneously, happily. I held my arms open, and Fern ran to me. Just like she had when she was a girl. And she grinned, happy to see me, happy to fall into my arms, which she did, and I held her tightly, I held onto her for dear life. I kissed her hair and told her I loved her. Soon David was hugging us, and then Hayword, Joanie, and then Hayword pulled Mark in. Until we all started laughing, and Joanie declared it was all too kinky for her.

In the near distance, we could hear sirens and fire alarms and car alarms.

"Man," I said, "I can't wait until this full moon is done and over."

"That was a big one," Joanie said. "I better go home and see what's up. I left Marie there all alone. She's been in a staring contest all day with a bear in our back yard." She blew us a kiss and then wobbled away.

"What now, Mom?" David asked. "I can't get any service on my phone. Do you think the world ended?"

The survivor on the plane had looked around, faced reality, and saw beauty, too. Beauty was part of the reality of survival. Was that what Gabriella had been trying to tell me?

Beauty does exist, even in awful times. Even in whackadoodle times.

"The world hasn't ended," I said. "Look around. We're still here, and we're still together."

"This is about the time in a movie when zombies would come out of the woodwork," David said, "or out of the woods."

"Not in my movies," I said. "In my movies, the zombies and humans all live happily ever after."

"Only after the zombies almost destroy the world," Fern said.

We all walked toward the house.

"Are we the zombies or the humans?" David asked.

"Only time will tell," I said.

"I vote for zombies," Fern said.

"You would," David said.

They ran toward the house.

"Wait for your dad," I said. "It might not be safe."

I watched the three of them cross the threshold and go into the house.

Mark stopped me and put his arms around me.

"That was intense," he said.

"The life of a repo man is always intense," I said.

He looked down at me. "What?"

"Oh god," I said. "You've got to start watching more movies. Didn't you ever see *Repo Man*?"

He smiled. "I was just teasing you," he said. "I knew what movie it was from. Now I need to call Ian and let him know I'm okay. I'll go see if I can get phone service anywhere."

"Okay," I said.

And then Mark was gone, and I was standing in my old backyard, alone. In the sunshine, under the blue sky. I looked at the grass where Fern had strewn Alberto's ashes. I waited for a beat. But no arm came bursting up through the sod.

Thank goodness. I would not want life to be like any of my movies.

"Love you, sweetheart," I whispered before turning around and going toward the house to join my family.

Turned out the earthquake was a pretty major one. Pundits started calling it the earthquake the animals predicted. Some even called it the Zombie Animal Earthquake, which I didn't really understand since none of the animals died and came back to life. After the quake, a tsunami hit our shores. It didn't reach the restaurant but it was pretty high and pretty bad.

LA was knocked off its foundations by the quake. Many buildings destroyed. Because of retrofitting and new building codes most people survived. Most buildings, too.

But the chaos was extreme for a time. We didn't have electricity for days. Fortunately the generator kept the food safe for us. We weren't able to get down to the village for almost a week because of damage to the road. Trees were down everywhere. We were lucky.

We all rallied around each other. We came out of our shells, out of our houses, and helped each other out. Our house—Hayward's house—had some damage, but it was structurally sound. The bungalow had absolutely no damage while other houses around it fell apart. The beach house and restaurant had some structural damage.

Despite all of this—or maybe because of it—my family and community seemed to grow closer. Mark and I stayed in the bungalow, and Fern moved in with David and Hayword since her apartment was all but destroyed. The five of us spent so much time together that we actually began to feel like we were a family. Even Mark's son Ian started joining our little crew.

It's only been a few months since the quake, but filming on the movie started on time. The financial problems at AFT either resolved themselves or else they stopped talking about them because Sally hasn't brought them up since. AFT will use part of the profits from the movie to help those who were affected by the earthquake.

Hayword and I decided that we're going to start a foundation in Alberto's name with the profits from *Beauty and the Zombie Part Two*. We're not sure what the foundation will do. David wants it to be used to save the world. We told him we needed to be more specific than that.

"Okay, save this world," he said. "Planet Earth."

We asked Fern if she wanted to run the foundation. She has a certain facility for business. Why not? So she's going to start taking some classes on running a nonprofit and see if she likes it. She's also promised to go back to therapy. We'll see. She wants to take acting lessons, and this fills me with dread.

Hayword and I haven't divorced yet. I'm not sure why. But Mark and I are actually talking about our relationship. I don't leave the room when these conversation start, no matter how much I'm tempted.

Hayword thinks we should tell Ryan Nichols about the foundation once it's up and running. Since it's in his son's name. I dunno. Alberto was never his son. He was always Hayword's.

David wants to call it the Alberto McMurphy Lightman Back from the Dead Foundation. We told him to think again.

They've already asked me to start writing the third *Beauty and the Zombie* movie even though they haven't completed filming on the second one. I've got an idea for it, though. It's called *Beauty and the Zombie Part Three: Whackadoodle Times.*

But first I'm looking forward to seeing Part Two. Especially the last scene. I want to see Colleen walking away from her son's grave. I want to see his arm come up through the Earth, I want to know he will live again. I understand he's part zombie, so he'll be part of the living dead. And he's fictional.

In other words, I know my son will never be coming back to life again.

Still, when no one is around, I stand in the backyard of Hayword's house—or our house—in the spot where Fern spread Alberto's ashes. I'm not waiting for Alberto to burst forth from the Earth or anything. Or maybe I am. Who knows? But I do talk to him. I do whisper to him, and I listen for his voice in the wind. Sometimes I close my eyes and see him as I did in the dream, with his fist raised above his head, and he is whispering to me, he is calling to me. "Momma. Run!" I'm ready. I'm ready to run. If that's what's needed.

Until then. Until then I'm ready. Until then, I'm ready to stay.

Kim Antieau's novels include Brooke McMurphy's first adventure, *Whackadoodle Times,* as well as *The Jigsaw Woman, Her Frozen Wild, Church of the Old Mermaids, Coyote Cowgirl, The Monster's Daughter, Butch,* and many others. Learn more at www.kimantieau.com.